Infamous

ALYSON NOËL

Infamous

A BEAUTIFUL IDOLS NOVEL

KATHERINE TEGEN BOOKS

An Imprint of HarperCollins Publishers

Katherine Tegen Books is an imprint of HarperCollins Publishers.

Infamous
Copyright © 2018 by HarperCollins Publishers
All rights reserved. Printed in the United States of America. No part
of this book may be used or reproduced in any manner whatsoever
without written permission except in the case of brief quotations
embodied in critical articles and reviews. For information address
HarperCollins Children's Books, a division of HarperCollins
Publishers, 195 Broadway, New York, NY 10007.
www.epicreads.com

Library of Congress Control Number: 2017943404
ISBN 978-0-06-232458-0 (hardcover)
ISBN 978-0-06-279645-5 (international edition)

Typography by Erin Fitzsimmons
18 19 20 21 22   CG/LSCH   10 9 8 7 6 5 4 3 2 1

First Edition

For Howard and Karen

The truth is rarely pure and never simple.

—OSCAR WILDE

Spotlight magazine exclusive!

We caught up with rising star Heather Rollins to discuss the latest developments in the Madison Brooks case. As you probably know, Heather was a close friend of Madison's, and she's also acquainted with the four teens recently arrested for their alleged involvement in Madison's disappearance. Read on for Heather's unique, insider perspective of the ongoing scandal!

Spotlight: *Heather, we know how busy you are with your new show—congratulations, by the way! We're honored you managed to carve out some time to speak with us today.*

Heather: *Thank you, but really, the honor's all mine. Like the rest of the world, I'm distraught over Madison's disappearance and I just pray she's okay. I miss her, and I want her to return home safely.*

Spotlight: *Certainly the latest news that the body found in Joshua Tree has been ruled out as Madison comes as a relief. But tell us, how are you holding up, and what are your theories? It seems everyone has one these days.*

Heather: *The news was certainly a relief, to say the least. As for theories, I can't say I have any. I'm mostly just glad to know Madison is still out there, somewhere, and I pray every day that we'll see her again—the sooner the better.*

Spotlight: *I'm sure we're all rooting for the same outcome. Though we're also wondering, as someone with connections to everyone involved, what do you think of the recent arrests of Aster Amirpour, Layla Harrison, Tommy Phillips, and Ryan Hawthorne?*

Heather: *Well, it definitely came as a shock, but I really hate to speculate. It seems like the public has already convicted them in their minds. And while I understand the need for justice, I think it's wise to take a step back and trust that the LAPD and our legal system will do the right thing.*

Spotlight: *Yes, but they were caught at the scene of the body, along with Madison's tracker—what do you make of that?*

Heather: *It certainly looks bad, doesn't it? I'm just reluctant to point any fingers until we know the full story. A reputation can be ruined in a second, and it can take a lifetime to restore it, if ever.*

Spotlight: *The body was found outside a cabin in Joshua Tree owned by Paul Banks. The same Paul Banks who's been linked to Madison, and whose office* *building recently burned down in what was since ruled to be arson. Since the body has been established as a middle-aged male, do you think it was him?*

Heather: *I really think that's up to the coroner's office to determine. Like you, I'm just glued to my phone, waiting for updates.*

Spotlight: *Did you know Paul Banks, or ever see him with Madison?*

Heather: *Uh, this is starting to sound more like an interrogation and less like an interview.*

Spotlight: *Apologies. I guess we're all a little high-strung around here.*

Heather: *Understandably.*

Spotlight: *Would you like to add anything in closing?*

Heather: *Believe me when I say that Madison is truly a star in every sense of the word. She's always the brightest light in any room, and she radiates this magical vibe that comes from within. And yet, there's a side to her that few people realize. She's super generous to her friends and fans, but there's also a part that's very private to the point of being impenetrable. While I know she'd appreciate the enormous outpouring of love and support coming in from all over the globe, I also can't help but think how much she'd hate the three-ring circus her life has become. People tend to forget that underneath all the glamour and fame lives a real* girl. *A complex human being with her own hopes and dreams, and yes, even regrets. Madison inspired me to become the person I am today. We met early on in our careers, but I knew right away there was something really remarkable about her. She has so much determination and drive—I've never met anyone else who could even come close to matching her sheer power of will. It's impossible to think she might truly be gone. I refuse to accept it. So, if she's out there, somewhere, and is able to read this, I just want her to know that like everyone else the world over, I'm rooting for her safe return and won't rest until I see her again.*

Spotlight: *We couldn't agree more, and we thank you for taking the time to speak with us. Before you go, any hints for what's next?*

Heather: *Filming on my new show,* Lacey's Castle, *is set to begin soon. And I'm sure you heard about my new lip kit. It's called* Tempt, *and I'm wearing the baby-pink gloss now! I worked alongside the chemists to get the formula just right. It's packed with nutrients that make it super hydrating and soothing but not at all sticky. I put it on first thing this morning, and so far it's lasted me through an intense Tracy Anderson workout, an entire bottle of Moon Juice Matcha Pearl, and now this interview—crazy, right? Anyway, I'm really* *excited about both projects, and there are more in the works, so stay tuned!*

Spotlight: *So exciting, and I have to say your lips really do look great. I need to get some immediately! Speaking of exciting new developments, what can you tell us about your budding romance with hot up-and-comer Mateo Luna, who just so happens to be Layla Harrison's former boyfriend? Any truth to the rumors?*

Heather: *Mateo is a kind and gentle soul and a truly good person. That's all I have to say.*

Spotlight: *Well, thanks for stopping by, Heather. We here at* Spotlight *wish you all the best!*

ONE

FATHER FIGURE

Madison Brooks was not alone.

The first thing she sensed when consciousness dawned was the presence of someone looming over her bed.

She froze. Keeping her breath even, her limbs still, she listened intently for any sort of clue that might provide some insight into who had taken her and why.

Weeks in captivity had left her with little to go on. Still, there was always a chance that her captor, thinking she was asleep, would get careless or lazy and possibly do something that might give them away. Madison was so desperate for answers she refused to waste a single opportunity, no matter how improbable it might seem.

"You awake?"

Madison startled. The voice was familiar—one she

knew well. It belonged to a man she'd trusted since she was a much younger girl.

Her eyes snapped open and zeroed in on the nondescript male hovering nearby. His hair was neatly combed and nearly the same shade of beige as his face. His lips were thin, his nose unobtrusive, his irises a dull, chalky brown. It made for a collection of features so unremarkable he was hard to describe and nearly impossible to recall.

And yet, even though she recognized him, knew him as her one true friend, she pulled the blanket defensively up to her chin and recoiled against the cold hard wall.

"Easy," he coaxed, tentatively raising both hands to prove he meant her no harm.

Madison remained leery. She knew him as Paul Banks, aka the Ghost, aka her mentor, protector, and friend, who'd acted more like a parent than her real parents had.

Paul had always been there for her, had risked his life for her more than once. So she shouldn't be the least bit surprised to find him there now. Still, the time spent in confinement had left her skittish and traumatized. She'd grown so accustomed to living in a constant state of paranoia and dread that the transition to her new reality, where she really was safe with nothing to fear, was difficult at best.

She blinked a few times, allowing a moment to adjust to the shift. Paul was not her captor. Thanks to Paul, she no longer had a captor. He'd taken care of that creep by ensuring he'd never mess with Madison, or anyone else for that matter, again.

It was hardly the first time she'd seen a dead body, but she'd never forget the fleeting look of surprise on her kidnapper's face as he was positioning himself, preparing to do her great harm, when he was interrupted by a momentary flash and a loud cracking pop, and then the side of his head exploded into bits, showering chunks of brain matter and flesh all over the walls.

Next thing she knew Paul was lifting her, holding her close, and whispering reassurances into her ear. While he disposed of the body and cleaned up the mess, Madison slept a deep, dreamless sleep. By the time she woke, other than the strong scent of bleach permeating the room, it was like it'd been nothing more than a terrible hallucination. Neither of them had mentioned it since.

Still, there had been another captor before him. One who'd acted with great determination. And the worst part was they were still out there, somewhere, faceless and unknown. The thought made Madison shiver as she gathered the blanket even tighter around her.

"You okay?" Paul's voice was gentle, his features blunted with concern.

Madison nodded, more for his benefit than hers. She wasn't okay. Not even close. As long as her first captor was out there, she doubted she'd ever achieve such a state.

Would they try to strike again?

Possibly finish what they'd started?

While she had no idea what their endgame might be, unlike the second guy, they'd never physically harmed her, hadn't even tried to rob her. Sure, they'd taken her purse, but as she'd recently learned, it had shown up in the trunk of her car, which was left outside Paul's office the night of the fire. Only one of the gold-and-turquoise earrings Ryan had given her had managed to survive, but she was still in possession of her expensive diamond-encrusted Piaget watch, so clearly it wasn't money they were after. Also, according to Paul, there hadn't been a single ransom demand, making the motive a frustrating mystery. Yet another reason Paul insisted on keeping her completely hidden from the rest of the world.

Funny to think how all the news outlets were breathlessly speculating on her demise, and yet, here she was, hiding out in some dead guy's shack in the middle of Death Valley, with a man many had seen but no one remembered.

Paul continued to hover, while in her head, Madison recited all the reasons she trusted him. Eventually the thoughts began to take root, her body relaxed, and she glanced around the small, shabby room they shared.

It was bare-bones, run-down, and offered only a minimum of comforts. There was the saggy bed shoved in the corner. The mattress was lumpy and stained, but Paul had covered it in clean sheets and a thin blanket, so it was hardly the worst thing Madison had ever slept on. There was a battered old coffee table that held a small hand-crank radio, a large flashlight, and a stack of survivalist tomes. Beside it sat an old couch Paul had claimed for himself by stretching a flannel sleeping bag across it. In addition to a weak air conditioner that didn't do much to dispel the searing heat, an array of fans were scattered around, their blades whirling furiously throughout the day.

There was no sign of the knife the man had shoved hard against her throat, but she figured Paul had gotten rid of it, along with the body.

Still, there was a bathroom with running water, didn't matter that it was cold, and a toilet that flushed. After weeks of severe deprivation, the simplest conveniences took on luxury status.

"How's the ankle?" Paul gently lifted the corner of the blanket that covered her leg. "And how are you?"

Her body was wounded and sore. She was malnourished and weak. And her flesh bore the deep cuts and scrapes that had resulted from her ill-fated run through Death Valley.

She leaned her head back against the wall and closed her eyes for a long, peaceful moment. When she opened them again, she looked at Paul and said, "How am I?" She ran her tongue along the inside of her cheek. "Uncomfortable, weak, and angry beyond belief." She reached for the cup of instant coffee he'd left on the small fold-up table beside her and took a small sip. It was awful, truly disgusting, but at the moment, a Starbucks run was out of the question.

Apparently, the whole time she'd been missing, Paul had purposely gone missing too. He'd simply dropped off the radar, as only someone as practiced as him was able to do. Although as a master of invisibility, he'd been there all along. Moving among the very people he suspected of playing a part in her disappearance, without a single one of them noticing he was lurking around.

He reached for a pillow and gingerly placed it between her back and the wall, then handed her a plate he'd lumped with Spam and canned pineapples, the best the cupboards had to offer.

"You shouldn't have." She glared at the disgusting mash of food.

"It ain't Nobu, I know, but it's sustenance all the same. Might even help remedy the uncomfortable and weak bits you were complaining about." He spoke without a trace of irony.

Madison took a tentative bite of Spam, then made an exaggerated gagging face, mostly for his benefit. In the weeks she'd been locked up, she'd eaten far worse. "And what about the deeply seething anger? What remedies that?" She stuck her fork in a piece of limp pineapple and lifted it to her mouth.

Paul dragged a chair to the side of her bed. Settling onto it, he said, "I find revenge is often a good and reliable cure."

Madison took a few more bites, then set the plate aside.

"You're not a doctor, you know." She winced as Paul went about surveying her ankle.

"Not by profession, but I've tended far worse."

She shrugged, but what she really wanted to do was scream. She wasn't kidding about being mad. Most days it was the only thing that fueled her. But she wasn't mad at Paul, or at least not entirely.

"Ow!" She leaned forward and swiped at his hand.

He pulled away. "You know what they say about sprains. . . ."

"That they're worse than a clean break."

He nodded. "Definitely true in your case. Though at least some of the swelling is starting to subside."

"How soon can I return to my Spin Cycle class?"

Paul lowered his glasses onto his nose and stared at her from over the thin metal rims. "Don't push it. It's not safe for you out there."

Her lips dragged to a frown. "I can't take much more of this," she said. "Tell me you've at least narrowed it down to a few suspects."

Wordlessly, Paul crossed the room and returned with a stack of magazines for her to read while he went about rewrapping her leg. She'd prefer the use of a phone or a tablet, but Paul had banned anything that could be easily hacked or traced back to them. On a good day, Paul was paranoid, but lately he'd taken it to a whole new level. His palpable unease did nothing to quell her own gnawing fears.

She flipped through the stack. Her face was on every cover, alongside pictures of Layla, Tommy, Aster, and Ryan. It was as though they'd become as famous as her.

Also like her, they were locked up now too.

Madison traced her finger across Ryan's mug shot. There was a time when she'd considered him a suspect, but the idea didn't stick. At one point, she'd mentally accused all of them. Thoughts were the only things she had to keep from going insane. But now that she was free, she realized none of those thoughts held any weight.

Though Paul was right about revenge. The elaborate retribution fantasies she'd plotted in her head were pretty much the only thing that had gotten her through. Well, that and her refusal to find herself on the losing end of whatever messed-up game she'd been cast in.

She pushed the magazines aside. She was in no mood to read them. "Do they still think it's you?"

Paul finished wrapping her ankle, then reached for her hand and inspected the pinkie finger she'd broken a few weeks earlier that he'd had to reset. "What do you mean—suspect or victim?"

"I suppose one will overrule the other, but have they identified the body?"

"They've determined it's not you." He let go of her hand and grabbed two pillows to prop under her ankle.

"Just a matter of time before they learn it's not you either. So who is it then?" She watched him carefully. The body had been found on Paul's property.

"Why would you think I'd know?"

She continued to stare.

"You honestly think I'm dumb enough to bury a body on my own property?"

He made a good point. "What about Ira Redman?"

"Alive and kicking, last I checked."

"No, I mean as a suspect."

Without missing a beat, Paul said, "He's on the list."

Madison wondered if he'd realized the irony of his words. Ira ran the hottest clubs in town, where everyone vied for a spot on *the list*, and now Ira had earned a spot on Paul's list. She looked at Paul's bland expression and determined the joke was lost on him.

"Okay, so if we don't know who, then how about *why?* Why would someone go to the trouble of setting up Ryan, Aster, Layla, and Tommy, and how is it connected to me? Who have I wronged who would do such a thing?"

The words echoed between them as Paul shot her a patient look.

"Fine." She huffed. "So I've made a few enemies along the way." She cast a sideways glance at Paul. As usual his expression was impossible to decipher. "But clearly it's either someone from my past, or someone who knows about my past as well as my connection to you. Against all odds they managed to uncover a picture of me as a kid. Same pic they sent you. Also, the walls of my first cell were papered with that image. There's only one person I can think of, but that's impossible, right? I mean, it couldn't possibly be—"

Before she could finish, Paul pressed a cool hand to her forehead and said, "Don't go getting yourself wound up now, okay? I'm handling it."

Madison shrank beneath his touch. It was the most she'd spoken at once in a very long while, and it left her feeling exhausted and spent.

Thanks to her injuries and overall traumatized state, Paul had kept her on a steady stream of pain pills that left her heavily sedated. Most of the time it felt like her brain had turned to mush. Madison was just starting to realize the huge toll that had taken. "I don't understand what this is all about," she finally said, her voice little more than a whisper. "What do they want from me?"

Paul shot her a sobering look. "It's about destroying you and everything you've worked so hard to build."

Madison was jolted by his words. It was the first time he'd said anything like that. Or at least that she could recall. She rubbed her eyes, forced herself to think, to try to capture remnants of past conversations they'd had. But from the moment that bullet whizzed past her face and into that creep's head, everything had been a muted, blood-spattered, medicated blur. And yet she was sure this was the first time Paul had ever said such a thing.

Did Paul actually know more than he was letting on?

Had he been holding out on her all along?

"But who would do that?" She spoke slowly, as though carefully handpicking each word. When really, she just wanted to prolong the conversation so she could better observe him. "Who would be so jealous and spiteful and bent on revenge?" She tried to see Paul without bias, as though it was the first time they'd met.

Was he involved?

Was there a clue she might've missed?

When he trained his focus on her, she immediately shifted her gaze toward the far side of the room. She couldn't risk him capturing even a twinge of doubt on her face.

The silence stretched between them, broken when he said, "That's what I'm trying to find out." He rose to his feet and pushed the plate toward her. "Now eat." His tone was paternal, but Madison was on edge. "We need to leave soon. It's just a matter of time before someone stops by, and we can't afford to leave any trace of us behind."

Dutifully, Madison picked at her food as Paul expertly

wiped down the room. She spied the gasoline can he'd left near the door. He'd probably use it to douse the place, then light a match and drive away. They'd watch the flames from the rearview mirror as he took her to one of the many safe houses he kept.

It was the same MO he'd used when he burned down her childhood home. It was only now she was beginning to think maybe that hadn't worked out quite as well as he'd led her to believe.

"Where are you taking me?" She watched through lowered lids as he approached with yet another pain pill and a tall glass of water. Briefly, she considered trying to refuse, but she was in no position to fight. For the time being at least, it was better to play along.

Paul stood over her, watching as she placed the pill on her tongue and pretended to wash it down. "The less you know, the better," he said.

Satisfied, he carried the glass to the sink and washed it clean of prints. After drying it in a way that left it glistening and smudge free, he smashed it hard against the wall and stared as it shattered into tiny, glittering bits.

With his back turned, Madison spit the pill onto her palm and mashed it between her fingers until it morphed into a thin, grainy paste she wiped onto the sheets. She was surprised it had taken her so long to question Paul's motives. Especially considering how hard it was for her to trust anyone. She'd learned from a young age that when it came right down to it, she had only herself to rely on. And yet, for the better part of her life, she'd depended on Paul with no questions asked. But now she couldn't help but wonder if that had been a mistake.

There was something off about him. Something he was purposely holding back. While she couldn't quite put her finger on it—the drugs had left her brain too cloudy for that—Madison had always relied on her instincts, and at that moment, every cell in her body was telling her it was time to take back control of her life.

"Did you find an ID for that man who attacked me?" Madison watched Paul's shoulders stiffen before he slowly turned to face her. "Do you know who he was?"

Paul held her gaze. "No," he finally said. "Just a bum. An opportunist, I guess."

Madison debated whether to mention that the man's voice had been familiar. One she still couldn't quite place but definitely recognized.

Instead, she simply nodded as though she believed him. Then she closed her eyes and pretended to sleep, knowing it was what Paul wanted to see.

Someone was out to harm her, and while she had no idea if Paul was involved, she was sure he was lying.

Whether his lies were meant to protect her or harm her, she couldn't be sure. All she knew was that as soon as she built up her strength and cleared her head, she'd track down whoever had done this to her and show them just how badly they'd underestimated her.

Madison had killed before.

If it came down to it, she wouldn't hesitate to pull the trigger again.

TWO

NOTORIOUS

Layla Harrison clutched the plastic bag stuffed with her belongings and quietly shuffled past the door her dad held open. She paused a few beats, adjusting to the punishing light, while fingering the tender bracelets of flesh that circled both wrists. The wounds served as a lingering reminder of the too-tight handcuffs that had been placed there a few days before. Back when she'd been arrested for an A-list celebrity's murder—a crime she wasn't convinced had actually happened until she'd stumbled upon the decomposing corpse.

"You okay?" Her father shot her a look of concern.

She took in his paint-splattered T-shirt, the soft, worn look of his jeans, which now sagged so low on his hips it seemed as though he'd borrowed them from a much bigger man. He'd lost weight. Weight he couldn't afford to lose. And Layla knew his weary, gaunt appearance was entirely due to her.

It hurt to see him this way, and yet, when she finally did meet his gaze, she was greeted with so much love and compassion, she clamped her lips tightly and quickly turned away.

In jail, she'd been caught in a constant cycle of utter defiance and absolute despair. One moment she was outraged, pacing her cell and shaking the bars of her cage, demanding justice to anyone close enough to hear. But eventually, like water left to boil too long, her rage desiccated to a silent, scorched anguish. Who was she kidding? No one was interested in proving her innocence. The whole world was rooting against her. Detective Larsen had a high-profile case he was eager to close, the media had a juicy story to breathlessly report, and fans of Madison Brooks were looking for a target at which to direct all their hate. It was an inferno of accusation she couldn't possibly penetrate.

"Sorry it's a bit of a hike." Her dad squinted into the distance. "Couldn't find a closer spot."

"It's okay," she said, suddenly realizing the truth of her words. It really was okay. In fact, it was absolutely okay. Maybe not for the long term (God knows, just thinking about what the future might hold put her on the verge of hyperventilating), but at that very moment her complaints were few. After several days in captivity, she'd been released. And though she had no idea how long her freedom would last, she intended to cherish each and every glorious second.

She walked alongside her dad, listening to the dull rhythm of her boots scuffling over the asphalt, the tiny black pebbles rolling and crunching beneath every step. She couldn't help but marvel at how much she'd changed inside over the course of the last few days, and yet the outside world was just the same as she'd left it. The sun was shining. A long strand of birds perched in tight bunches on the telephone wire strung taut overhead. Their incessant chirping seemed to promise that the world would continue to hum and churn despite what happened to her.

There was no place for regret. And though Layla wasn't one for spiritual leanings, she firmly believed every life had a mission, a driving impulse toward a greater destiny. That wasn't to say that everyone made good on their mission, or even acknowledged its existence. But for Layla, her desire for truth and justice had thrummed through her veins for as long as she could remember.

It was the only explanation for why she'd put her own life at risk in order to help a girl who'd gone out of her way to act like a total bitch the first time they'd met. And yet, so much had happened since then, and Layla was done holding grudges. Aster had been set up. She was innocent of every crime leveled against her. And because of it, Layla felt compelled to help prove her innocence. Even if she'd been given a peek into the future that warned how she'd only end up implicated alongside Aster, Layla wouldn't have chosen any differently.

"Here, I almost forgot." Her dad pulled a pair of dark-lensed sunglasses from the pocket of his hoodie and thrust them into her palm.

Layla gratefully slid them onto her face, then tucked her chin to her chest and continued trudging alongside him.

She was exhausted. Hadn't slept for days. And her mind was in torment, refusing to allow even a moment's rest. Every time she closed her eyes, a reel of horrifying scenarios unspooled in her head.

Aside from her father and a handful of friends, no one seemed willing to give her a chance. And as someone who'd dreamed of being a serious journalist for most of her life, she was horrified to find herself the subject of countless sordid headlines. The media had portrayed her as a hateful person bent on revenge, and soon her fate would rest in the hands of twelve jurors who'd probably already made up their minds well before opening arguments were over.

If the verdict was guilty, she'd spend the bulk (if not all) of her life trapped behind bars. Her dreams would never be fulfilled, and the close relationship she'd once shared with her father would be reduced to awkward, guilt-laden visits, where Layla would watch helplessly from behind a smudged Plexiglas window as her father aged and withered before her.

It was the worst outcome imaginable, and the scary thing was, it was entirely possible.

"Layla! Hey, Layla—over here! Where's Madison? Tell us what you did to her?"

Great. Just what I need. Paparazzi.

Layla hiked the plastic bag high to cover her face as her father slung a protective arm around her and pulled her in close.

"Don't look. Ignore them." He pressed the words into her hair and rushed her toward his waiting car.

Layla leaned into him, allowing his momentum to carry her along, all the while fighting the impulse to cry at the sheer frustration of it all. With so many cameras centered on her, she couldn't afford to give in to tears. The press thrived on capturing vulnerable moments. They were all in pursuit of the same thing—the rare instant when the mask dropped and the celeb inadvertently revealed an alarming humanity. Beyoncé had a pimple once, and the internet nearly exploded.

While Layla's popular celebrity-bashing blog, Beautiful Idols, had fueled her financial independence and helped lessen the burden from her struggling artist father, she had no doubt that what was happening to her now was karmic payback for once being a player in the very industry that now stalked her.

She swallowed hard and burrowed deeper into her father's side. She felt shaky, oversensitive, but she couldn't afford to show any weakness. The breakdown would have to wait until later.

"Hey, H.D.! Over here! Are you standing by your daughter even though she's a murderer?"

Layla's father grew tense—a sure sign that the primal fight instinct had kicked in. Layla would prefer he chose flight.

Dad, she started to say, *don't, it's not worth it.*

But before she could get to the words, he was already turning away and securing her inside the car.

"Tell us whose body it is!" another pap screamed, his voice muted when her dad shut the door, shielding her from the onslaught.

"What's he talking about?" Layla watched her dad settle in.

"It wasn't Madison."

It took a moment to process the words. She repeated them back to him just to make sure.

"Wasn't her." He shook his head and slowly maneuvered through the retreating throng. "That's why they released you. I'm sorry, I assumed they would've told you." He turned his focus back to the road.

Layla gnawed the inside of her cheek, trying to decide what the news meant. "I figured you'd posted bail."

Her dad pressed his lips together and gripped the wheel hard. "No bail. They refused it."

Layla screwed her eyes shut and allowed the good news to sink in. Her chest loosened, her breath flowed with less restriction, as the eternal flame of optimism began to burn through what had come to seem like an impenetrable fog of despair.

If the body wasn't Madison's, then the LAPD could no longer charge her with murder.

The fact that they'd let her go probably meant they'd deemed her entirely innocent.

She rolled the thoughts around in her head until they gathered enough strength to edge the darker ones out.

"Did they ID the body?" She studied her dad, realizing that while it might not be Madison, there was still a dead body. "Was it Paul Banks?" The body had been found on his property, so it was entirely possible. Maybe she wasn't in the clear, after all.

"It's an adult male. That's all so far."

"And the others—Aster, Ryan, and Tommy—are they out too?"

Her dad shrugged. "I got the call to come get you, that's all."

Layla slid her fingers beneath her sunglasses and rubbed the delicate skin around her eyes. The good news—it wasn't Madison—was delivered in potentially bad news—it could still be Paul, who was connected to Madison—and Layla had no idea how to read it. All she knew for sure was that for the moment she was free. She just hoped it would last.

The rest of the ride home was spent in silence. H.D. had never been one to dodge the important conversations, but for now, Layla figured he was giving her space. The talk would come later.

Her dad pulled into the driveway and waited for the garage door to roll open as Layla nervously scanned the street, searching for signs of paparazzi. Deeming it clear, she seized the moment to slip free of the car and tilt her face directly into the sunlight.

"What're you doing?" Her dad's worried tone prompted her to laugh.

"Making good on my promise," she said. "I'll never take my freedom for granted again."

She lowered her gaze to meet his. The beginnings of a smile were lifting her lips when her phone chimed from inside the plastic bag she carried, and the latest text, in a long stream of them, popped onto her screen.

There was an image of a cartoon cat, this one with a deep, jagged gash that stretched across his throat. Just below were the words:

You're more stubborn than most
And though I don't like to boast
I meant what I said
And now, because of you, someone is dead
While you were away
I took the liberty of having my say
M's diary is now live on your site
Just a matter of time before the world sees it and bites
Will they bite you?
I haven't a clue
Though I can't take all the glory
Seeing as how I used your own story
But before you feel bad
Or even start to get mad
Don't forget it's your refusal to play
That brought you to this day
If you want this to end
Then consider me your best friend
Only I hold the key
So whatever you do, do not disappoint me
Further instructions will come
And I'm warning you to keep mum
If you share any of this with your gang
I promise, someone will hang.

Her heart pounding, Layla scrolled to her blog. An unvoiced cry died in her throat as she skimmed the post she'd written and had been dumb enough to leave in the draft folder instead of deleting.

BEAUTIFUL IDOLS
Through the Looking Glass
By Layla Harrison

Her stomach churned. It was all there, every word. Her gaze fell to the most incriminating part. If it turned out to be a hoax, and the entry wasn't really pulled from Madison's childhood diaries, Madison, or even Madison's estate, could sue her for slander.

But of course, just as she feared, the words were now posted for the whole world to see.

> . . . without further ado, I present to you the first installment of Madison Brooks's journal.
>
> Make of it what you will, but please note that I did not make this up, this is not a work of fiction, and it came to me via a reliable source.
>
> As always, feel free to exit through the comments section on your way out.

October 5, 2012
I'm so over it!!!!
So over absolutely EVERYTHING!
Including my so-called friends, my family, my stupid fake boyfriend, but mostly, this stuffy, boring, stick-up-its-ass town.

Layla could hardly breathe as her gaze skimmed the words.

The Ghost saved me—spared me from a future too horrible to contemplate. . . .
I guess you could say I owe him my life.
Then again, he owes me his too. . . .
If I ever go down, he's going down with me. Though I'm pretty sure that only works one way. Because if P goes down first, he'll go down alone. And he'll take all my secrets with him as well. He already proved it six years ago when he made a choice to save me. Which is why I guess, in a lot of ways, I consider him my real father.
Anyway, tomorrow is the day I board the bus to LA and never look back. . . .
It's crazy to think how next time I write in here, I'll be living an entirely different life!
☺ ☺ ☺

Layla's hand flew to her mouth. "Omigod," she whispered through trembling fingers.

"Everything okay?"

Her dad watched with concern from inside the garage.

"Mmm . . . Yeah. Of course." She sank her phone into her pocket and followed him inside.

She'd been hacked, that much was clear. And though her first instinct was to delete the post, the chilling text convinced her to leave it untouched.

According to whoever had sent it, her failure to play along before had landed them all in jail, possibly even getting someone killed.

Her dad ushered her down the hall and urged her to get some rest. "Later I'll make dinner. Or we can order in, up to you. Also, I spoke with Ira. He said not to worry about coming to work. He wants you to take some time— whatever you need."

Layla gave a distracted nod, headed into her room, and sank onto her bed. Gazing at the portrait her father had painted of her as a child, she wondered if she'd ever be able to smile as genuinely, spontaneously, and unselfconsciously as that again.

At the moment, it seemed inconceivable.

As wound up as she currently felt, sleep seemed inconceivable too. And yet, there were long days ahead, and she knew better than to face them in a state of exhaustion.

After a hot shower, she pulled on an old Stevie Nicks concert T-shirt and slipped beneath the covers.

Briefly, she thought of Tommy and the night they'd spent together. The sex had been amazing, but they'd sworn to each other there would be no strings attached. They were busy pursuing their dreams and couldn't afford the distraction. That would only amount to a mistake neither of them was willing to make.

At the time, Layla had been willing to agree to just about anything to ensure that Tommy's lips continued to press against hers.

But now she was glad for the pact. No matter how much she missed him, no matter how much she longed to check in and see how he was doing, the note had sent a clear warning. And in light of everything that had happened, she was done playing stubborn.

When she woke, the mess would still be there, calling her name. But for the moment, she closed her eyes and allowed sleep to claim her.

THREE

CAN'T REMEMBER
TO FORGET YOU

Aster Amirpour climbed out of Ira Redman's customized Cadillac Escalade and strolled into the lobby of
the W residences, only to find Ryan Hawthorne sitting by
the elevator bank.

Beside her, Ira paused, acting as though he was equally
surprised to find the former teen idol hanging around,
which left Aster feeling even more off balance than she'd
initially felt.

First there was Ryan: gorgeous, sexy Ryan. With his glittering green eyes, personal-trainer-honed body, and that
damn perfectly tousled hair glinting under the lights.

And then there was Ira—domineering, commanding,
all-powerful Ira—acting as though he wasn't really at the
controls of absolutely everything that went down in LA,

including that very moment. It made Aster suspicious.

"Looks like you no longer need me." Ira nodded toward Ryan, who pushed away from the bench and made a tentative approach. His expression shifted from warm and welcoming to cautious and wary as his gaze moved between them. "I'll leave you to it then." Ira gave Aster a perfunctory hug, and she returned it with two dutiful pats to his back.

Outside of a romantic relationship, Aster wasn't much for hugging. She always found those moments when someone came at her, arms wide and teeth flashing, to be clumsy and embarrassing at best. But hugging Ira was always a double dose of awkward. She was never sure what to make of it. It never felt entirely paternal, and yet it never felt inappropriate either. Not to mention, he was usually so distant and imperious, it seemed wildly out of character that he'd even try such a thing.

Ira gave them each one last look. Then, with a sharp turn of his heel, he headed for his ride, calling, "Let me know if you need anything," over his shoulder.

Aster studied Ira's retreating form. So far, she'd chosen to trust him, mostly due to the fact that he was the only one who'd shown up for her precisely when she needed it most. Ira had given her a place to live when life with her parents became unbearable. And not just any old place—he'd generously handed her the keys to a luxury condo and had so far asked for nothing in return.

He'd also supplied the top-notch team of lawyers who were set to defend her in her upcoming trial. And while she tried to be grateful, she never deluded herself into believing that when it was all said and done, his generosity wouldn't come with a very hefty price tag attached.

Ira Redman wasn't the altruistic type. But Aster was so far gone, all she could do was wait and see and hope against hope he'd wind up proving her wrong.

She watched as Ira was whisked away by his driver, then shook her head and trained her focus on Ryan's stupidly beautiful face.

He had stupid long-lashed eyes.

Stupid sculpted cheekbones.

An absurdly stupid square heroic jawline.

And the most stupid part of all was that ridiculously stupid smile he now wore that seemed so disarmingly genuine that Aster defensively crossed her arms against her chest.

She frowned. Waited for him to make the first move. He'd said some unkind things about her to the press just after Madison had gone missing, and yet Aster had still taken a leap and decided to trust him after he'd pleaded for a chance to do better.

The way he stood before her now, hesitating to speak, reminded her of an actor waiting for someone offstage to feed him his lines so he'd know what to say.

She let out a weary sigh. She really hoped he didn't turn

out to be yet another mistake on what was becoming a very long list.

"You okay?" Ryan took an uncertain step forward, followed by another.

Aster lifted her shoulders in reply. She had no idea how to put her conflicting thoughts into actual words, so she didn't bother to try.

Despite her growing doubts, she felt supremely lucky just to be standing right in that spot. Occupying that square of red carpet in the lobby of her luxury building felt like some sort of small miracle had been worked on her behalf.

Although the State of California had done its best to keep her locked up throughout her upcoming trial, through a bit of magic (or more likely, knowing Ira, through the weight of his considerable influence, with a pinch of dark sorcery), Ira had managed to spare her that fate. And so far, all he'd asked in return was that she stay in touch and not flee the state.

Ryan reached forward and traced a finger along the curve of her jaw. The move was so comforting, so tender, before Aster could stop herself she was falling into his arms.

She pressed her body hard against his, as he clinched her tightly at the waist and whispered into her ear. "I'm so glad you're okay. . . . I was so worried about you." He pulled away, sweeping her hair from her temple to better study her face. His gaze was brimming with such warmth and concern that Aster could barely bring herself to meet it. For a girl who'd been richly rewarded for her stunning good looks, she wasn't sure what to make of Ryan's admiring gaze.

She hadn't had a proper shower in days. Couldn't even remember the last time she'd brushed her teeth, popped a breath mint, or even glanced in a mirror that wasn't spiderwebbed with cracks. Her long dark hair was greasy and unkempt. Her normally flawless complexion was mottled with zits. Her brows were an unruly mess. And she refused to take a closer look at whatever remained of the intricate nail art manicure she'd once rocked. She was at her absolute most unglamorous, and yet, Ryan looked at her as though he saw something far beyond all that.

It made her feel weird, and she wished he would stop.

She didn't have time for this nonsense. Maybe later, after the trial, if somehow the verdict managed to work in her favor, but certainly not now, not . . .

She struggled against him, did her best to pull away, but Ryan only tightened his hold.

"Don't." His gaze deepened, demanding she meet it. "Please don't. You have no idea how good it is to see you."

Her laugh was derisive, but again, he stopped her cold.

"I mean it. You have no idea how much I . . ."

Don'tsayitdon'tsayitdon'tsayitdon'tsayit—Don't you dare say it!

To stop him from speaking the words she was neither ready nor willing to hear, she kissed him.

The move was reckless. Yet another promise she'd made to herself now broken.

And yet she pressed hard against him, no longer caring that she was standing out in the open, kissing Ryan Hawthorne as though she had no intention of ever doing anything else.

For those few glorious moments when his lips were sealed against hers, his arms clasped snugly around her, Aster felt safe, secure, protected, and wholly insulated from a hostile world.

Then the elevator doors swooshed open and a group of gawkers stood staring at her.

Instantly, Aster broke the embrace, ducked her chin low, and marched past the group and into the second elevator waiting beside them.

Seconds before the doors closed, Ryan slipped in and joined her.

"Aster—" Ryan started, but Aster nodded toward the camera pointing down from the corner and discreetly shook her head.

While it was definitely a relief to be out of jail, she was under no illusion as to how the rest of the world viewed her. As the most hated girl in America, she knew there was no shortage of people who were willing to sell her out to the nearest tabloid. Kissing Ryan in an elevator was out of the question. Talking was too.

She turned her back to the camera, waited for the car to arrive at her floor, then strode purposefully down the hall, keeping a safe distance from Ryan, who slowly followed along.

Tears stung her eyes as she let herself inside. How much longer would she have to live like this—overly cautious and paranoid?

One look at her apartment told her there was no end in sight.

The cops had gone there right before she'd been arrested in Joshua Tree. They'd found her little brother Javen and hauled him in for questioning; then they took the opportunity to ransack the place. Though Ira had assured her the maids had since cleaned up the mess, the thought of that creepy detective Larsen picking through her belongings left Aster uneasy.

Had he gone through her underwear drawer?

She briefly considered burning everything she owned and starting over.

"You okay?" Ryan regarded her with concern, but Aster had no idea how to answer. Her only real goal was to remain upright and breathing. Aiming for *okay* seemed like too big a reach.

"I think I'll take a shower," she said, heading for her

bedroom. "Make yourself comfortable, order from room service if you want. I'll be out in a bit."

With the bedroom door shut, she tugged off her clothes, eager to rid herself of any physical traces of her time spent in jail. She removed her jeans and kicked them into the far corner. They'd once been her favorites, but no more. She was busy pulling off her T-shirt when she noticed someone had written on the mirror that hung over her dressing table.

From a distance, the words were a scrawled pink blur. Her heart racing, she made a tentative approach.

Someone had used her favorite Charlotte Tilbury lipstick and left the empty gold tube discarded on the dresser.

At the sound of her scream, Ryan barged inside her room and stared in confusion.

Aster gazed down at herself. In her panic, she'd forgotten she'd stripped down to her bra and underpants, but there was no time for false modesty now.

Wordlessly, she pointed at the mirror. She had no idea what to make of it, much less who might've done it. There was no telling how many people had been there while she'd been in jail. Even Ira had a key that allowed him to come and go as he pleased.

It was a rhyme—like the ones in the threatening notes Layla had received. Only instead of a cartoon cat, someone had drawn a circle of broken hearts all around it.

Aster heaved a tremulous breath and began to read.

Your friend wouldn't play
So you all had to pay
Now I'm counting on you
To see this thing through
As a show of good faith
Take a look in your safe
If you abide by my rule
All will be cool
Where you ultimately land
Now rests in your hands.

The second she finished, Aster raced for the closet and punched in the code to unlock the safe. When the door sprang open, she was met with a spray of confetti.

Undeterred, she rummaged through it. As bits of pink cellophane hearts spilled to the floor, she removed her jewelry, an envelope filled with cash, her laptop and iPad. So far all her valuables were exactly as she'd left them.

When she reached the bottom, she found a plain manila envelope that hadn't been there last time she'd checked.

She met Ryan's gaze, then slipped her hand inside, retrieving a DVD with a note taped to its side.

Yes, it's exactly what you think
The sight of it probably brought you to the brink
There is only one more out there

*As you might've guessed, only I know where
If you do as I say
There'll be no price to pay
There's an artist you need to meet
She lives on a flower-named street
She knows Madison's secret
So don't let her keep it
We both want the same thing
For justice to ring
Don't share this with Javen or your mates
Or you'll all meet some very sorry fates.*

Aster stood unsteadily, her mind a whirl of all the horrible possibilities. She didn't have to watch the DVD to know what it contained. She'd been secretly filmed while she was in a blackout state the night Madison went missing. She'd performed an embarrassingly awkward striptease that would no doubt set the internet aflame if it were ever released.

The thought of that was bad enough, but Aster's real fear was for her family. Javen had been threatened, and if her parents ever learned about the tape . . .

She hugged herself at the waist and shivered. She couldn't bear to think how they'd react. Though they'd definitely disown her, of that she was sure.

It was hard to be around them knowing how much she'd

shamed them, so she'd done what she could to distance herself. On her last visit, they'd surprised her with their show of support. But when they tried to talk her into accepting a plea bargain, she'd left in despair.

Aster was adamant about not pleading guilty to a crime she hadn't committed. She'd take her chances with a jury. But now, with only two weeks left until trial, she sometimes wondered if she'd made the wrong choice.

If they didn't find Madison soon, there was a good chance she'd go away for the rest of her life.

She was so busy spiraling into the abyss of her thoughts, she'd lost track of what Ryan was saying.

"You know, the ones in Madison's house—near the stairs?"

Aster blinked and tried to catch up. But she was too upset to follow the thread. "I'm sorry, what?"

"The photographs. The ones with the old couch and the gun on the coffee table?"

Aster paused as she fought to recall them in detail. "Layla thought they seemed odd," she said. "Like they might be a clue pointing to Madison's past." She shook the note in her hand. "Do you think that's what this is about? The artist on the flower-named street who knows Madison's secrets?"

Ryan shrugged, his face setting in a way that made him look older. "Do you remember the name of the artist?"

"Layla might." Aster frowned. "But I won't contact her.

I'm not taking any chances."

"I'll look into it while you shower." Gently, he removed the DVD and the note from her hand and propelled her toward the bathroom.

"But you're not going to contact Layla, right?" Aster gave him a searching look. "I'm worried about even you knowing. The note made it clear that—"

Before she could finish, Ryan said, "Trust me. And when you're done with your shower, I want you to pack a bag."

He met her gaze, and Aster, suddenly remembering she was half-naked, was overcome with embarrassment. But Ryan was a gentleman and kept his focus firmly on her face.

"Until we figure out who's behind this, you're staying with me. It's not safe for you here."

She was about to refuse when she took one last glance at the message scrawled on the mirror, and headed into the shower instead.

FOUR

SHARP DRESSED MAN

Mateo Luna stood in the doorway and peered inside. The space was large, cavernous, and a long way from finished. With its plywood floors and unpainted walls, it offered no clues about the exclusive nightclub it was destined to become.

It was the last place Mateo wanted to be, and he seriously considered leaving before anyone noticed he was there. Every passing day it seemed his life belonged less to him and more to everyone else.

"Oh, you're here!" Heather bounded across the room, her brown eyes flashing, blond hair bouncing over her shoulders. "How long have you been standing there?"

Mateo glanced at Ira as he walked alongside her. With his dark jeans, sharply pressed untucked black shirt, and unreadable expression, there was something vaguely ominous about him.

"Welcome to RED." Ira chased the words with the kind of tight grin that set Mateo on edge. Then again, Ira often had that effect.

Heather nudged Ira with her elbow and rolled her eyes. "He calls it RED, even though he's planning for an all-white decor." She laughed at the absurdity of it all.

Mateo picked at the woven bracelet he wore on his left wrist—a gift from his little sister, Valentina, a few birthdays back. At the start of the summer he'd never given it much thought. Now it served as one of the few reminders of the sort of blissfully simple life he'd once lived.

"How's your sister?" Ira squinted through a veil of construction dust their footsteps had kicked up. "Valentina, right?"

Mateo squinted back. He'd met Ira before, most recently at Ira's tequila launch party, but Mateo couldn't remember ever having a conversation about Valentina. Had Layla, or even Heather, mentioned it to him? Mateo briefly considered it. It seemed improbable, but not impossible.

"Cancer's a bitch." Ira's gaze sharpened, as though he'd just said something profound and was expecting Mateo to commend him for his brilliance.

Instead, Mateo focused on Heather and said, "You ready?" She'd sent him a text, claiming she needed a ride.

But now that he was there, she seemed content to hang around.

"What's the hurry?" she said. "Don't you want to see the new club?"

Mateo shook his head. "I'm not much for clubs." He wasn't much for Ira Redman either and saw no point in pretending otherwise.

"Aw, yes." Ira's eyes glinted with amusement. "I seem to remember your bit on Trena Moretti's show. Something about club owners not giving a crap about the kids who are making them rich." He tilted his chin and peered at Mateo from under a lowered brow. "Or something to that effect."

It was weird how Ira had quoted him verbatim. Had he actually been insulted by Mateo's words? You'd think he'd be used to that sort of criticism, or at least better equipped to handle it. But like many in the Hollywood crowd, Ira's praise-seeking narcissism made him surprisingly thin-skinned and easily offended. He was also rumored to keep a growing list of enemies. Mateo idly wondered if he was on it.

Ira stared at Mateo as though he expected an apology. Mateo embraced the silence. The description fit and he had no intention of taking it back.

"At any rate," Ira said. "Sorry to hear about your brother Carlos. Though I assure you, I've never had anyone overdose at one of my clubs. If I did, I would never dump them outside and leave them to die."

"No," Mateo said, his voice full of venom. "Maybe no one's overdosed, but someone did get roofied. You remember what happened to Aster the night Madison went missing? She was drugged right there in your club. From what I heard, you poured the champagne."

If Mateo had blinked, he might've missed the flash of seething anger that crossed Ira's usually impenetrable face. It vanished almost as quickly as it appeared, but Mateo had caught it, and the way his lip curled in response told Ira as much.

It was a risky move, baiting the beast. But Mateo had reached a point where he no longer cared. He was one of the few people in his small group of friends who was not reliant upon or indebted to Ira in any way. He planned to keep it that way.

"Well!" Heather clapped her hands together and pasted an exaggerated sitcom smile onto her face. "Maybe this wasn't the best idea after all."

Mateo stared in confusion. As far as he knew, he was there to provide a ride and nothing more. He should've known Heather had something else planned, otherwise she would've ordered an Uber.

He had no idea what he was doing there. Actually, scratch that. He knew exactly why he was there. He was just too ashamed to admit it.

His sister was sick. His mom was a wreck. His ex-girlfriend was in jail for a crime she didn't commit. And Mateo was stuck in a job he hated but was lucky to have.

The huge sums of money he was paid to smolder for the camera helped to cover Valentina's astronomical medical bills. Still, he couldn't help feeling embarrassed every time he passed a billboard that featured his face.

It was Heather who'd helped him get started. Without her his family would be a lot worse off. There was no denying he owed his good fortune to her. Still, that wasn't the only reason he'd jumped at the sight of her text.

He was lonely—a relationship guy who sucked at being single. And in the midst of his life falling apart, Heather had become his favorite go-to distraction.

Problem was, while he knew why he was with her, he was beginning to suspect her reasons for seeking him out weren't quite as pure as she pretended they were.

"I guess I should've been more up-front." She bit her bottom lip in that adorable way that she had. Only lately, Mateo was beginning to find it far more manipulative than cute. "Thing is, Ira wanted you to swing by and see the new place and possibly set up a time to shoot."

Mateo gave her a confused look.

"The club." Heather lifted her shoulders up toward her ears. "Trena Moretti's doing a show about Ira and the empire he's built. He asked me to take part in some of the promos. I'm slotted to be the celebrity guest DJ on opening night. Anyway, we both thought it might be fun for you to join in."

Mateo swiped a hand through his hair and switched his gaze to Ira. "Really? You thought it would be fun? Because it sounds more like you want to continue to capitalize on Madison's disappearance by using two people remotely connected to it, since everyone else is in jail."

"They're not in jail," Heather said.

Mateo was knocked speechless by the news.

Since when? And more importantly: Why hadn't Layla called to tell him?

Just because they were no longer a couple didn't mean he'd stopped caring about her. Most days, he found he cared a lot more than he should.

"They were released a few hours ago. I assumed you knew." Heather shrugged as though it were no big deal, which left Mateo wondering if she actually cared about anyone other than herself.

"Listen," Mateo said, eager to leave. "If you still need a ride, we're good. As for everything else—" He gestured toward the unfinished club. "Count me out."

Heather shot Ira an opaque look, then stalked away in search of her belongings. While she was gone, Ira looked at Mateo and said, "You do know I'm helping Aster, right?"

Mateo returned Ira's gaze, but refused to respond either way.

"I didn't drug her."

"But you know who did?"

Ira assumed a pensive look, as though choosing his words. When Heather returned, he simply said, "All the best to your sister."

Mateo turned away.

"Let me know if I can help," Ira called.

"I think curing cancer is a little out of your jurisdiction," Mateo spat.

"You'd be surprised how far my reach extends."

Mateo shrugged it off and kept going. He was nearly at the door when Heather said, "I'm really sorry. I didn't think it all the way through. It won't happen again. I promise."

Mateo reached for the handle. Now was as good a time as any to start weaning himself from her. When he sensed she wasn't following, he turned to find her standing before a dust-covered mirror propped against a wall. She was drawing a large heart with the tip of her finger.

She glanced over her shoulder and shot him a questioning look. When he hesitated, she started to trace a crack down its center.

God, she was so dramatic. Mateo sighed, and swiped a hand through his hair. Then again, what had he expected, getting involved with an actress?

She thrust her lower lip into an exaggerated pout, and against his better instincts, Mateo started to laugh.

"C'mon," he said, watching her face brighten as he offered a hand. "Let's get out of here. It's been a long day."

Heather cast a last look at the heart she'd drawn and brushed the remaining dust away, leaving no evidence of the crack that had been there a second ago.

If only it were that easy. Then, refusing any further thoughts of Valentina, his mom, Layla, or anyone else on his long list of heartbreaks, he entwined his fingers with Heather's and headed into the night.

FIVE

UNCERTAIN SMILE

Trena Moretti P @trenamoretti—13s

Everything you need to know re the body linked to the Madison

Brooks case—TONIGHT on #InDepthWithTrenaMoretti

#WhereIsMadisonBrooks

Trena Moretti reread her latest tweet, then tucked her phone away and looked over her notes. The decision to film the show live had seemed like such a good idea at the time—but with the moment fast approaching, her stomach was a tangle of nerves.

Her career had started in print. But thanks to a move from DC to LA that coincided with Madison Brooks's disappearance and Trena's decision to focus on it, she'd become the face America trusted most when it came to all things Madison. In light of the recent developments, her producers had agreed that a live broadcast was the best way to deliver the story and, more importantly, maintain their number one spot in the ratings.

She looked up from her script and gazed into the large mirror before her. From the outside, she looked good: calm, poised, professional, and perfectly put together. People often commented on what a natural she was. Plenty of journalists longed to make the leap to the higher-paying TV spots, but few had the right combination of smarts, chops, and charisma to pull it off. Trena was one of the lucky ones blessed with the innate gift to look into a camera and convincingly relate a story, no matter how banal, that people could not turn away from.

Credibility. Integrity. Authority. They were all qualities she'd worked hard to maintain, and in her line of work she'd be nothing without them. But at the moment, Trena was feeling shaky and unsure. With the cameras set to roll soon, that just wouldn't do.

She dropped her notes to her lap, placed her right hand to her belly, closed her eyes, and forced herself to take a series of deep, calming breaths. It was an old trick she'd learned as a child from her beloved Noni Moretti, back when Noni's attempts to teach Trena to meditate had failed to catch on.

As a kid, the idea of stopping her thoughts seemed both

ridiculous and impossible. But now, haunted by the troubling images that lurked in the darkest recesses of her brain, Trena couldn't help but wish she'd tried a little harder back then.

Usually, a nice long run was all it took to shed her anxiety. But the six miles she'd logged on the treadmill just a few hours earlier hadn't done much to calm her.

She returned to the script. She'd memorized every word, but Trena was a perfectionist who left nothing to chance, and so she dove in once more.

ANNOUNCER: Tonight—on our special live edition, catch the latest, up-to-the-minute news on the body found in Joshua Tree and its connection to the disappearance of Hollywood A-lister Madison Brooks, on *In-Depth with Trena Moretti.*

[Cut to clips of the shallow grave in Joshua Tree surrounded by crime scene tape, a billboard featuring Madison Books, an aerial view of Hollywood Boulevard, the Night for Night facade, and the mug shots of Aster Amirpour, Layla Harrison, Tommy Phillips, and Ryan Hawthorne]

TRENA MORETTI: Good evening and welcome to *In-Depth.* Tonight, we delve deeper into the investigation of Madison Brooks's disappearance, and the four teens recently arrested for their alleged involvement. We'll hear from the suspect's friends:

SAFI NASSERI (from video): I've known Aster for as long as I can remember. We even had those best-friends necklaces at one point, you know those hearts that are cracked down the middle? Aster was obsessed with Madison. She even kept a file on her, filled with pictures and articles and stuff. I didn't think much of it at the time, but now . . . (she visibly shivers). Once she started promoting Night for Night, she totally changed. She started seeing Ryan Hawthorne, and it seemed like she was trying to claim Madison's life. That's also about the time we stopped hanging out, and I'm glad I got away when I did. To think I was best friends with a possible murderer . . . (closes her eyes and shakes her head). The whole thing gives me the creeps.

AMY STREETER (from video): I dated Tommy Phillips back in high school. What's to say? He was cute, talented, and a total player who only cares about himself and never stops to think about the sort of heartbreak he causes. Without any warning whatsoever, he told me he was moving to LA, and then, less than twenty-four hours later, he was gone. He acted like he was too good for our small town. (Rolls her eyes.) Nothing about him would surprise me.

TRENA MORETTI: We'll hear from rising young star Heather Rollins, who will be live in our studio. Heather was a close friend of Madison's and knows all the suspects involved.

[Clips from Heather Rollins's sultry photo shoot with up-and-comer and former boyfriend of Layla Harrison, Mateo Luna]

TRENA MORETTI: And of course, at the center of it all, Ira Redman, the enigmatic owner of the Unrivaled brand, which includes a recently launched tequila label, along with a string of exclusive nightclubs that Madison was known to frequent. Ira is also rumored to be financing Aster Amirpour's legal defense team.

IRA REDMAN (from video): Listen—don't be so quick to judge here. These are good, hardworking kids with a healthy entrepreneurial spirit. But instead of being lauded for their endeavors, they're being demonized for having big dreams. Sure they're ambitious and willing to do what it takes. So what? That doesn't make them criminals! This is America—it's part of our national

DNA to yearn for a bigger, better life. Since when did that become illegal?

TRENA MORETTI: We'll also discuss the explosive journal entry posted just hours ago on Layla Harrison's Beautiful Idols blog, which got the whole world talking. As you remember, Layla was one of the four teens recently arrested in Joshua Tree for her alleged connection to Madison's disappearance. Moments after being freed from jail earlier today, the incendiary post, titled "Through the Looking Glass," appeared on her site. Was it an act of revenge? Only Layla knows. If the words truly are Madison's, then it leaves us to question everything we ever thought we knew about the young star. If not, then it's a risky move on Ms. Harrison's part that could be met with serious legal action. Stay with us, as we keep you updated on the latest developments regarding the disappearance of Madison Brooks on tonight's special live edition of *In-Depth with Trena Moretti*.

[COMMERCIAL BREAK]
[*In-Depth* logo]

It was all there. Nothing Trena didn't already know. Of course, Heather was a wild card, since there was no way to guess how their on-air interview would go.

Then again, Heather had so far proved herself to be a consummate pro who seemed eager to attach herself to the scandal, if for no other reason than to build her own platform. Trena frowned at the thought until she realized she'd done the same thing. Standing on another's back for a faster rise to the top was the very foundation Hollywood was built on.

She'd tried to get Mateo, but he'd been quick to deny her request. It was too bad. With his laid-back vibe and his obvious disdain for the very spotlight that seemed to adore him, he would've made a perfect addition. Still, Trena hadn't completely surrendered. There was always the possibility of filming a segment on childhood leukemia. She'd already put out feelers to the hospital that was treating Mateo's little sister. A big donation to accompany it just might make for an offer he wouldn't refuse.

Ira had claimed he was too busy to provide anything more than a video clip, but Trena didn't buy it. Ira was never one to turn down a chance at free publicity. It was as though he was trying to distance himself from the very scandal he'd used to propel his own brand. It didn't make sense.

She reached for her phone and tried once again to reach Layla. Trena hoped she had a good reason for making that blog post, because if not, she'd soon be facing serious consequences. When Layla's phone went straight to voice mail,

Trena left another message, her third that day. She was about to review her script one final time when her assistant, Priya, opened the door a crack, poked her head in, and said, "You have a visitor."

Assuming it was one of the producers, Trena tossed the script onto the table and ran a hand over her wild mane of bronze curls. It was important to look her absolute best, both on and off camera.

"Been a while."

The mere sound of his voice was enough to make Trena freeze. Turning slowly, she watched James advance as Priya shut the door behind him.

"You don't write. You don't call. Not even so much as a text." He stood before her, all dark gleaming skin and well-honed muscles. His brown eyes flashed as his lips slid into a wide feral grin.

"I have to be on camera soon." Trena rose to her feet and brushed a hand down the front of her dress, straightening the seams in a way that enhanced her lean curves. She might not trust him, but she was still vain enough to want to impress him.

James peeked at his shiny gold Rolex. "In exactly six minutes," he said. "Give or take."

"What're you doing here?" Trena fussed with the random items strewn across her dressing table, trying to appear unconcerned about being alone in a room with him.

"I thought I'd try for a better ending. I got a strange vibe last time we said good-bye."

It was then that Trena noticed he clutched a long, rectangular box behind him.

She swallowed hard, fought to compose herself. Last time she'd received a similar package before a show, it contained a threatening message that continued to haunt her.

"Wow, you're a tough one." He laughed softly when she hesitated to take it. "You're really going to make me earn my way back, aren't you? Tell you what—I'm up for the challenge. But can't a guy at least give you flowers?"

As long as they have their heads. She bit back the words and, with a shaky hand, accepted the package and opened the box.

"Did someone die?" She glanced in dismay between the dozen long-stemmed white roses and James.

"What? No!" He looked perplexed. "The woman behind the counter told me they stood for new beginnings."

Or endings. Trena held the box, unsure how to proceed. James was sexy, mysterious, and quite possibly dangerous. Last time she'd seen him, she felt lucky to have gotten away. But maybe she'd overreacted. Maybe the flowers really did have two meanings.

The list of reasons to keep him at bay was seemingly endless, and yet she found herself saying, "Is that what this is, an offer for a fresh start?"

James pressed his lips together and hitched his shoulders high.

"I have a show to do." She kept her voice firm, wanting him to think she remained in control. That his mere presence hadn't set off her alarms.

James consulted his watch. "In three minutes," he said. "Which allows you just enough time to answer my question."

Trena turned away and placed the roses on the dressing room table. Then she stalled for as long as she could under the guise of checking her makeup.

"I was hoping maybe we could meet up after the show? Grab a late bite and just talk?"

She knew she should decline, and yet there was a good chance James had insider knowledge about the Madison case, that he knew the kind of things that could really cement her standing as a big-time journalist. In the interest of furthering her career, she figured she might as well. . . .

"What did you make of Layla's blog entry? You think it's legit?" She trained her focus on James, watching for even the slightest hint of deception.

He flashed his palms wide and said, "Nothing surprises me in this town."

She was about to follow up, when there was a knock at the door. "Two minutes!" someone called.

She looked at James. They could sort it out later. Maybe

over that late bite he'd offered. "You can hang out here." She kept the tone as professional as she could, considering the deeply interested look he gave her.

He grinned and settled into the same chair she'd just vacated. "Break a leg!" he said as she passed him.

Immediately, she turned and stared. He'd just recited the words from the threatening note she'd originally suspected him of sending.

"That's what they say before a performance, right? Break a leg?" He cocked his head and shot an appreciative glance over her body.

She pressed her lips tight and made for the door. She'd just reached the threshold when her phone chimed with an incoming text, and she glanced over her shoulder at James. Had he sent it? She could've sworn she heard that telltale *swoosh* seconds before she'd received it.

He lifted his gaze to meet hers and flashed a flirtatious grin that could mean just about anything.

Was James helping her or harming her? She couldn't be sure. But she knew better than to read too much into his response until she could gather enough evidence to prove either way. Without another thought, she left him alone in the room and went in search of Priya.

"You okay?" Priya reached an arm toward her, but at the last second, quickly pulled away.

"I need them to run that clip with the nurse at Eileen

Banks's convalescent home," Trena said, her voice a bit shaky from her encounter with James. "Tell them to cut the clip of Ira if they're worried about time."

Ira wouldn't like it, but too bad. That was what he got for refusing a live interview in order to manipulate her into doing a piece on his empire. He'd get his segment, but for tonight, he was on the cutting room floor.

"Did something happen?" Priya seemed surprised by the change.

Trena considered sharing the text, which included an image of Madison's birth certificate, revealing her real name, as well as the true identities of her parents. After all, it was Priya who'd discovered that Madison, aka MaryDella, had lived with Paul Banks's mother, Eileen Banks, between the time Madison lost her parents in the fire and when she moved in with her adoptive family.

Paul had been the first on the scene when Madison's childhood home burst into flames, ultimately claiming the lives of her parents. He'd been there to help when Madison moved to LA, and he'd been looking out for her every day since. Paul had been impossible to track down. They didn't call him the Ghost for nothing. But Trena was convinced that if anyone knew where Madison was, it was him. She just needed to find him.

She studied Priya. Something about her covetous expression convinced Trena to hold back. Let her watch the show and learn the same way as everyone else.

"Just see that it's done!" she called over her shoulder.

She had a show to shoot. And thanks to that text, she had no doubt there was an Emmy waiting in her future.

SIX

WAITING ON THE WORLD TO CHANGE

Tommy Phillips stood in the entry of his luxury apartment and looked all around. After nearly a week in jail, he could hardly believe his good fortune to land in such a place. But with the way things were going, he couldn't help but wonder how long he'd get to stay.

He grabbed a beer from the fridge and headed out to the balcony, where he pressed against the glass banister and gazed at the flickering LA skyline beyond. For most of his life he'd dreamed of that view. He'd driven all the way from Oklahoma in a piece-of-shit car with a cracked windshield in pursuit of it. Just another small-town hotshot with dreams of making it big—yet another LA cliché to add to the heap.

Funny how the city ended up being everything he'd

thought, and nothing like he'd hoped.

When he first arrived, he got the impression that while LA wasn't exactly welcoming, it was still full of possibility for those who worked hard and refused to give up.

Now it reminded him of one of those flaky internet life coaches the city churned out by the dozen. The kind who seduced you into confessing your wildest dreams, only to sell them back to you at a price you never saw coming.

Tommy had dreamed of fame and he'd scored. There wasn't a tabloid out there that hadn't featured his face on the cover. As the last person to see and kiss Madison, he'd been the headline on trash rags all over the world, though his record label warned that as a walking, talking PR crisis, they needed to find a way to cut through the noise and persuade people to give him a chance.

Malina had even dreamed up a strategy she laughingly referred to as Project Ghost. The idea was to pay a big-name director to create a video scored by one of Tommy's songs without ever actually featuring Tommy. The video would be so beautiful, the song so irresistible, it would immediately go viral and only later, after it had hit number one on iTunes, would they reveal that Tommy was the voice behind it.

It sounded gimmicky, disingenuous, and Tommy instinctively hated everything about it.

But he also realized that in the current climate, it might

be the only way he'd ever get a fair shot.

He closed his eyes and took a long swig of beer. The last few days had been rough. He'd used his one phone call to talk to his mom, wanting her to learn the bad news from him instead of one of her tabloid-reading friends. It was the toughest call he'd ever made. She'd spent most of it crying and pleading with him to come home.

"I told you not to work for Ira Redman," she'd said, her voice choked with tears.

Tommy had gripped the phone tightly, waiting for her to finally put a reason to the refrain she'd been repeating since he moved to LA. To finally admit that the man she pretended was his father didn't exist, though his real dad, Ira Redman, did.

The long, dark hours in jail had been spent wondering where he'd be if Ira Redman had never walked into Farrington's Guitar, spotted him behind the counter, and passed him the flyer advertising the Unrivaled Nightlife contest. He guessed he would still have the job, since Ira was a big part of why he'd lost it. He would've struggled to get gigs, meet a girl he could truly connect with, and make friends in a new city that wasn't nearly as friendly or inclusive as it pretended to be.

Despite Tommy's growing list of regrets, despite everything bad that had happened to him because of his involvement in Ira's competition, it had also played an integral role in propelling him out of his former shithole apartment and into his current luxurious digs.

It was also largely responsible for scoring him the deal with Elixir Records. Malina might complain about his notoriety being a burden, but Tommy suspected his infamy was one of the main reasons she'd signed him.

And, of course, if it weren't for Ira and the contest, Tommy probably never would've met Layla.

Still, there was no denying Tommy was better off now than he had been at the start of the summer.

He'd arrived in LA with two goals—become a rock star, and finally confront the dad who didn't even know he existed.

If he ended up in jail for a crime he didn't commit, neither of those things would happen.

And if it turned out his dad was responsible for landing him in prison, well, what then?

The more Tommy thought about it, the more he grew convinced Ira was somehow involved.

Layla had received a stream of messages—strangely worded rhymes—always accompanied with a creepy cartoon cat suffering a multitude of injuries: black eyes, gunshot wounds to the head. There was even one that featured a noose around its neck.

Tommy had seen that same cartoon cat on a piece of paper in Ira's office. The paper had slid off his desk and fallen to the floor, but before Tommy could get a closer look, Ira had stepped on the image, effectively hiding it from view.

Had he done so on purpose?

Possibly.

Probably.

Worst-case scenario: his dad was a murderer.

Second-worst-case scenario: his dad had set them all up so he could get tons of PR for his clubs.

Either way, it didn't look good.

Tommy took one last look at the view and headed inside. His friends didn't know about his connection to Ira, and he planned to keep it that way.

If a miracle was going to save them, then it would have to be one of their own making.

From inside his pocket, his phone chimed with an incoming text, and he immediately thought of Layla. He'd wanted to contact her the second he was sprung from jail, but he needed time to collect himself.

He and Layla had a deal. No strings. No complications. As though it were really that easy. But just the thought of her beautiful face with her lovely gray-blue eyes and inviting lips had him longing to kiss her.

He shook free of the thought and read the screen.

The battery was low. It could die at any second. But the text wasn't from Layla. It came from Malina.

I know you're out. We'll talk soon. For now, get some rest. You have an interview in 2 days (Tues) w/Rolling Stone. LMK if u want me to send someone from our team to join you. If not, call me the second it's over. Details TK.

Tommy knew that *someone from our team* was code for babysitter. Clearly Malina didn't trust his ability to handle an important interview. He needed to prove he could do it on his own. His whole life he'd dreamed of a piece in *Rolling Stone*. Actually, he'd dreamed of landing the cover, but he'd take what he could get. Besides, he had two days to rest up and get his head together.

Got it. No worries. Talk soon.

He sent the reply and was in search of a phone charger when his doorbell rang.

Again, his first thought was Layla. Maybe she'd stopped by?

He opened the door to find a package placed just outside. His name was typed on a label affixed to the front, but there was no return address, and whoever had left it was already gone.

A second envelope tucked inside contained a series of black-and-white photos. The images were grainy, clearly taken from a surveillance camera, though there was no mistaking that the subject was Tommy.

What the—?

He gaped in disbelief. The photos were of him standing

outside Night for Night. The time and date stamp showed they were taken the night Madison had gone missing, moments after she'd entered the building.

The photos slipped through his fingers as a wave of panic washed over him. It wasn't what it looked like. He had only followed her because she'd accidentally left her keys with him and he wanted to return them and make sure she was okay. He'd never even made it inside.

Up until that moment, Tommy had been sure Ira was the only one who'd known about it. He'd even promised Tommy he'd erased the images in a move to protect him.

At the time, Tommy had felt conflicted. He was grateful Ira had spared him the grief of Detective Larsen ever learning of the surveillance footage, and outraged that Ira could think Tommy capable of harming anyone, much less Madison.

He swiped a trembling hand through his hair and fought to steady his breath. His pulse raced, his body sheened with sweat. He felt like a hunted animal, like he was on the verge of a full-blown panic attack. Clearly Ira hadn't really handled it, and if there were more photos out there . . .

Shit! Angrily, he paced the room. He was out of jail. He had an interview with *Rolling Stone* lined up, and now *this*. Just when things were finally looking up, the universe slapped him back down with something new to worry about.

He was scooping the photos into a pile when he noticed a note scrawled on the back of one of the pictures.

> Only a few of us know these exist
> They were taken moments after you and Madison kissed
> It looks as though you could be to blame
> But you'll have nothing to fear if you agree to my game
> The rules are easy to abide
> If you follow them, you'll have nothing to hide
> Though I warn you not to let on to your friends
> If you do, they'll meet some very sad ends
> Best if you do as I say
> Otherwise there will be hell to pay.

The words were written in a thick, black felt marker. No cartoon cat or curlicue scrawl like on the notes Layla had received, but the tone was similar, and he knew he'd better take it seriously. Whoever had sent it had considerable power and reach, which only convinced Tommy that Ira was behind it.

Ira was a world-class manipulator and control freak. A game like this was right up his alley. This was his way of letting Tommy know he was willing to protect him, but only if Tommy did what he wanted. Clearly Ira had to be stopped before this went any further.

Still, Tommy needed to proceed with care. If Ira so

much as sensed Tommy was onto him, he wouldn't hesitate to make good on his word. Ira was way more powerful, connected, and immoral than Tommy and his friends combined.

For now, Tommy would play along, which meant steering clear of Layla. As much as he missed her, he wouldn't risk putting her in any more danger than she already was.

He carried the pile of photos to the fireplace and spread them over the bed of fireglass. Then he stood back, clicked the remote, and watched the flames shoot up, licking away at the edges, leaving nothing but ashes behind.

SEVEN

BLUE AIN'T YOUR COLOR

Compared to the last several weeks of her life, her new room with its single brass daybed, wall-to-wall shag carpeting, and en suite bathroom with the rust-stained tub and Pepto-Bismol pink tiles was nothing but luxury.

Still, Madison couldn't wait to break free.

Paul had a plan; a lead even. According to him, he was working hard on tracking it down and would divulge all the details if and when it panned out.

But Madison was tired of depending on Paul. It was his job to protect her from the very thing that had happened. She'd paid him a lot of money over the years to handle every aspect of her security detail, and her trust had never once wavered. She'd actually felt lucky to have the best in the business at her disposal. And yet, he'd gone and failed her in the worst way imaginable. She was far from healed, but she would no longer surrender her will.

She scowled at her ankle. Paul swore she was on the mend, but to her mind, it wasn't healing quickly enough. She missed her mobility, missed her luxurious home with its fantasy closet and infinity pool. She wondered idly what had become of it.

Were the gardeners still coming once a week to trim the rosebushes that lined the long drive?

Was the pool man keeping the saltwater levels properly maintained?

Or was it wasting away from neglect—becoming decrepit and overrun with weeds and fallen palm fronds languishing in the deep end?

And then there was Blue. Paul had assured her that her assistant, Emily, was looking after him, but the news didn't sit well with Madison.

Madison looked at Paul and said, "I want my dog back."

It wasn't the first time she'd said it, though it was the first time she'd voiced it in a way that was more insistent than whiny.

Paul lowered his phone and shot her a considering look.

"And don't even try to deny me. I'm in no mood to listen to your endless list of excuses for why I can't have him. No one loves him like I do, and I'm sure he misses me as much as I miss him. I want you to get him."

It may have been a bit melodramatic, but Madison set her face in a way that proved she'd meant every word. Her rescue mutt Blue was everything to her. Her dog, along with Paul, were the only things that connected her to her true self—the girl she kept hidden—the one no one would guess at. Which explained the nagging guilt she felt over the way she was using him.

Paul considered the request. "About that, I've been thinking . . ."

Madison sat up straighter, watching as he swiped a meaty hand across his chin. At first sight, he resembled an ordinary schlump stuck in a boring midlevel job. The kind of guy who after yet another long, soul-sucking day at the office returned home to a crappy apartment and an indifferent cat, only to eat a microwaved dinner in front of the TV. Though the quilt of scars crisscrossing his knuckles hinted at a much darker existence.

"Maybe you're right."

Madison froze, afraid to so much as move lest he sense her real reason for asking. As good as she was at reading him, he was far better at reading her.

"I'd like to stay put until you're back on your feet. So as long as you promise to stay out of sight, I can't see why you shouldn't be reunited with Blue."

"Seriously?" Even though she had other motives for asking, the thought of seeing her scraggly mutt brought tears to her eyes. Though sadly, the reunion would have to wait. Madison had more urgent matters to deal with. "Because if you're not serious, if you're just trying to—"

Paul raised a hand to silence her. "You have my word. I was thinking I'd pay Emily a visit anyway. May as well return with Blue."

"Emily?" Madison frowned at the mention of her assistant's name. "I thought you said you didn't know where she was." Her voice rose with suspicion.

"I didn't. She went AWOL for a bit. But I just heard she landed a new assistant gig."

Madison was in no mood for the hesitation she sensed in his reply. "Yeah, with who?" She studied him shrewdly.

"Heather Rollins."

Madison started, her face taking a comic turn with popping eyes and a dramatically dropped jaw. If she'd tried that on a film set, any director worth his salt would yell *Cut!* and pull her aside to talk. But in real life, she truly was shocked. "Seriously. Emily is working for Heather?" She shook her head. Most of the world considered her dead, and yet Heather was still competing against a ghost, trying to claim bits of Madison's life for her own.

Once upon a time, they'd been friends, though it didn't take long to notice how Heather was always trying to best Madison by going after the same parts, the same clothes, the same agent, the same boys—what a bore. Of course Heather never actually attained any of those things, and Madison had chosen to ignore her lame attempts, even felt sorry for her. How exhausting it must be to always yearn for the peak when the spot was clearly reserved for someone more deserving. It wasn't long before Madison grew tired of her games and cut Heather off.

And now Heather was poised to claim the space that had once belonged to Madison. She had Emily, access to Blue . . . it stung in a way Madison refused to tolerate.

"I want my dog. Now." Madison fixed her gaze on Paul. "I don't want her anywhere near Blue."

The thought of Heather so much as petting Blue was intolerable. Then again, Blue had much higher standards and probably wouldn't allow it. He'd never learned to like Ryan, and always used to growl whenever he came around. Blue was a dog of great discernment. The thought brought a fleeting smile to Madison's face.

"Rumor has it Heather is now dating Mateo Luna."

Madison watched as Paul slipped a tweed blazer over his pale blue button-down shirt. Outside, the temperature soared to the triple digits, and yet Paul dressed like he was off to the bank to ask for a loan.

"Am I supposed to know who that is?" Madison frowned. She was mainly surprised Heather wasn't dating

Ryan Hawthorne. It would only make sense.

"Mateo used to date Layla Harrison, who is now dating Tommy Phillips."

Madison turned the information around in her head. It was interesting, in a minor, D-list, gossipy sort of way. But it hardly seemed worthy of discussion. Was Paul interested in this stuff? Because Madison no longer was.

"Heard she's working on getting him a part on her new show."

"How do you know all this?" Madison observed him from under a skeptical brow.

"It's my job to keep abreast of anything connected to you. However tangentially."

Madison cocked her head and gathered her hair into her fist. "Cable or network?"

Paul looked at her.

"The show—is it on cable or network?"

Madison starred in movies—big-budget Hollywood movies. She had no time for small-screen nonsense. And yet, it was no secret that the paradigm had shifted, and now loads of A-list actresses were clamoring for the good, juicy roles that the smarter TV shows offered.

Was it possible Heather had scored such a role?

One that might've gone to Madison had she not been abducted?

She was seriously working herself into an agitated state

and was growing increasingly annoyed with the way Paul was hedging the answer. It was a simple question. What the hell was he up to?

When she caught his amused expression, she flushed with shame. Yep, he could read her like a book. Heather wasn't the only one who got competitive. His look reminded her as much.

"Network," he said, chasing it with the kind of teeth-baring grin he rarely indulged in.

Madison rolled her eyes and mumbled unintelligibly under her breath. She knew she was acting awful and spoiled, but she hated the way her life was on hold and seemingly no longer hers to control. Still, it was a relief to know Heather hadn't scored a big, splashy cable gig. If nothing else, it assured Madison that she hadn't fallen too far behind while she'd been off the radar.

"So, back to Blue." She adopted a steadier, more serious tone. "How soon can I see him?"

The question was more loaded than it seemed on the surface. Paul kept a number of safe houses stashed in remote areas of California and beyond, including a few in and around LA. On the drive over, he'd made her hide beneath a blanket in the back, thereby prohibiting any chance she might've had to see where they were going. From the moment they'd arrived, she wasn't allowed out-side. She hoped his answer would provide some insight into their general whereabouts.

If Blue was with Emily and Emily was working for Heather, then that meant Blue was in LA. The amount of time it would take Paul to make the round trip might clue her in as to how far away they currently were.

"I have a few other things to take care of first, so it might be a while."

That didn't help.

"Though I promise to have you two reunited by the end of the day."

Madison fought to maintain her composure. "That would be great, really great." She cringed a little when she said it. It sounded false and ingratiating, but Paul didn't seem to notice. "Just as long as you're sure you can pull it off without raising suspicion."

Paul lifted a brow, and Madison fell silent. Not once since she'd known him had he ever had a problem getting what he wanted.

Madison rubbed her fingers over the burn scar on the inside of her arm. There was a new scar just above it, from where the tracker had been torn from her flesh. Whoever had done it had clumsily stitched her up again. So by the time Paul had found her, an infection was setting in. Luckily, Paul knew his way around such things and got her cleaned up and restitched. He must've done a good job, since all her various wounds seemed to be healing a lot faster than her ankle was.

The tracker had wound up next to a body so ravaged by coyotes that everyone had at first mistaken it for hers. Apparently, Layla, Tommy, Aster, and Ryan had been out looking for her. How funny it would be when she managed to track them down first.

"You going to be okay, staying here alone?"

Madison struggled to a sitting position, making it appear so much harder, and much more painful, than it actually was.

"I'll be fine." She spoke through gritted teeth. "But maybe you can give me another pill?"

Paul rubbed at his chin, looking conflicted. "They're highly addictive."

Madison groaned. "Fine, then. Leave me alone for hours on end with nothing to do but think about how much pain I'm in so I can relive all the terrible things I've been through."

Without a word, he brought her two tablets and a tall glass of water. "Four hours between these. No sooner."

"You're going to be gone that long?"

Where the hell were they?

"Probably not," he said. "But just in case."

She placed the tablet onto her tongue and went through the motions of pretending to swallow.

When he finally grabbed his laptop, pocketed his keys,

and headed out the front door, Madison reached for her crutches and rushed toward the window, where she watched through the curtains as the tires crunched over the gravel and the car backed down the drive. Once he'd pulled onto the unpaved road and driven out of sight, Madison hurriedly changed into one of the disguises Paul had brought along in the event they needed to go out in public.

With her wig adjusted and makeup in place, Madison stood before a mirror and searched her reflection. She had no idea if it would work, but she was committed to trying.

She made for the safe and punched in the code. All that time pretending to sleep had paid off. Paul grew careless when he assumed no one was watching, making the combination easy to crack. Inside, just as she'd hoped, she found an envelope stuffed thick with cash, the key to the old Jeep he used for local errands and stored in the shed, a burner phone, and a gun.

She reached for the pistol and curled her fingers around the grip. The weapon felt big, weighty, but reassuring all the same. She lifted her arm, aimed the barrel toward the opposite wall, and feigned pulling the trigger. Thanks to Paul's training, she was more than capable of handling it. Madison was far more adept than most people realized when it came to such things.

She was just securing the money and gun into her bag

when she noticed a plastic ID card hidden under a stack of fake passports.

It was from West Virginia, and at first she wondered if it might be her own, or even Paul's.

But as soon as she flipped it over and saw the face and name labeled on the front, she had all the proof she needed to know she'd been right all along. Paul had been lying when he claimed he didn't know the first thing about the man he'd murdered.

Madison studied the man's face and realized she'd never really forgotten him. What memory—perhaps in an effort to protect her—had relegated to a blur, was now staring right back at her.

This was the man who'd found her in the middle of Death Valley.

The one who'd dragged her back to his shack and tried to assault her, until Paul came along and planted a bullet in the side of his head.

Even on his ID, he looked dodgy, seedy, and yet vaguely familiar.

Although she didn't recognize the name, she knew better than to pretend the West Virginia ID was a coincidence.

Now more than ever she was convinced that everything that'd happened to her was directly related to what had gone down one decade before.

The past never really stayed buried.

And now hers was rising up to haunt her.

After memorizing the face and corresponding stats, she carefully placed the ID in the center of the safe, so Paul would know without question that Madison was onto him.

She struggled to her feet and took a few tentative steps. Her ankle was tender, but she was determined to manage without any sort of crutch, literal or figurative. Slinging her bag over her shoulder, she limped out the front door, more than ready to reenter the world.

EIGHT

LONG ROAD OUT OF EDEN

Layla pulled into the parking lot, slipped free of her car, and searched for Trena's dark red Lexus coupe as she found her way to the entrance of Lake Shrine. She'd made a point to arrive early, thinking it might give her the upper hand, or at least help to restore some of the confidence she'd recently lost.

From the moment she'd woken from her nap, she was inundated with texts, emails, and voice messages. It seemed every major news outlet had gotten wind of her blog post and wanted an interview.

Wearily, she deleted them all and gave her father strict instructions to hang up on anyone who dared to call and ask about it.

Trena's was the only call she'd returned, though she still

wasn't sure why, other than the fact that she and Trena shared a connection. They'd met the first day Madison was presumed missing, and as much as Layla had grown to distrust and resent Trena, there was a time, not long ago, when Layla had believed in, and even admired her.

Now she viewed Trena as yet another morally ambiguous sellout in a city that specialized in them.

Still, Layla was smart enough to know when she was in over her head. She hoped Trena could help her make sense of the mess she'd found herself in.

Layla walked along the sun-dappled pathway. With the swan-filled lake on one side, and a fragrant garden tangled with blooms on the other, she took in the golden lotus archway, the houseboat, the statue of Krishna playing his flute, and the sarcophagus said to contain Gandhi's ashes, and made her way past the windmill to the small, quiet cove with low marble benches.

As a kid, she'd visited frequently with her dad, but years had passed since she'd last made the trip. It was the perfect spot to meet, one of the few places in LA she could count on to remain paparazzi free.

"Well, this is unexpected."

Layla's heart sank when she saw that Trena had arrived early. Then again, Trena was always one step ahead. Resigned to the situation, Layla claimed the opposite bench.

"What surprises you most, the location or my willingness to meet?" Layla asked.

"Wasn't sure you'd show." A slight breeze kicked up and Layla watched as Trena lifted a hand in an attempt to keep her wild mane of bronze curls from blowing into her face.

"Why? Because you implicated me in a crime I didn't commit?" Layla was tired, but not too tired to call her out. But again, Trena was a pro and took the harsh words in stride.

"How you holding up?" She studied Layla with concern.

Layla sighed. There was no point in pretending she was any better off than she was. "I watched your show last night."

Trena arched a perfectly groomed brow. "You and a million other people." Though the words reeked of smug self-satisfaction, the delivery was the opposite. Trena was merely stating a fact.

"How'd you get ahold of Madison's birth certificate?" Layla figured Trena would hedge on the answer.

"My source came through." Trena lifted her slim shoulders and crossed her legs at the knee. "How'd you get ahold of Madison's diary? Or at least I hope that's her diary, because if not . . ." She left the sentence unfinished. When Layla didn't take the bait, Trena said, "Last time we met, you asked about libel laws. I'm guessing that's why?"

Layla gave a quick nod and waited for a hand-holding

couple to move well out of earshot. Maybe she'd made a mistake choosing such a public place to meet?

Sensing Layla's concern, Trena leaned toward her and lowered her voice to a whisper. "I guess your post means you've determined it is in fact Madison's?"

Layla screwed her eyes shut and slowly shook her head. When she opened them, she said, "My blog was hacked." One look at Trena's sardonic smirk was all it took for Layla to know her words had not landed the way she'd intended. "I mean, yeah. Obviously, the post was mine. I wrote the opening. Only I left it in my draft folder. I guess someone got tired of waiting."

"Who got tired?" Trena's voice took on a confessional tone.

"I don't know. I don't have a clue who's behind this. Some anonymous person has been sending me packages that contain stuff about Madison, mainly diary entries, and they always include a threatening note."

"What kind of threats?" The cautious look on Trena's face made Layla wonder if she knew more than she was letting on.

Layla shrugged. "Some that came true." She focused on the shiny Cartier watch encircling Trena's wrist. A recent upgrade from the Timex she'd once worn.

Trena caught Layla looking and flashed the diamond bezel in a way that caused the stones to catch the light and glint. "A gift from my producer," she said. "One of the perks of bringing in the highest ratings in the network's history."

"Guess your producer owes us all a watch then. Seeing as how you couldn't have told the story without the access we gave you."

Layla shot Trena a look that dared her to refute it, but Trena didn't so much as flinch. She just smiled seamlessly and said, "For the record, you're not the only one who's received threatening notes. It's why I was with Larsen the night you were arrested. I wanted there to be a record in case I went missing. I think you know how the night unraveled from there."

"Any suspects? Regarding the sender, I mean."

Trena bit her lip in a way that seemed false. Like she was trying to appear conflicted, when in fact, she felt just the opposite. "At first I thought it might be James." She worked her lip and paused. "You know, the bouncer at Night for Night?"

"And now?" Layla prompted, striving to keep her face free of suspicion. No point in letting Trena know she doubted her story.

Trena adopted a faraway gaze. Lifting her shoulders, she said, "Why don't you delete the blog post?"

"It's a little late, don't you think?"

"So what're you going to do?"

Layla sighed. "Whatever they tell me to."

"That doesn't sound like you."

"I can't even tell you how many death threats I've received. I feel unsafe just sitting here now."

"Some people are immune to facts," Trena said. "No matter what kind of proof you show them, they'll always default to their personal paranoia and bias. But while your fear is understandable, make no mistake: this is exactly the moment you decide who you're going to be. When your back's against the wall, that's when you discover what you're really made of."

Trena spoke in earnest, but Layla responded by rolling her eyes. "Pretty sure I saw that exact quote on an inspirational meme."

To her surprise, Trena laughed. "Listen, I think I know you well enough to know you don't sit around waiting for people to tell you what to do. You're smarter than most, and your vision cuts right through the bullshit. Don't deny that part of yourself—use it! Now more than ever, you've got to put your strengths to work so you can clear your name. As a journalist, your credibility depends on your reputation. You lose the trust of the people, you lose everything."

Layla grew quiet, allowing the words to sink in. "It's not just the notes and the death threats. Whoever's behind this always knows right where to find me. They have access to everything."

"So, who has direct access to your life outside of Aster, Tommy, and Ryan?"

"My dad." Layla shrugged. "Mateo—or at least he used to. Ira." Her gaze leveled on Trena's.

"So perhaps we should take a closer look at some of them."

"Aster, Tommy, and Ryan were arrested too."

"And what about Mateo? Where was he?"

"He wasn't there."

"But he knew you were going?"

"Forget Mateo," Layla snapped, surprising herself. "Not because of any lingering feelings for him, but . . ." Before she could finish, Trena shot her a knowing look that annoyed Layla to no end. "Just because a relationship ends, doesn't mean—" She caught herself before she could go any further. Overexplaining was only making it worse. "Whatever, just . . . no."

"That leaves Ira. Also, your dad, but let's just stick with Ira."

It wasn't like Layla hadn't always considered Ira a suspect, but she had no idea where to begin.

"Problem is, I haven't been able to uncover much of anything. Certainly no ties to West Virginia, though there was a stint in Oklahoma that for some reason he keeps under wraps."

"Oklahoma?" Layla jerked to attention.

"He went to university there, though not for long. It was right before he moved to LA."

"Do you know when that was?" Layla fought to keep her cool and seem only mildly interested.

"Nearly two decades ago, but there's no connection to Madison. Thing is, if Ira is behind this, which I really believe he could be, then there's got to be a connection somewhere, something that links him to Madison. So far, all I've managed to uncover is the stuff you already know. . . ."

Trena went on to list Madison's lies. How she wasn't really a tragic yet well-bred East Coast prep, but rather little MaryDella Slocum, born and raised in West Virginia until the night her parents mysteriously died in a fire and she was reborn as Madison.

Layla tuned her out. She'd heard it all before. It was Ira's stint in Oklahoma that intrigued her the most.

Tommy was from Oklahoma. And though Trena had been vague about the dates, Tommy was eighteen, soon to be nineteen. Ira having been there around two decades ago gave new insight into something that had always bothered her, a sort of nagging truth she could never quite grasp.

Tommy possessed an uncanny understanding of Ira's motivations. Once, when Layla questioned him, Tommy had been quick to dismiss it, claiming he simply liked to know who he worked for.

At the time, Layla let it pass. But now, if what Trena said was true, then Layla was sure Ira Redman was Tommy's father.

"I found a news report claiming two dead and two injured in that fire. Madison burned her arm, as we all know, but I got the impression the article wasn't referring to her. . . ." Trena droned on while Layla pretended to listen. Truth was, her mind was in a whirl.

Tommy Phillips was Ira Redman's son!

The more Layla thought about it, the more it made sense.

Their nearly identical navy-blue eyes only served to seal it.

Layla looked at Trena, wondering if she should tell her.

"Before MaryDella was adopted, she lived with Eileen Banks, Paul Banks's mother." Trena's voice was a whisper. "Paul was first on the scene the night of the fire. He was head of the drug task force unit before he abruptly quit and moved to LA."

If Ira was somehow behind it, and Tommy was involved, did that mean Tommy was part of it too?

Layla shivered at the thought, causing Trena to misread her reaction. "I know," she said. "It's like the pieces of the puzzle are beginning to take shape; only the inside is still missing, so we can't yet determine the face."

Layla decided to keep the revelation to herself. Information was power, and she'd yet to meet the person who could keep a secret as potentially explosive as that.

She pushed her thoughts aside and focused on Trena.

"In the diary entry, she mentioned she owes her life to P," Trena said. "Clearly P stands for Paul. I've been unable to locate him, which led me to believe the body found in Joshua Tree was his."

Layla's gaze narrowed.

"LAPD's holding a press conference today—they identified the body." She paused dramatically, as though imagining the at-home audience leaning closer to their TV screens.

Layla found it extremely annoying.

With a shake of her curls, Trena said, "Not him."

Just like that, Layla felt a block of tension dissolve. Paul had served her a restraining order demanding she stay clear of Madison. It was a connection Layla couldn't afford. Larsen would read it as motive. "Who is it?" she asked.

"Kevin O'Dell."

The name meant nothing to Layla.

"A white male, forty-one years old, with an extensive criminal record. All petty crime, nothing that points to kidnapping or murder."

"Then why was Madison's tracker found with his body?"

Trena shrugged. "I'm sure he's a suspect. But I also

heard the body was purposely dumped there long before you arrived, so there's a good chance he'll be cleared. If you ask me, someone set the scene, then lured you there on purpose." She glanced over her shoulder, as though she didn't quite trust her surroundings. "We need to find Paul. He'll lead us to Madison."

"You think he kidnapped her?"

Without hesitation, Trena said, "Technically, I guess he could have, but I doubt it. I think he's protecting her."

"What makes you say that?"

Trena hooked a stray curl behind her ear. "He's spent a lifetime doing exactly that. Why stop now?"

"A thing does what a thing is known to do."

Trena quirked a brow.

"Something I read once. It stuck because it seemed simultaneously dumb and insightful. Anyway, in this case it applies. But don't you think we should look into this Kevin O'Dell person?"

Trena nodded. "That's how we find Paul. My gut tells me they're linked. And when my gut speaks, I've learned to listen." She gave a short laugh. "Well, most of the time."

"So why include me?"

"Because you're coming on my show, of course."

Layla sat with the news. She should've guessed as much. "And what do I get in return? Aside from being on your show, which isn't actually as valuable as you might think."

Trena's expression was patient. "Don't kid yourself," she said. "But if you need more, how about a letter of recommendation to the journalism school of your dreams?"

Layla paused a few beats to consider. "It's a start." She knew better than to display even the slightest hint of appreciation. "So, where to begin?"

"With Javen. Unless you know of a better hacker we can trust."

"I can't go near him. I won't take the chance, not after the text I received."

"Okay, so I'll deal with Javen. And you?"

Layla lifted her chin. "I'm going after Ira." She rose from the bench and straightened her skirt. Now that she'd decided, she was eager to leave. "Thanks for the talk," she said, surprising Trena with her sudden departure. "It really did help."

Before Trena could respond, Layla retraced her steps to her car. About to climb inside, she noticed a small envelope wedged under her windshield wiper, though of course there was no one around. Whoever was responsible for these things made a point of never being caught at the scene.

She ran a finger under the flap and retrieved a note written on high-quality card stock with a rhyme that read:

Seems like you've learned your lesson
So I won't keep you guessin'

Meeting with Trena puts you on the right track
Though she has never truly had your back
She's hiding a clue
And has no plans to reveal it to you
You can beat her at her own fame-seeking game
Or risk looking lame
It's up to you to discover
I shall remain undercover
If you make me proud
I will sing your praises out loud
If not
I will make sure you rot

Without hesitation, Layla slipped the note into her bag, reached for her phone, and called Javen.

NINE

CAKE BY THE OCEAN

Aster Amirpour gazed out the passenger-side window and stared longingly at the pretty postcard view of Laguna Beach. With its iconic lifeguard tower and crowded pedestrian walkways, everyone looked so happy and trouble free, skating, strolling, and surfing their way through another hot summer day.

At the start of the season, Aster would've defined luxury as a closet full of designer dresses, handbags, and shoes. It was only now that she understood just how misguided she'd been.

Real luxury, true luxury, was having the freedom to embrace a beautiful day relaxed and unbridled from the sort of threats she currently faced.

"I can't believe I don't visit more often." She sounded

distant and dreamy, like they were merely enjoying an afternoon drive, and not on a mission to unearth the sort of clues that could change everything.

"I blame the traffic. That long stretch of freeway is a formidable barrier no matter what time of day." Ryan exited Coast Highway and navigated a series of hilly, narrow paved streets, as Aster tracked the numbers on the haphazard row of mailboxes alongside the road.

The neighborhood was beachy and cute, pretty much what she expected to find in a small coastal town, though its quaint appearance was deceiving. Those small, charming cottages were known to consistently fetch an easy seven figures whenever one came on the market. The neighboring Tuscan-style two-stories fetched even more.

"You sure this is the right street?" Aster frowned.

"Camellia—that's a flower, right?"

Aster gave a distracted nod.

"But more importantly, are you sure you want to go through with this?"

Aster balked, surprised by his words. They'd driven all this way and he was still questioning her intentions? "Of course I'm going through with this! Unless you have a better idea?"

She didn't mean to sound so edgy, but luckily, Ryan took it in stride. "Actually, I have a lot of ideas. Not necessarily better ones, just—"

From out of nowhere, a band of skateboarding teens blazed down the middle of the street, immune to any oncoming traffic concerns.

Ryan swerved to avoid them, then rolled his eyes and groaned, "Kids."

Aster was about to laugh, when she noticed the house just up ahead. "That's it." She jabbed a finger in that direction. "Number fifty-eight. Quick, pull over!"

"Um, where?" Ryan glanced up and down the street, crowded with cars lining both sides.

"Right up there."

"That's someone's driveway."

"Well, I don't know." Aster was flustered. "Double-park— or drop me off while you figure it out."

She was antsy, shaky. Now that they'd arrived, she could barely contain her excitement. It was entirely possible the clue she needed most was right within reach.

"Hey—" Ryan reached for her arm in an attempt to keep her from jumping free of the still-moving car. "You can't just run in there. We need to come up with a convincing story."

Aster grumbled in frustration and reached for the door handle. "I have a convincing story. I told you all about it on the drive down."

"Okay, then we need a *more* convincing story." Ryan switched between the side-view mirror and his backup monitor as he struggled to parallel park without scraping his bumper against the Tesla in front of him or the vintage Porsche angled awkwardly behind. "Listen," he said. "I'm just . . ." He frowned at the small, well-kept cottage with its painted yellow shutters and wild English-style garden. "What exactly are you going to say? You can't just storm in there and start grilling her about Madison."

"Have a little faith." Aster spoke with more confidence than she felt. "I'm going in as an interested buyer. I'll admire her work, inquire about her process, and then I'll just happen to mention . . ." She paused.

"That you saw her work on a missing A-list actress's wall when you broke into her house?" Ryan righted the car and killed the ignition. "Call me crazy, but I highly advise against it."

Aster steeled herself against him. "I'm going to wing this. I'm going to march right up to that front door, ring the bell, and see where it leads. So if you'd rather stay behind and keep a lookout for . . ." She glanced around the safe and pretty neighborhood, which seemed impervious to any sort of immediate danger. "Whatever," she said, already tiring of the argument. "Just—are you in or are you out?"

Ryan sighed in a way that let her know he remained unconvinced. "We're both easily recognized. I doubt she'll be fooled."

"Well, at this point, I have nothing to lose." Agitated,

Aster popped out of the car, unsure if he'd follow.

Ryan raced to catch up and entwined his fingers with hers. "This okay?" He raised their joined hands. "Are we a couple?"

Aster stalled. Was he asking in regard to the story they were going to tell? Or did he mean on a more personal level? Although he'd invited her to stay with him last night, she'd ended up sleeping alone in his guest room.

His gaze glittered on hers, and she gave his hand a reassuring squeeze. Following the arrowed signs leading to the studio tucked behind the small cottage, they came across an older woman busily tending the garden.

"We're looking for Roland? Roland Jennings?" Aster said.

Gripping a pair of pink-handled clippers in her right hand, the woman slowly rose from a kneeling position and glanced between them. "I'm Roland."

Aster fought to hide her surprise. She wasn't sure why, but she'd expected the artist to be younger. In the bright sunlight, the woman appeared to be well into her sixties. But what she lacked in actual youth, she made up for in vibrant energy.

With her petite frame, short-cropped white hair, Breton-stripe T-shirt, and distressed skinny jeans, she reminded Aster of a chic combination of a female Andy Warhol and a more mature Jean Seberg.

"Do you have an appointment?" Roland anchored her dark sunglasses onto the top of her head and squinted against the glare of the sun.

Ryan looked worried, but Aster kept her composure and said. "I'm sorry, we didn't realize we needed one." Then, hoping to keep from being turned away, she was quick to add, "We just drove down from LA."

"Well, aren't you brave soldiers?" The woman's lips widened and lifted in a way that sent her blue eyes sparkling and lit up her whole face. "Are you on holiday?"

Aster glanced at Ryan, then quickly shook her head. Roland was talking to them like they were just a normal couple enjoying a beautiful late summer day. Like she hadn't seen a tabloid or turned on the news since last spring.

"Uh, no. Just a day trip," Aster said.

"Too bad." Roland placed a hand on her hip. "There are loads of interesting things to do and see. And here's a well-kept secret: our beaches are much prettier than yours."

"Can't argue with that." Ryan grinned, causing the woman to narrow her eyes and study him in a way that made Aster nervous.

"You a surfer?" Roland asked.

Ryan nodded, and Aster turned in surprise. She hadn't known that about Ryan. Then again, there was probably a long list of things she still had to learn. Or maybe he was just acting. It was impossible to tell.

"I try to catch a few sets every morning," the woman said. "If you stay, let me know. I'll let you in on some of my favorite spots." She set her clippers on a small mosaic-topped table and wiped her hands down the front of her jeans. "So what can I help you with?"

"We're interested in seeing your work," Aster said.

"Oh, well, that's easy. I'm currently showing at a gallery just south of here on Coast Highway."

"We'll be sure to check it out," Aster said. "But I heard you also allow private studio visits."

Roland nodded. "By appointment only."

"Oh, okay, well, we were hoping—"

Before she could finish, Ryan jumped in. "We were also interested in possibly commissioning a piece." He squeezed Aster's fingers, warning her not to say anything to the contrary.

Roland lingered in silence. Then, without a word, she turned on her heel and motioned for them to follow.

She opened a door and led them inside a small but surprisingly warm and cozy space. Large windows punctuated the walls, and generous-sized skylights allowed a stream of natural light to pour in. There was a small kitchenette off to the left with a mini-fridge, a poured concrete countertop, and some pretty customized cabinets below and overhead. And a charming tiled fireplace was tucked away in the corner, surrounded by some comfortable-looking chairs and a carved wooden table piled high with various art tomes.

Although the room was cheery and bright, to Aster's dismay there was no sign of either a camera or a darkroom.

Warily, she eyed the two easels in a far corner, both featuring similar works. One was a landscape of the beach at daybreak; the other a still life of an old, rustic shed with a surfboard propped alongside it.

While Aster was no expert when it came to art, the two pieces hardly seemed like the work of the woman responsible for the photos that hung on Madison's wall.

The note she'd received had specifically said: *There's an artist you need to meet / she lives on a flower-named street / she knows Madison's secret / so don't let her keep it.*

She and Ryan had been so sure they'd cracked the code, but had they somehow gotten it wrong?

Was there another piece of art by another artist they should've gone after instead?

"Everything okay?" Roland studied Aster's face. "You look a little uneasy."

Aster shook her head and forced her lips into a half-hearted grin.

"No, I'm good. It's just—"

Before she could finish, Roland headed for the electric teakettle she kept on the counter and pressed the switch. "I'm about to make some tea. Would you like to join me?"

Ryan was quick to agree. Aster nodded wordlessly.

"I'm sorry," Aster tried again. "But I thought you were a photographer. I didn't realize you were a painter."

She watched as Roland measured precise amounts of loose-leaf tea into a mesh infuser basket, which she then placed inside the ceramic pot.

"Can't I do both?"

"Of course. Absolutely. It's just . . ."

"I teach painting." Roland hooked a thumb toward the easels. "Those are works by my students." She turned to Aster with a smile. "But you wanted to commission a photograph, is that it?" Her gaze switched to Ryan. "Listen, you two are great-looking kids, but if it's head shots you want, I don't do that sort of work. Though I can recommend someone who does."

Aster stole a glance at Ryan. Was it possible the woman didn't recognize them? "No, no head shots. Nothing like that." Aster waved the thought away as Roland motioned for them to sit, and Aster sank so deep into the cushion it forced her knees to heave up awkwardly as she struggled to reposition herself.

"Don't waste your energy." Roland laughed. "That's a war you won't win. Those chairs are older than you, and they don't give up easily. Better just to surrender until it's time to leave." She grew silent as she waited for the water to boil and the tea to steep. Once it was ready, she placed a teacup in front of Aster and Ryan, claimed her own seat, and looked at them expectantly.

Aster sipped from her tea. Then, setting the cup aside, she said, "We're here because we saw some of your work."

Roland stared in a way that made Aster nervous.

"It was at a . . . at a friend's house. The pieces were really unique."

Roland warmed her hands with her cup but kept her gaze blank.

"They were photographs," she started, before Ryan stepped in.

"They were part of a series," he said.

Roland offered no clue as to whether she knew the photos he referred to.

"The pics were dark and edgy. Sort of domestic scene. You know, downtrodden living rooms, old, secondhand furniture . . ." He rubbed his lips together. "A shiny gun on a battered coffee table."

Roland rocked back in her seat and studied them at length. "Aw, yes," she said. "The trailer park series. I shot that a couple years ago."

Instinctively, Aster reached for the gold-and-diamond hamsa hand charm she'd once worn at her neck. Her fingers fumbled awkwardly against her bare collarbone when she remembered what had become of it. "That's it," she said, trying to contain her excitement. Was it her imagination, or was Roland suddenly acting cagey and suspicious? "I was really drawn to it. It had such a gritty, authentic feel."

Roland's face pinched, her gaze narrowed until her eyes were barely visible. "Funny." She sipped her tea and nodded toward Aster's expensive designer handbag. "Gritty is not something I'd think you'd be attracted to."

Aster stilled, unable to breathe.

"Then again . . ." Roland's face softened, adopting a more thoughtful expression. "Art often speaks to what lies within."

The sentiment was similar to what Layla had said when she first saw the pictures hanging on Madison's wall.

Aster shifted uncomfortably. "Um, anyway—" She cringed at the way her voice pitched. "I'd like to talk about the series. If you don't mind, that is."

Roland took another sip of tea. While she didn't seem thrilled with the conversation, she'd yet to turn them away. It was enough to convince Aster to continue.

"I was wondering if the pieces were commissioned or were they purchased from a gallery?"

"Is that really what you wanted to ask?"

Aster tried not to fidget, but it was hard not to react when Roland regarded her with an all-seeing gaze.

"Seems a bit silly to drive all this way when you can just ask your friend."

Aster gulped and looked searchingly at Ryan. She'd totally blown it. The only question left was how to make a quick but graceful getaway before Roland decided to alert the authorities.

"We can't ask her," Ryan said, which only deepened Aster's worry.

Roland turned to him with a patient face, like she had an entire afternoon to waste on such nonsense.

"The commission is for her," Ryan lied so easily Aster didn't know whether to be relieved or alarmed. "We know how much she loves your work, and so we thought we'd . . ."

Without a word, Roland rose from her seat and went to fumble in a drawer.

Aster took advantage of the moment to shoot Ryan her best *what the fuck* face.

Ryan shook his head as though there was no reason to worry. It was all part of his plan.

Roland returned with a folder she spread across her lap. Lowering a pair of reading glasses onto the bridge of her nose, she flipped through a messy pile of papers. "MaryDella," she said, as Aster froze and waited for more. "That's your friend, right? MaryDella Slocum?"

Aster sucked in a breath, then nodded vaguely.

Roland tossed a stack of pictures onto the table between them. Aster practically leaped from her seat to get at them.

"She was very specific. Definitely one of the most interesting clients I've ever worked with," Roland said.

"In what way?" Ryan asked, as Aster began to shuffle

through the deck of Polaroids.

"I hardly had to do anything. She'd prepared the entire set. She even handled the lighting. Not necessarily how I would've done it, but it was her commission, and she paid good money for it."

"Where was the shoot?"

Roland squinted as though sifting through a backlog of memories. "Bit outside of LA. Ojai area, if I remember correctly. An old trailer. One of those Airstreams, but vintage. It was off by itself, really remote. She claimed it belonged to her."

"What do you mean by 'claimed'?" Ryan took a casual sip of his tea, as though they weren't onto something big.

"Just a feeling. Seemed more staged than lived in. It was fully outfitted with a working kitchen and bathroom, but it didn't appear as though she spent any real time there."

Aster flipped to a photo of a pretty girl with long blond hair and violet eyes who she instantly recognized. Though everything else, from the ripped stockings to the short denim cutoffs, was decidedly un-Madison-like.

"That's her." Roland gestured toward the picture.

Aster held it up for Ryan to see and watched as his eyes went wide with recognition.

"I wanted to take more pictures. I found her quite captivating. She had such an interesting, contradictory energy." Roland's expression grew thoughtful, as though she was lost in the memory. "She had one of the most exquisite faces I'd ever seen. Strangely, she seemed very displeased by my request to photograph her and only agreed to the one you've got there."

"Why did that seem strange?"

Roland paused for a lingering breath. "Well, you'd think she'd be used to such requests. I mean, we are talking about Madison Brooks, after all."

Aster swallowed.

Ryan froze.

"You're not really interested in commissioning a piece, are you?" Roland's features sharpened. The kind-older-lady facade had dropped. She'd been playing them all along.

Aster stared wordlessly, having no idea how to respond, so Ryan spoke for both of them. "You know who we are, then." Aster cringed when Ryan said it, but quickly realized there were no other options, no way to start over.

Roland gazed at them shrewdly. "I recognized you immediately."

"I'm sorry," Aster started. "We just—"

"You're just looking for clues, I suppose. I knew it was Madison back then. When I watched *In-Depth*, Trena Moretti confirmed it."

"Has anyone else come by?" Ryan rested his arms on his knees and leaned toward her.

"Surprising as it may seem, you're the first," Roland told

him. "But then, most people don't really think about the deeper implications of what attracts people to the art they choose to surround themselves with."

"Did you and Madison keep in touch?"

"She never knew I recognized her as Madison. I wanted the commission and knew better than to let on. If you're asking me if I know where she is, the answer is no." Aster started to return the pics, but Roland motioned toward the one of Madison and said, "You keep it. I have no need of it." She dug deeper through the file and handed over an old photo of a similar scene, only this one didn't seem staged.

"She gave me this for reference. Though it wasn't necessary, seeing as how she'd arranged the scene exactly how she wanted. It's rare to work with a client with such an exact vision. Made me wonder why she didn't just get herself a nice camera and take the pics herself. But again, I needed the money, so I did my best to give her what she wanted. Tell me, how do they look—hanging on her wall?"

Aster stared at the pic. It looked a lot like the ones Roland had taken. After a moment, she flipped it over. The word *Home* had been written on the back, the letters awkwardly formed as though written by a child. "The pictures are striking." She looked at Roland. "Though they seem a bit out of place among the glitzy surroundings."

"Doesn't surprise me." Roland nodded. "Like I said, the girl was full of contradictions."

"Can I keep this as well?" Aster asked, surprised when Roland reached toward her and snatched it right out of her hand.

She tucked the photo into her pocket and stood, signaling she'd run out of patience.

"I'm sorry for the trouble," Aster said. "We appreciate your help."

"Seems you need all the help you can get about now."

Ryan grinned gamely. Aster fell mute.

They made their way back through the gate and were rounding onto the street when Roland called out behind them. "In case you change your mind about that commission." She handed Ryan her card, then disappeared back inside.

Ryan glanced at the card, tucked it into his palm, and ushered Aster toward his car.

"I'm not sure how I should feel about that," Aster said, once they were safely inside. "I'm left with more questions than answers."

Ryan pressed his lips together and pulled onto the road. "I'll tell you how you should feel about it." He handed her the card. Seeing Aster squint in confusion, he motioned for her to turn it over.

Aster flipped it, then gaped at Ryan in shock.

"Looks like we're taking a trip to Ojai," he said.

TEN

FAKE LOVE

"When are you going to introduce me to your mom?"

Mateo blinked his eyes open to find Heather propped up on her side, gazing at him.

"You serious?"

Lazily, she traced the tip of her finger around the curve of his ear. "Of course, silly. Why else would I ask?"

Mateo gazed up at the beaded chandelier hanging over the foot of the bed and tried to imagine such a thing. The vision didn't get very far before it fell apart.

Heather hummed quietly with a hint of impatience, letting him know she was waiting for an answer.

"My mom's pretty simple." Mateo regretted the words the second they left his lips. Still, it was true. His mom was hardworking and down-to-earth. And while he knew she'd be nice and polite (she was that way with everyone), the first thing she'd ask once Heather was gone was if he'd lost his mind bringing home such a frivolous girl.

"Are you saying I'm not simple?"

Mateo glanced her way. "Simple is not a word I'd use to describe you."

"Hmmm . . ." Her bottom lip nudged forward as the corners of her mouth tugged into a full-blown pout. "So what words would you use?"

He took his time to consider. He was wading into dangerous waters, where anything he said could, and most likely would, be used against him. "Driven, perfectionist, successful, self-motivated . . ." It seemed like a solid list to him, but before he could finish, Heather heaved a dramatic sigh and made a point of rolling her eyes.

"All wonderful traits in a job interview, sure. But isn't there something else you might want to add? Maybe something like, oh, I don't know, something more to do with my physical attributes. Like the way I look, perhaps?" She inched the sheet lower to refresh his memory. "'Cause it seems like you've already forgotten. Then again, it was nearly an hour since we last . . ." She grinned and slithered closer, rendering Mateo unable to resist her.

At some point, he knew he had to put an end to whatever it was they were doing. He'd planned on doing exactly that just after they'd left RED. But then they'd grabbed dinner, and headed back to her place, and before he knew it, they were in bed together. If he hadn't seen the point in resisting her then, he saw absolutely no point in starting now. Next thing he knew he was kissing her.

He guessed they were in a relationship, since he wasn't seeing anyone else, and as far as he knew, neither was she. But it was undefined and could end at any point. While he'd miss certain things, he wouldn't necessarily miss her. He didn't kid himself into thinking they'd share a future together. And he'd certainly never taken her seriously enough to consider bringing her home to his mother. To his surprise, Heather took it a lot more seriously than he did.

Or maybe she was just playing him. It was impossible to tell sometimes where the actress left off and the person began.

All he knew was at that particular moment, with her talented hands wrapped around him, none of those things really mattered. He was merely open to receiving whatever she was willing to give.

"So," she murmured, her lips trailing the length of his torso. "Now that you've had some time to think about it, is there anything else you want to add to that list?"

She paused, her lips parted, just shy of her hands.

In a hoarse voice, he said, "How about irresistible—does that work?"

Heather flashed a seductive grin. "It's a good start." She

tipped her tongue toward him. "Anything else?"

He forced himself to think, but it was hard to stay focused when she teased him like that. "Beautiful. Hot. Smokin'."

"I like those too. . . ." She swirled her tongue over his flesh.

"Sexiest fucking girl on the planet," he groaned.

Heather laughed softly. "You're about to be richly rewarded."

Mateo closed his eyes and sank back onto a pile of pillows as Heather made good on her promise.

Still wet from the shower with a plush blue towel wrapped low on his hips, Mateo went in search of his clothes.

He was heading into the den, remembering how they'd drifted from the couch to Heather's bed, when he found himself face-to-face with a girl he didn't recognize.

"Oh, hey. Sorry." Her eyes traveled from his face to his feet, then back up again, leisurely drinking him in. "I didn't realize you were still here."

Mateo stood awkwardly, unsure what to do.

"I'm Emily. Heather's assistant." She thrust a hand forward, then quickly retracted it when she saw Mateo struggle to keep his towel from falling. "Anyway, um . . ." Her gaze lingered on the place where he ended and the towel began. "I'm guessing those are yours?"

She was blatantly staring, and at first Mateo thought she was referring to his abs, but then he noticed she'd hooked a thumb over her shoulder, motioning toward a pair of jeans and a T-shirt that had been neatly folded and placed on the same couch where Heather had yanked them off the night before.

Emily moved to retrieve them and quickly handed them over. He balanced the pile in one hand and held it before him, while he kept his towel in place with the other.

"Heather ran out for a bit. I guess you were in the shower when she left, going by . . ." She made a vague gesture toward the beads of water still clinging to his shoulders and chest.

"Is everything okay?" he asked in confusion. Just after climbing out of bed, they'd made plans to grab breakfast before he went to the hospital to see Valentina. It seemed strange that Heather would leave without telling him.

"What?" Emily forced herself to look away from his body and focus on his face. "Yeah, I mean, I guess. Do you remember Madison's dog, Blue?"

Mateo shrugged. Layla might've mentioned it. But back then, he was so sick of all the Madison-related drama, he'd ignored most of what she'd told him.

"Well, I've been taking care of him. I guess I grew attached. Heather too. Then from out of nowhere, Paul calls to say he wants him back."

"Paul?" Mateo knew exactly who Paul was.

Emily frowned. "Legally, I know I have no right to keep him, but I'm not sure Paul does either. Have you ever met him, Paul, I mean?"

Mateo shook his head.

"Well, he's pretty scary. Not in the way he looks. In that department, he's beyond basic—all lumpy and beige, like a piece of cardboard left out in the rain. It's more in his attitude. There's just something vaguely threatening about him. Madison adored him, though. He's the only one she really trusted. But I never liked being around him. And honestly—" She lowered her voice and leaned closer. "I'm still not convinced that whatever happened to Madison isn't his fault." Her gaze held steady on his. "But, please don't tell anyone I said that. I don't want to get involved. I prefer to steer clear of anything having to do with it at this point. I mean, look what happened to your girlfriend."

Mateo was taken aback, wondering what she meant.

"Sorry, I mean ex-girlfriend, Layla. Anyway." Emily shook her head and flushed in embarrassment. "Heather was so upset when I told her about my meeting with Paul that she decided to go in my place. That's why she ran out of here without telling you. Hopefully she'll succeed and we can keep Blue." She ran a knowing gaze over Mateo. "God knows she's a master at getting whatever she wants."

The smile she flashed him saw Mateo mumbling a quick

good-bye and retreating to Heather's room. He dressed in a hurry and was about to leave, when he decided to jot a quick note. Not a breakup note—since they weren't exactly a couple, there was no relationship to break. But it was time to put some distance between them. And though Mateo hated to admit it, it was a lot easier for him to do that when Heather wasn't in front of him.

Heather was fun, and he'd meant what he said when he told her she was sexy as hell. But aside from their mutual lust, he didn't feel any real and lasting connection to her. He'd thank her for all that she'd done on his behalf, and avoid making mention of possibly meeting again.

He'd just found a pen and was searching for paper, when a picture slid free from a binder and swooped onto her desk.

Speechless, Mateo desperately searched his mind for a way to explain the photo now lying before him.

It was a picture of Layla, standing in the middle of the Jewel dance floor, kissing Tommy.

Mateo instantly recognized it as the same picture someone had anonymously sent to his phone, which had prompted him and Layla to split.

So what was Heather doing with it—unless she was the one who sent it?

Did she manipulate their breakup just so she could move in on him?

He was trying to decide what to do when his phone

chimed with an incoming text.

So sorry I had to run. Promise to make it up to you!

Attached was a photo of Heather's promise.

Mateo glanced between his cell and the picture on the desk, wondering what the hell kind of mess he'd gotten himself into.

Instead of leaving a note, he slipped the picture back inside the binder and quietly let himself out.

ELEVEN

WORLD SPINS MADLY

There was a little less than half a tank of gas in the Jeep. Probably enough to make the drive, but Madison wouldn't risk it. Driving in LA was less about actual distance, and more about flow of traffic. If she got caught in the dreaded stop-and-coast snarl, she'd burn through the fuel in no time.

She pulled up to the pump and killed the ignition. With a wallet full of cash and no credit cards, she had no choice but to pay inside.

The whole world was searching for her—her face was on every TV screen, every magazine cover—and yet, she was about to march straight into that mini-mart and take her place at the end of the line. Her entire future now hung on the hope that no one would see through her cover.

Her sunglasses were dark and oversize. The wig was of the highest quality, made from real hair. And while she'd always been thin, it was more in a lean and sinewy personal trainer kind of way, as opposed to the gaunt and bony look she had now. Weeks of poor nutrition and little to no exercise had left her looking haunted and stark. Although she was eager to return to a healthier, stronger version of herself, she had to admit it did lend a certain authenticity to her current disguise.

It'd been a while since she'd worn this particular getup. The frayed denim mini and black lace camisole were the opposite of what her fans would expect, which was why they had never once failed her.

Though thanks to her injury, the usual shoes she paired the outfit with had to be swapped for a flip-flop on one foot and a big, black medical boot on the other. At the last minute, she'd pulled on a long-sleeved army jacket, figuring it would help her feel less exposed, and also cover the telltale burn scar on the inside of her arm.

She had a lot to lose, and the game she was playing was risky at best. One false move and the entire thing would backfire, resulting in the sort of headlines that could end her career, or worse—wind up getting her killed by whoever was out there hunting for her.

Still, she needed to make her move before Paul found her. There were a few places she knew he would look; she just didn't know in what order.

She climbed out of the Jeep and headed inside. Figuring she might as well pick up a few things while she was at it, she filled her arms with two large bottles of water, a family-size bag of M&M's, aspirin, toothpaste, a toothbrush, body lotion, and small bottles of cheap shampoo and conditioner.

"Next!" the cashier barked, her eyes squinting in disapproval when Madison stepped forward and dumped her supplies on the counter. The clerk tallied her purchases, all the while directing the occasional condemning glance at the plunging neckline of Madison's sheer lace camisole. "Anything else?" She chomped her gum, acting as though Madison was taking too long even though there was no one behind her.

"Um, yeah. Twenty on pump number five."

"And?"

The clerk quirked a brow in annoyance, but Madison was too busy staring at the front page of the *LA Times* displayed on the rack just beside her.

Instead of the usual *Where Is Madison Brooks?* headline, this one screamed: *Who Is Madison Brooks?*

"Hello? Anything else?"

With a shaky hand, Madison added the paper to the pile, handed over the money, and got the hell out of there.

After filling her tank, she drove a few blocks, pulled into an empty parking lot, reached for the paper, and began to read.

Breaking News:

Madison Brooks's True Identity Revealed!

By Trena Moretti

In a town built on make-believe, it should come as no surprise that missing Hollywood A-lister Madison Brooks just might turn out to be as fictional as the characters she portrays in her movies.

The story of her ascent from poor little orphan girl to Hollywood's most highly paid and sought-after star is nothing more than a glossy facade meant to hide a much darker tale.

In a stunning revelation on *In-Depth* Sunday night, I revealed a birth certificate, believed to be that of Madison Brooks, that states her real name as MaryDella Slocum, her place of birth as West Virginia, and her parents as the deceased Henry and WillaJean Slocum—two small-time hustlers with an extensive criminal background.

A far cry from the bio Madison sold us.

Hours before my show went live, Layla Harrison, writer of the Beautiful Idols blog, and one of the four teens recently arrested in Joshua Tree in connection with Madison's disappearance, posted an entry allegedly torn from the diary of Madison/MaryDella that would've placed her at fourteen years old at the time. The piece, shared below, reveals the young star to be far more calculating and conniving than her pristine persona ever let on.

Numerous mentions of P seem to point to Paul Banks, who . . .

Madison's gaze raced down the page. By the time she reached the end, she could barely breathe.

It was all there. Her birth certificate, the fire, even the diary entries she'd written as a much younger girl.

Her whole life was exposed.

Well, maybe not *all* of it. Though it was just a matter of time before they uncovered those secrets too.

And then what?

What would become of her once the ugly truth was revealed?

Where could she possibly go once her secrets were known all over the world?

Was she supposed to live out the rest of her life hiding behind dark sunglasses and a wig?

She gazed around wildly, trying to make sense of what was happening. Someone had pulled back the curtain on her life, and apparently Paul had known all along. He'd even hinted as much when he said, *It's about destroying you and everything you've worked so hard to build.*

Had he seen the article? Her guess was he had. He'd probably planned to keep her in the dark until it was handled.

Well, it was too late now. The article was merely a trickle in what promised to become an epic flood.

Question was: *How the hell had Layla Harrison gotten hold of her diary?*

Whatever the answer, one thing was clear: Between the journal entry, the birth certificate, and the original article about the fire, Madison was screwed.

Really, truly, and royally screwed.

And yet, just as Paul had taught her to always peer past the surface, that everything was capable of serving more than one purpose, he'd also taught her how to control her own narrative. She had no idea how she'd begin to spin this, but she knew she eventually would.

When it came to the story of her life, the ending would be hers to write.

She sank a hand into her bag and patted the gun for reassurance. Then she tossed the paper into the backseat, started up the Jeep, and headed for the secret hideout she kept tucked away on the outskirts of Ojai.

It'd been a while since her last visit, but Trena's article had thrown her off balance. She'd take the night to figure out a new plan of attack, sure of only one thing: whatever decision she made would not be easily reversed.

TWELVE

GUYS MY AGE

Trena pulled up to the curb, propped open the passenger-side door, and let Javen in.

"Your sister would kill me if she found out about this," she said.

Javen tugged at his seat belt and settled beside her. "Only if my parents don't get to you first." He stared through the windshield and frowned. "Then again, I haven't even heard from her. She's been out of jail since yesterday and won't even answer my texts."

"I think I might know why." Trena told him about the threatening notes Layla had received. "Maybe Aster got one too?"

Javen considered. "Well, it would make sense. At least, it better be the reason. After all I've done for her . . ."

"And all you're still planning to do?" Trena pulled out of the school parking lot and merged into traffic.

"Yeah. Sure." Javen shrugged and took in the passing scenery.

Trena stopped at a light and used the moment to study him. He was avoiding eye contact, had barely so much as looked at her. Normally she was skilled when it came to reading people, but in this case she hadn't a clue as to what might be motivating his cagey behavior.

"You know, you don't have to do this," she said, figuring if he was worried about getting into trouble, it was her job to reassure him. "You're under no obligation. Last time, you got off easy. Not sure that'll be the case if Larsen catches you again."

Javen focused his brown eyes on hers. "Well, let's make sure he doesn't catch me then."

Trena held the look, then returned to driving

"You know, you really send a lot of mixed signals."

Trena cracked a half smile. "How so?"

"You seemed pretty scary when you barged into my sister's apartment that night."

"No, not me." Trena shook her head in a way that sent her curls bouncing. "I didn't barge. The barger was Larsen, one hundred percent."

"Well, you were part of the barge." Javen was not about to give in. "You were right there with your notepad in hand, looking for someone to incriminate."

"No notepad either. I forgot to bring it." Trena stopped at an intersection and scrutinized him. He seemed to be warming up. She took it as a good sign. "Perhaps I misjudged you. Maybe you don't have the eye for detail I thought you did. Should I drop you at the mall, or the library instead?"

He rolled his eyes, and it reminded Trena so much of Aster it was like they were twins. Never mind that Javen was three years younger, and slightly prettier, which seemed impossible, even though it was true. "Fine," he huffed. "A metaphorical notepad. Whatever. At any rate, I'm in. If it'll help Aster, it's worth it. And I hate to say it, but this is turning out to be the most exciting thing that's happened all week." He frowned. "Which, by the way, is off the record. You put that on your show, I'll lose half my Snapchat followers once they get a true glimpse of how tragic my life has become."

Trena maneuvered through traffic, taking surreptitious looks at him. With his smooth olive complexion, wavy dark hair, sculpted cheekbones, and large brown eyes with those ridiculously long lashes, he had a face that was made for the spotlight. Though strangely, unlike most beautiful people she'd met in LA, Javen had no interest in fame. Unfortunately, because of the mess involving his sister, infamy had found him.

No wonder he preferred a low profile. Couldn't be

easy being gay in a family like that. From what Trena had gathered, the parents were traditional, conservative, and extremely strict. For a moment, she considered turning around and dropping him back at school where she'd found him. But she needed him, and he wanted to help. And so, she kept driving.

"Clearly you're not here to chat or lure me into an episode of carpool karaoke, so what's really going on here?"

Trena grinned. Now he reminded her of Layla.

"I need help," she said.

He gazed out the passenger-side window. "Obvi."

Trena laughed. It'd been a while since she'd spent time with a fifteen-year-old. "The kind of help that will hopefully help your sister as well. I need you to go deep on a few people."

"Listening . . ." He drummed his fingers on the armrest.

Trena swerved into the underground parking structure of her building, claimed her designated space, and said, "I need a few background checks."

"Something a little more than a Google search, I'm guessing?"

"I need you to dig up whatever you can on Paul Banks and Kevin O'Dell." She turned off the ignition. "See if their paths converge. If they come together at some point."

"I know what 'converge' means." He shook his head. "I'm in honors English, you know. Thing is, those are pretty common names. Any way to narrow it down?"

"Not to worry." Trena climbed out of the car and led him toward the elevator bank. "I'll give you everything I've got, along with a few suggestions on where to start. You can take it from there."

"What about MaryDella Slocum? You forget about her?"

"Her too," Trena said. "I know it's a lot to ask." She pressed the call button and frowned.

"Generally speaking, it's not. But since I'm guessing you're expecting me to hack into a protected database or three, then yeah, it kinda is."

"Well, if you can't do it, or don't want to . . ."

Javen stared openly. It took Trena a moment to catch on to the fact that he'd just switched to negotiating mode.

She entered the waiting car and pushed the button for the thirty-fifth floor. She never should've underestimated the kid. He lived a pampered, somewhat sheltered life, but he still had his share of street smarts. Not only was she on the spot, but also annoyed with herself for being so slow to catch on.

Still, might as well get to the point. Trena turned to him. "What is it you want?" The second it was out, she realized she'd blown it. She'd basically tossed him the ball and told him to run with it. She'd negotiated a killer contract with the network's top brass, but when it came to a teen, she was out of her league. She'd just forfeited the game before it even started.

"First and foremost," he said, his tone professional, brisk, "I want to be clear that this is about helping Aster."

"Of course." Trena nodded, watching as the doors opened to a short hallway, just a handful of steps to her apartment.

"Because Aster is innocent, and she's in desperate need of our help."

Trena readily agreed and ushered him inside.

"In fact, maybe we should take a moment of silence for—"

"Don't push it." She needed his help, but she still had her limits.

Javen crossed the spacious room to the floor-to-ceiling windows and took in the expansive city view. "I know you're eager to get started," he said. "And I'm guessing you plan to share whatever I find on your show so you can raise your ratings, broaden your audience, and further promote your agenda." He looked over his shoulder, and when she failed to confirm, he continued, "In which case, I think it's only fair I get something out of it too."

"You mean aside from helping your sister avoid a guilty verdict?" Trena placed her hands on her hips and steeled herself for whatever came next.

"Well, yes." Javen turned away from the window.

"And what is it you're looking for?" She was worried he'd overestimated her. Her spike in ratings had also led to a spike in power and clout, and had undoubtedly padded her bank account. Still, there were limits to the sort of things she could offer.

"My parents monitor all my comings and goings."

Trena watched as he wandered the apartment, plumping the couch cushions and running a finger across her shelves, inspecting for dust. He was the world's worst mother-in-law disguised as a beautiful adolescent boy.

"Sometimes I feel like they have eyes everywhere. It's like there's not a single space in the city where they're not spying on me."

Trena rocked back on the heels of her Jimmy Choos. Her bullshit radar had just kicked into high gear. "Let me guess." She looked him over. "Your parents have eyes all over the city—everywhere but *here*."

Javen nodded solemnly, though the gleam in his eyes assured her she'd just been masterminded by a fifteen-year-old. "Exactly," he said. "Which is why I'm thinking I might need to visit a few more times in the future. You know, for follow-up work."

Trena grew silent. This was not at all what she'd planned. "I'm sure that can be discussed at some point," she finally said, her voice tight.

Javen grinned happily. "You know, I've always wanted

to live in a penthouse apartment." He stood before a framed black-and-white print—a gift from Trena's ex-fiancé that she still couldn't bring herself to part with. "My parents' house is huge, don't get me wrong, but sometimes it feels too big, you know?"

Trena folded her arms across her chest. He was seconds from being evicted. He just didn't know it.

"But a place like this is pretty much the stuff of my dreams."

"Really?" Trena cocked her head and squinted at the beautiful, manipulative, savvy boy she'd wildly underestimated. "You dream about real estate?"

Javen gave a casual lift of his shoulders. "That. And a few other things."

It was time to take back the reins before this went any further. "You're not moving in."

"Wouldn't consider it. Pretty sure I just mentioned I live at home with my parents. Now that Aster's gone, I have an entire wing to myself. Still, every now and then, I do find myself in need of a little more privacy."

Their eyes met. If she agreed, she'd be aiding and abetting a minor in who knew what kind of teenage debauchery. If she didn't, she might never get what she needed.

Deftly avoiding an answer, she said, "I figured I could set you up right over here." She gestured toward the breakfast bar that separated the kitchen from the den.

Javen pursed his lips and tapped a finger to his chin, looking as though it didn't quite live up to his standards. Trena was just about to blow, when he said, "That'll do." He grabbed a stool, propped open his laptop, and went to work.

"You know what would be good?" He glanced at her, his hands hovering over the keyboard.

Inwardly, Trena groaned. She was already regretting her decision to involve him. "Let me guess, you want me to go on a fro-yo run?"

Javen rubbed his chin as though considering the offer. Deciding against it, he said, "No. But a little road trip might be fun."

"Javen," she said, ready to let him have it, when he turned his computer toward her. She leaned over his shoulder and peered at the screen showing a document for a property in Ojai registered under the name of MaryDella Slocum. "Is this legit?" Trena skimmed the page again, sure that it was. "You found that just now? After less than a minute of typing?"

Javen laughed. "No, I just placed an order with Post-mates. It'll be here in twenty-five to thirty minutes. This I found right after you revealed Madison's birth certificate on your show."

Trena stared. Clearly, she'd been played by a pro.

"I'll text you whatever else I find. But for now, I think you should go. Don't worry about me. I'll let myself out when I'm done."

THIRTEEN

SURFACE ENVY

"I hope you brought tacos, because that's what I ordered."

Layla breezed past Javen and moved toward the center of the room. "Did she believe you?" She turned in a circle, taking in the bright, open space.

"What do you think?" He shot her a mock-offended look. "Sure took you long enough to get here. I was starting to think you weren't coming."

"I watched her leave." Layla roamed Trena's spacious apartment. It was a large open-floor plan with stunning city views and sleek modern furnishings. Aside from a few framed pieces on the walls, the personal touches were kept to a minimum, leaving Layla to wonder if Trena preferred a more anonymous, spare look, or if she'd simply been too busy to add her own stamp to it.

It was a recent acquisition, and though Layla had never visited her last place, she was willing to bet it wasn't nearly as nice as this new one. Clearly, her hit TV show had come with a considerable leap in the pay grade.

Glancing at Javen, Layla said, "I wanted to make sure she stayed gone." She lifted a hardcover book from the coffee table authored by an esteemed journalist Layla admired. She inspected the front and back covers, flipped to the title page, and confirmed it was indeed signed and personalized. Then she placed it right back where she'd found it and joined Aster's brother.

"Again, you're doubting my skills." Javen scowled.

"Or overestimating Trena's. Two sides to everything, right?" She peered over his shoulder and peeked at his laptop. From what she could see, he was writing a school essay.

"It's part of my escape plan." He nodded toward the screen. "I need to maintain my grades so I can graduate early and attend an East Coast college. I don't even care which one, just the farther away the better."

Layla could relate. There was a time, not long ago, when she'd made a similar plan. Now it seemed like nothing more than the quaint dream of someone who'd never been arrested, never seen the inside of a jail cell, never been chased by paparazzi, never received death threats that flooded her in-box until she'd stopped reading all incoming comments, direct messages, and email. She was living each moment as it came. There was no looking ahead, no telling where she'd end up. Planning seemed like a luxury she could not afford.

To Javen, she said, "It's a good goal."

"So." He looked at her. "What now?"

Layla pursed her lips. "We snoop."

"And are we looking for anything in particular?"

It was a good question, but Layla had no solid answer. "I guess just anything remotely connected to Madison, your sister, Ira, Paul . . ." She finished with a shrug. "Does Trena keep an office here?"

Javen directed her down the hallway and into a back room, where Layla stood in the doorway, stunned by the sudden jolt of jealousy that overcame her.

Normally, she made fun of people who crammed their wall space with framed certificates and photos of all the famous people they'd met. But now she understood that her former urge to poke fun had more to do with her own glaring lack of accomplishments than the pride Trena took in hers.

It was an impressive collection of achievements, and there was no denying Trena had worked hard to get where she was—nothing had ever been handed to her. But this latest accomplishment—the penthouse apartment and the prime-time slot—was entirely due to a story Layla had helped her create.

Though instead of feeling bitter, Layla was left to wonder if journalism was something she still wanted to pursue. After playing a major role in one of the world's most scandalous stories, she was no longer sure she had it in her to be the hunter after having spent so much time as the prey.

Writing for a major news publication was the only solid dream she'd ever really had, and now, even that was in jeopardy. The summer had robbed her of nearly everything she'd ever cared about.

"Are we starting in here?"

Layla turned to find Javen leaning against the door frame.

She looked away, needing a moment to compose herself. "You start in the bedroom," she said.

Javen's reply was swift. "No. No way."

Layla heaved a frustrated sigh.

"Not a chance. You go looking in her underwear drawer. I'm not going anywhere near it. This is not what I signed up for."

He was so adamant there was no use pushing it. "Fine," Layla said. "I'm sure if there's anything to find, it'll probably be in here anyway."

"Or on her laptop," he said. "Only it's not here. She took it with her."

Layla pressed her lips together, trying to decide where to begin. "Is there any way to tap into her network—or her cloud—or whatever?" Might as well encourage him to use one of his most valuable skills. "The note said she was hiding a clue, but it wasn't specific as to where."

"There's always a way." He smirked, disappearing down the hall as Layla made for Trena's desk.

Trena had left the *Washington Post* to head up the *LA Times* digital division, which probably meant Javen was right. Anything important was stored on her computer.

Then again, Layla specifically remembered seeing Trena carrying a notebook back when they'd first met. Finding her stash of notebooks would be a good start.

The desk was modern, sleek and white—exactly the sort of desk Layla might choose for herself. The top drawer didn't offer much more than a stack of sticky notes, some paper clips, and a book of stamps. The side drawers revealed a tube of hand lotion, a pricey lip balm, and a pile of hair bands.

Layla ran her hands underneath and all along the sides in search of secret compartments. Realizing she was reenacting every spy movie she'd ever seen, she stepped away and surveyed the room. If she had important documents she didn't want anyone to find, she'd store them in a place no one would ever think to look.

The bookshelf was tightly packed, though it was obvious from the pristine condition of the individual book jackets that Trena harbored a real affection for her collection.

She'd never choose to deface one.

Magazines, on the other hand . . .

There was a stack of *Vanity Fair* and the *Hollywood Reporter*, a few in particular that appeared especially lumpy and thick.

Pulling them from the stack, Layla claimed a space on the rug and spread them all around. Arranging them by the dates on the cover, she started with the June issue of *Vanity Fair* and immediately confirmed that her hunch was correct. The pages had been torn out and replaced with meticulous notes Trena had kept on Ira's Unrivaled Nightlife contest, including a rundown of the rules and the names of those who were cut—there was a full dossier on every one of them.

Layla was tempted to see what Trena had written about her, but not wanting to waste time on something with the potential to upset her and throw her off track, she pushed the magazine aside and moved on to September.

She rifled through the papers. Trena's writing was loopy and wide, and at times it was hard to make out every word. Most of it consisted of stuff Trena had already told her, and Layla was ready to give up when she came across a photocopy of an old news clipping Trena hadn't mentioned.

After skimming it, Layla knew why.

She reached for her phone and took a quick pic. Trena was on her way to Ojai, which meant there was no hurry to leave. But now that Layla had found what she needed, there was no reason to stay.

"Find anything?" Javen moved into the office and glanced over Layla's shoulder.

She briefly considered telling him, but decided the less he knew the better.

"Well, I've got something," Javen said. "It's an address, in Ventura County. A different one from where I sent Trena. According to Google Maps, it's about an hour's drive."

Layla hoisted her bag on her shoulder and went to stand beside him. "You actually sent her somewhere legit?"

"I sent her to a tiny parcel of land with a trailer on it." He shrugged. "This, on the other hand, is a house. And from what I've seen, it's the sort of place Madison would choose to hang out."

"And if I run into Trena while I'm out there?"

"Out of my jurisdiction. I'm just the hacker. Though you should know, the only side I'm taking is Aster's, and mine, of course."

"Duly noted," Layla said.

She was heading for the door when he called, "Oh, and before you go, can you bring me my Postmates? Pretty sure it was just delivered."

FOURTEEN

FUNERAL FOR A FRIEND

For the first time in a long time, Madison Brooks was having fun.

Maybe not *fun* in the usual pampered, VIP sort of way with all the highly coveted freebies and perks regularly showered on a star of her caliber. But she was out on her own, free to move about as she pleased. After weeks under lock and key, that alone meant everything.

She was also taking the first meaningful step toward revenge. The thought was enough to coax that world-famous grin to her face.

Though she still felt guilty about Blue, Madison knew her beloved mutt would be well looked after. Despite whatever suspicions she might have about Paul, he had a code he'd never deviate from. Paul would kill a human without a second thought, but when it came to animals, he would do no harm. He considered them sacred, and far superior to most people he knew. Madison tended to agree.

She cruised up Hollywood Boulevard and headed toward Sunset. The day was bright and sunny, another scorcher in the making, and it seemed like everywhere she looked she caught a glimpse of her face.

The billboards for her movie were still up. According to Paul, it was the biggest hit of the summer. There was even talk of an Oscar nom for best actress, which meant she'd probably be up for a Golden Globe too.

Of course, she was featured on Trena Moretti's *In-Depth* billboards as well. Only on those, Trena's picture was bigger, leaving no doubt that she was the star of her show.

So much had changed since Madison had been taken. While the frenzied news coverage she'd received didn't surprise her, it was odd to witness firsthand the sort of cottage industry that had grown in the wake of her disappearance.

She passed a handful of souvenir shops hawking T-shirts that featured her image. The ones that said *Missing* seemed sweet. The ones that said *In Memoriam* gave her the creeps.

There were Madison masks, Madison key chains, Madison prayer candles. It was like she was haunting the city, serving as a grim reminder of how a person could be blessed with every conceivable gift—beauty, talent, riches, and stardom—and yet, they could still end up as tragically as any junkie on the street.

For those who had little, her disappearance provided a sense of justice, proving they weren't the only ones vulnerable to the whims of the universe.

For those who had much, it filled their hearts with terror. If it could happen to Madison Brooks, then no one was safe.

There was no shortage of people looking to make a buck off her story, and she couldn't help but wonder what would happen once she stepped out of the shadows and reclaimed her place in the spotlight.

Most likely, it wouldn't make much difference. The leftover merchandise would be sold at a discount while they waited for the next scandal to occur. It was Hollywood, after all. It wasn't like there was a shortage of celebrity meltdowns.

She drove past the Vesper and Jewel without so much as a glance. But as she approached Night for Night, against her better judgment she eased the Jeep into a nearby parking spot and gazed at the sprawling memorial set up near the entrance.

A sizable crowd gathered around a jumble of stuffed animals, flowers, and crosses nestled alongside several poster-size pictures of her. *Tourists*. She frowned with derision, a little miffed to find not a single peer among them.

They might've spared a few minutes the first week, maybe even shared a charming story about the time they'd run into her at Soho House. But as soon as the cameras moved on, they'd return to their regularly scheduled life of detoxing, Botoxing, and fighting their way to the top.

But these people, with their thick-soled sneakers and sunburned shoulders—they were the true fans. The ones who read every interview, who dedicated entire weekends to binge-watching her films and buying every product she was ever paid to endorse, never seeming to notice that she rarely used those products herself. Hell, she didn't even wear the perfume that featured her name on the label. She preferred a more exclusive brand.

They even bought into her overhyped romance with Ryan. When he'd given her the gold-and-turquoise hoop earrings, you would've thought he'd surprised her with the Hope diamond the way they went on about it.

They believed wholly in the gospel of Instagram, Snapchat, and *People* magazine. PR teams all over the city relied on their continued gullibility.

Madison had burst onto the scene with the necessary good looks and talent to succeed. But it was these very people who'd projected their dreams onto her who had propelled her to the top of the heap.

She watched as a frizzy-haired girl in a garish sundress broke into such a dramatic display of tears, several people nearby moved in to console her.

The girl had probably bought all Madison's posters—memorized all her movies by heart. If anyone were to recognize her, it would be that girl.

Madison popped open the door and slid from the seat. It was only the second time she'd ventured out in public. The first time, at the gas station, the girl working the register was so busy judging Madison's skimpy outfit she'd barely bothered to look at her face.

But this time was different. This was the test that would determine how she'd move forward from here. These people had devoted countless hours of their lives to watching her, reading about her, studying her, discussing her, dissecting her every Instagram post as though each pic held the key to her soul. If the disguise failed, it could prove catastrophic. And yet, she had no real choice but to see it through.

She smoothed a hand over her long blond wig, readjusted her sunglasses, and limped toward the memorial.

The first thing that struck her was how many were crying. It felt weird, like she was crashing her own funeral.

She moved toward the frizzy-haired girl and shot her a tentative smile, even made a point to pat her lightly on the shoulder. The girl would totally freak if she knew Madison Brooks had just tried to console her. As it was, she thrust a crumpled tissue to her face and blew her nose so loudly Madison cringed and slipped away.

It seemed every square inch was crammed with stacks of cards and letters—countless declarations of devotion, admiration, and love. These people adored her. They longed for her safe return. Madison was eager to grant them their wish, but there were things she had to do first.

Wanting to leave them with a symbol of hope, she reached into her bag and retrieved the single hoop earring from Ryan that had managed to survive. She'd just placed it beside a stuffed teddy bear with angel wings, when two girls came to stand beside her, and one of them said, "Oh, look at all the pretty flowers!" She angled her cell and started filming.

Her friend snickered and shook her head. "What the hell are you doing?"

"Shhh . . . video in progress!" And then in a mock-serious tone: "We're on Hollywood Boulevard outside Night for Night, where MaryDella Slocum was last seen." The girl couldn't even finish the sentence without breaking into hysterical laughter, prompting her friend to take over.

"And we sincerely hope she turns up dead, because that's what she deserves for lying to us all these years! RIP, bitch!"

Madison froze. She felt like she was about to be sick.

She looked to her fan in the hideous sundress. Surely she'd jump in to defend her. But she didn't. Nobody did. And that was when Madison realized they weren't there to memorialize her. They were there to condemn her and all the lies she'd told through the years.

"I can't believe what a phony she turned out to be," someone said.

Another chimed in, "Well, she may be a fake, but I still like her movies."

"I'm not surprised," said a girl in an off-the-shoulder T-shirt. "Everything about her seemed bogus. I heard she gets tons of Botox, and those aren't even her real eyes—they're contacts."

Botox? Madison shook her head. She was eighteen, what the hell did she need with Botox?

This had been a mistake. If someone recognized her now, it wouldn't end well. She ran a serious risk of being attacked by the mob, and from what she could see, there wasn't a single person willing to jump in and help.

She stood on shaky legs, determined to make a quick getaway, when someone shoved into her so hard, it nearly sent her crashing into a huge poster of herself. Under any other circumstances, the scene would be comical. As it was, Madison was on the verge of a full-blown panic attack.

"You okay?" a girl asked.

Tentatively, Madison nodded. She wasn't used to feeling so vulnerable, and she hated every moment of it.

"Tragic, isn't it?"

Madison turned. The girl was probably around her age

and had long brown hair, styled in long, beachy waves. Same way Madison often wore hers.

"All that time I spent admiring her." The girl scowled. "I can never get that time back."

Madison was incensed. She'd made the movies they loved, promoted the products they clamored for. She'd allowed glimpses into a lifestyle they all dreamed of living. What more did she actually owe them?

"Really?" Madison spat. "*That's* your idea of tragic? Maybe you should try stepping away from your Instagram feed long enough to read a newspaper so you can see what real tragedy looks like."

The second it was out, she was overcome with regret. But it was too late to walk it back.

Enraged, the girl spun on her and unleashed a tirade of hate that left Madison with no choice but to get the hell out of there as fast as her ankle allowed.

She limped toward the Jeep and had just swung open the door when a hand caught hold of her. The fingers pinched at the spot where the tracker had been ripped from her arm.

The moment sent her mind reeling back to the two previous times, at Night for Night and in Joshua Tree, when some unknown attacker had come out of nowhere and grabbed her from behind.

She whipped her body around. It was broad daylight, on a crowded street. She would not go down easily.

A scream rose up her throat, only to die on her tongue when she locked eyes with a guy holding a T-shirt bearing her image.

"Fifteen dollar," he said.

Madison stared in astonishment and fought hard not to laugh. It was one of the more surreal moments of what had become a very strange life.

Above her picture was the word *Wanted*. Below, it read: *MaryDella Slocum, goes by the alias Madison Brooks. If seen, contact ~~LAPD~~ Trena Moretti.*

Unfreakingbelievable. The world had known for two days, and a T-shirt had already entered the marketplace. It was capitalism at its best.

"I'll give you six." She reached for her wallet.

"Ten," he shot back, looking offended.

"Seven," she said. "Best and final."

After a moment of false deliberation he agreed, and Madison climbed into the Jeep and drove away from the scene. Her crumpled image on the seat beside her, she went in search of Tommy Phillips.

FIFTEEN

THINK A LITTLE LESS

By the time Aster and Ryan made it to Ojai, it was too dark to locate the trailer. After a string of dead ends, Ryan booked them a room at the Ojai Valley Inn, so they'd have a nice place to sleep before they tried again the next day.

"Separate beds?" Aster stood inside the doorway, overcome with shyness as she nervously surveyed the room.

"Didn't want to assume anything." Ryan shot her a cautious look. "Also, I'm respecting your wish to take things slowly."

At the time, Aster had been sure she'd never be able to sleep with Ryan lying in the very next bed. Turned out, she was so exhausted from the day and all that she'd been through, she was out the moment her head hit the pillow and didn't so much as stir until Ryan returned the next morning with a large bag from the gift shop and a small tin bucket filled with two cartons of fresh orange juice.

"Supplies." He tossed the bag onto the bed and handed her a carton of juice.

Aster twisted off the top and took a long, thirsty swig.

"They left the juice outside the door, along with this." He tossed a copy of the *LA Times* onto the bed.

Aster stared at the front page. The headline—*Who Is Madison Brooks?*—blazed across the front page. The byline, of course, was Trena Moretti's.

Quickly, she skimmed the article. It was basically a recap of everything Trena had revealed on *In-Depth* Sunday night, with one notable addition.

"Do you think Trena is working with Layla?"

Ryan drained his OJ, then came to sit beside her. "What makes you say that?"

Aster stabbed the paper with an unvarnished nail. Her rigorous schedule of salon appointments had taken a hit, but in light of her situation, she no longer cared. "Remember the newspaper article we saw, the one that mentioned two dead and two injured in the fire?"

Ryan nodded.

"She mentions it here. I mean, I guess she could've found it on her own. Just makes me wonder, that's all."

"Do you miss her?"

"Layla?" Aster scrunched her nose in distaste. "Mostly I miss Javen, and my parents. But I won't take the risk of contacting them. I just hope once this is over, I can find a way to explain." She fell silent, her fingers idly picking at a thread on the sheets. "Okay, fine. I miss Layla too." She heaved a grudging breath. "It feels a little weird to be left out of the loop."

"Don't you think maybe they got notes too, and that's why they haven't contacted you?"

With a shrug, Aster folded the paper and pushed it to the floor. She was sick of reading about it. Sick of Trena recycling the same old stories that never failed to drag Aster through the mud. She nodded toward the bag. "Souvenirs?"

Ryan laughed and reached a hand inside, retrieving a matching set of his-and-hers hotel logo T-shirts. "Thought it might be nice to at least change our shirts. There's a couple toothbrushes and toothpaste as well, along with a few other essentials. I figured we could shower, order some breakfast from room service, then head out and try to find that trailer."

"What if there is no trailer?" The words hung between them.

"You think Roland was lying?" Ryan stood uncertainly before her.

Aster shook her head. "It's just—it's a trailer, which means it's mobile. So what if it's no longer there? What if the reason we couldn't find it is because it no longer exists, or she moved it somewhere?"

"Are you saying you don't want to try?" Ryan's voice was tentative.

Aster bit down on her lip to keep from crying. She didn't know what she was saying. All she knew was she was caught in a spiral of panic, and when that happened, nothing good ever came of it. She needed to stop thinking so much, stop overanalyzing every little detail, and just go down the list, item by item. "I'm running out of time," she said. "And so far, I've got more questions than answers."

In an instant, she found herself wrapped in Ryan's arms. Her cheek pressed against his warm chest, as he whispered a string of assurances into her ear.

Against her better judgment, she melted against him. It felt good to have someone looking after her, caring for her, putting himself on the line for her. Ryan had gone above and beyond. He'd proven himself in more ways than she'd ever expected or even required.

"When this is over," he started.

But before he could finish, Aster pulled away and dabbed at the tears that had spilled onto her cheeks. "Don't," she said. "Don't project into the future. It's too uncertain for me."

She rose to her feet and headed for the shower, her own words reverberating in her head.

The future *was* uncertain. And yet she felt like she was speeding right toward it in a car with no brakes. There were less than two weeks before her trial began, and at the end of it, a lifetime spent in an orange jumpsuit seemed likely. If they locked her up, she might die a virgin. Her once amusing adolescent fear would come true.

It wasn't the reason she paused short of the bathroom. Fear was always a reliable motivator, sure, but in this case, Aster couldn't think of a single good reason for waiting any longer than she already had.

Ryan was only a few feet away. He was gorgeous, kind, supportive, and patient. He was the only one she'd ever wanted to fully share herself with. And yet, because of her, they'd wasted an entire night sleeping chastely in separate beds.

From where she stood now, it seemed like a terrible waste.

Slowly, she turned and extended a hand. When he met her gaze with a questioning look, she said, "You know, there's a serious water shortage out here."

He stilled, as though afraid of misinterpreting her words.

"In which case, it's probably best if you join me. You know"—she grinned bravely—"for conservation purposes."

In a flash he was beside her. "You sure?" He cupped her cheeks with both hands. The look he gave her told her he truly wanted the decision to be on her terms.

She was about to respond with another dumb quip about the drought, but the earnestness she found in his expression saw her pressing her lips against his, leaving no room for doubt.

"No point in wasting any water then," he said, and sweeping her onto the bed, he slid his body over hers.

SIXTEEN

SISTER GOLDEN HAIR

Finding out about Tommy was easy. He'd made quite a name for himself while she'd been missing.

Getting ahold of him was another matter entirely. He'd recently moved into a swanky new building that was too risky to even try to approach. So Madison took a chance and called the PR department at his record company. Posing as a reporter for *Rolling Stone*, she was surprised to learn he already had an interview scheduled that day with a writer named Dahlia. For the first time in a long time, it seemed the universe was working in her favor. She asked if they could move the meeting up a few hours, and just like that, it was done. Clearly, Tommy was eager to make it happen. Madison wondered what he would think once he discovered what she really had in store for him.

Despite her determination to put her plan into action, Madison wasn't fully convinced it would result in the desired outcome. Still, she was in desperate need of a friend. And since no one qualified outside of Paul, she was left with no choice but to go after one of the very people who stood to benefit from her discovery the most. She just hoped she could convince Tommy not to reveal her whereabouts before she was ready.

In the end, she'd make it worth his while. Still, there was no guarantee he'd agree.

She roamed the aisles of the record store where the reporter was supposed to meet Tommy, searching for him from behind her dark lenses. Tommy had exactly the kind of lean, sexy look Madison would go for if she wasn't, well, *Madison Brooks*. Sure she'd kissed him, and while it'd been fun while it lasted (and while she wouldn't necessarily be opposed to repeating it), it was little more than a harmless flirtation. Or so she'd thought. The moment she'd gone missing, Tommy hadn't hesitated to brag about it to just about any tabloid willing to listen.

While she had every intention of confronting him on his eagerness to sell her out, for now she brushed it aside. She needed to stay focused and in character. She took the role as seriously as those she was paid millions of dollars to portray.

She spotted him over in the alternative rock section,

where he casually rifled through the stacks as his gaze darted around.

His fingers skipped through a thick row of vinyl until he found something of interest and retrieved it from the pile.

When was the last time she'd actually stalked a guy?

Or, more appropriately, when was the last time she'd had to?

Madison had grown so used to being hunted it was nice to play the predator for a change.

Favoring her bad ankle, she worked her way toward him. No use in pouncing unexpectedly, when it was far more fun to catch his eye from across the room and work a leisurely flirtation until they ultimately found themselves standing next to each other.

Did Tommy like blondes? She tugged at her wig, deciding she'd yet to meet a guy who didn't.

"Nirvana's *Nevermind*?" She nodded toward the album cover. "If you don't already own it, you should buy it. I guarantee you will not regret it."

The grin he gave her was nothing short of dazzling. He pulled his lips wide, showcasing a display of white teeth straight enough to imply they might've once been behind braces—while just crooked enough to suggest he'd lost the retainer a few years back. Madison lingered on those teeth, relieved to find they bore absolutely no resemblance to the overly perfect porcelain veneers of every Hollywood actor she knew. She took it as proof she'd been right about him. Normal teeth, normal guy. She just might be able to trust him after all.

"Are you—?" He cocked his head, hesitating in the way of a guy who didn't want to be mistaken for flirting. Was he really dating Layla, or was he just trying to appear respectful?

"Dahlia." She lifted her chin and favored him with a watered-down version of her own world-class grin. "Nice to meet you, Tommy." She offered a hand, pleased to find he received it firmly in his.

Tommy rubbed his lips together and glanced nervously around the room. "So," he said, "I'm new at this. Where should we go?"

Madison took a moment to look him over. "Surely you're no newbie." She shifted her weight between her flip-flop and her boot. "Not after spending the bulk of the summer as the tabloid king."

She was pleased by the way he flushed in response. It showed a respectable level of shame for the part that he'd played.

"Not sure I'd refer to *Rolling Stone* as a tabloid," he said, barely able to keep the excited gleam from his navy-blue eyes.

Madison felt guilty. Setting him up seemed almost cruel. The next moment, the feeling passed, and she said, "How about we go for a drive?"

Tommy ran an uncertain hand across his chin. A moment later he'd agreed, and they were just leaving the store when his phone began to ring.

He paused in the sunlight and peered at the screen.

Madison hoped it wasn't someone from his record company, or worse, the actual writer from *Rolling Stone*.

"If that's your girlfriend, you might want to get it." Madison's voice was peppered with amusement. "This could take a while."

Tommy shook his head and let the call ring into voice mail. Turning to her, he asked, "Who's driving?"

Madison studied him. She'd accidentally left her keys with him the night she was taken, only to have her car end up outside Paul's office with her purse locked in the trunk. Was Tommy somehow responsible?

What she said was, "I ask the questions. You drive."

She was relieved when he readily agreed. Last thing she needed was to drive Paul's car for any longer than necessary. He was probably in search of her at that very moment. Hell, for all she knew, the car had probably been outfitted with some kind of tracking device.

A chill skittered across Madison's flesh. She couldn't

believe she hadn't bothered to consider that. It was the sort of sloppiness that could bring the whole thing crashing right down. Paul was a pro when it came to deception, which meant Madison couldn't afford to be anything less than vigilant.

Tommy was staring. She'd been silent too long.

"So where you parked?" she asked, her skin sheening with sweat as he deepened the stare.

"How'd you hurt yourself?" He motioned toward her ankle.

"Balance beam accident." She shrugged. "It happens." It was an obvious lie, but at least it worked to make him laugh. "Is that really what you wanted to ask?"

Tommy chewed his lip. "It's just—"

She waited.

"You remind me of someone."

Her breath hitched in her chest.

"Can you do me a favor and . . . I know this sounds weird, but can you just like . . . take off your glasses?"

"Seriously?" She stood frozen before him.

He nodded. "Sorry, but yeah."

She pressed her lips into a thin, grim line and did a mental countdown from three. "Well, okay then." Without another word, she lifted her glasses onto her forehead and peered at him through a pair of dark brown contact lenses. "Would you like to see my ID too?" She shoved a hand into her oversize bag. It was the sort of bluff she couldn't afford to lose. If he said yes, she was screwed.

She retrieved the cheap nylon wallet and slowly pried it open. It was a game of chicken she was determined to win.

"No, you know what, it's fine." Tommy flushed and waved it away.

Madison waggled the wallet before him. "Maybe it'll make you feel better about getting into a car with a strange girl who's at least half your size."

Tommy gave an embarrassed laugh. "No." He shook his head. "Really, it's okay."

Madison dropped the wallet back in her bag and shuffled alongside him as they made for his car.

SEVENTEEN

iSPY

Sipping from their to-go cups, Aster and Ryan stood outside the trailer and considered their options.

"You sure this is it?" she asked.

"It's not like there's a mailbox, so it's impossible to know, but considering it's the only thing out here . . ." He finished the statement with a lift of his shoulders.

"It's just . . ." Aster ventured forward until she stood uncertainly before the door. "It's nicer than I expected. The pictures made it seem like a dump. Not some cool, vintage Airstream with a well-tended plant by the door."

"It's a cactus," Ryan said. "Doesn't require a whole lot of TLC. But I guess it makes sense. Madison would want it to look nice from the outside at least, seeing how image-conscious she is."

Aster detected a note of bitterness in his tone, and it left her wondering if maybe Ryan still carried the tiniest bit of a torch for his former flame. But just as quickly, she shook the thought away. Ryan had assured her plenty of times he was totally over her—that he'd never really been all that into her to begin with. At the start of the summer, it would've been impossible to believe that any guy could be so blasé about having dated Madison Brooks. But a lot had happened since then, and Aster had no reason to feel insecure about Ryan's superstar ex-girlfriend. Not after the morning they'd just spent together.

Ryan made for the door and knocked a few times. When no one answered, he tried the latch, but of course it was locked.

"It's metal," Aster said, stating the obvious. "So it's not like you can kick it in."

Ryan flexed his hands and considered his options. "True. But maybe there's a way to jimmy the window wide enough for you to slip in?"

Aster wanted in there as badly as he did, probably more. But she wasn't entirely sold on the idea.

"I'll give you a boost." Ryan handed her his cup and slipped a credit card from his wallet, which he then ran between the window glass and the gasket. "Luckily, there's no screen." He spoke between gritted teeth as he worked to pry it open.

When that didn't work, Aster watched in amazement when he pulled a screwdriver from his back pocket and set about disconnecting the crank bars so he could maneuver them to pop open.

"Let me guess, you were a Boy Scout." She gestured toward the screwdriver.

"Sadly, not for long." He shot her a quick smile. "I missed too many meetings when I got cast as a regular on my first series, so I had to quit." With the bar where he wanted it, he pulled the window wide open. "There." Satisfied, he motioned that it was her turn.

Aster glanced nervously between the window and Ryan. This was no time for second-guessing. Besides, it wouldn't be the first time she'd broken into one of Madison's residences.

Setting the cups on an unseen surface inside, she placed her hands on the ledge and said, "On three . . ." The next thing she knew, she was halfway inside, gazing in wonder at the space before her.

"Anything?"

"No spoilers." Aster pulled herself in, then swung her legs around until her feet hit the ground. She stared in amazement as she made her way across the dark hardwood floor and slid open the dead bolt that unlocked the front door. "Welcome." She arced her arm wide and stepped aside to make room for Ryan.

He stopped in the center and looked around, his expression as uncertain as she currently felt. "Not what I expected."

Aster readily agreed.

The space was narrow, long, and extremely well organized into separate individual areas. At the nearer end, there was an alcove with a bed covered in a plush shearling throw and an abundance of expensive-looking decorative pillows. In place of a door, there was a screen of shimmering crystal-beaded curtains.

There was a surprisingly nice bathroom featuring just the sort of deluxe, high-end fixtures you'd expect to find in an A-lister's trailer.

Aside from the small kitchen with the custom table and eating nook, there was a den set up at the far end, with large cushions for lounging, and a low carved table littered with books, candles, and an assortment of crystals.

"It looks like some high-end fortune-teller's trailer," Ryan said. "The only things missing are tarot cards and a raven."

"It's the perfect place for a secret, romantic getaway. You sure you've never been here?" She flashed him an accusatory look. There she was, feeling jealous again. She shook her head and started over. "Anyway, it's nothing like the photos she commissioned."

Ryan moved toward one of the tables and checked out

her collection of art books. "Even though it's nothing like her house in LA, this definitely represents another side of her. Maybe her real side, for all I know. Hard to say what's real and what's pretend. Sometimes I wonder if she even knows."

"Meaning?" Aster watched as Ryan picked up a large chunk of polished rose quartz crystal and turned it over in his palm, before setting it back down.

"A lot of actresses are more comfortable playing someone other than themselves. And since Madison created a fictional past, sometimes I wonder if she maybe started to believe it. You know, like if you repeat the same lie so many times, it starts to seem real."

"Like in those diary entries," Aster said. "Where she mentions how she's always playing a role. She was just a kid when she wrote that."

Ryan scratched at his jaw. "Interesting as it is to speculate, none of it really gives us what we're looking for, though, does it?" He frowned as his gaze searched the room. "There's no saggy couch, no stained rug, no messed-up table holding a smoking gun."

Aster worried he was ready to call it quits, because she was just getting started. She wandered the different areas. Taking a closer look inside the bathroom, she cried, "She was here!" Her hands shook as she stood in the doorway. She'd never once doubted Madison was alive, but having the proof laid out before her momentarily robbed her of breath. "She was here—look!" Her legs trembled so much she grasped at the door frame to steady herself.

Ryan squinted past her shoulder. "I don't see it."

"Look, right there—in the sink. Madison was here! Recently, too!"

Aster's voice pitched high, her heart slamming wildly against her chest. She'd always thought that sort of good news would make her feel jubilant, triumphant. Not like she was on the verge of cardiac arrest.

"Look—the sink is wet and the towels and bath mat are damp! Also, there's stuff in the trash."

Ryan remained unresponsive, and Aster couldn't tell if it was because he didn't believe her, or because he did.

She pointed toward the bowl of the sink, where there was a dab of toothpaste stuck to the side. "She was here. I'm telling you." She plucked the toothbrush from the ceramic cup. The bristles were wet. She turned to Ryan. "This proves it."

Ryan remained unconvinced. His features were arranged in what she'd come to recognize as his go-to *I hate to break it to you but* face.

"Do you seriously not see what I do?" She knew she sounded hysterical, but the evidence was right there in front of them. Why was he so blind to the facts?

"Aster, I'm sorry," he said. "But damp towels and a glob

of toothpaste don't exactly prove anything. Maybe someone else has been staying here. It's entirely possible now that she's been missing so long."

"Like who? Who's been staying here?"

"I don't know." He squinted. "A squatter—someone who broke in, liked what they saw, and decided to hang around for a while."

"You're joking, right?"

He pressed his lips together. "I just don't think it's enough to go on."

"Okay, well, then how about this?" She picked up the hairbrush that was lying on the counter. It was tangled with both dark and light hairs. "Pending a DNA test, I'm going to go out on a limb and declare these hairs came from Madison."

Ryan's skeptical gaze met hers. "Even the blond one?"

"Could be from a wig. Just like the one she wore in the photo."

"So, what do you suggest? Should we bag it for evidence?"

Aster frowned. "Why are you being like this?"

Ryan looked uneasy.

"You're acting like you don't believe me—like I'm some desperate crazy person trying to turn the slightest thing into proof." She reached inside the trash can, batted aside the used tissue, and retrieved an empty water bottle along with a crumpled M&M's bag. "Here," she said. "In case you need more proof."

"It's a water bottle." Ryan frowned. "Someone's water bottle, but not necessarily Madison's." He pried the bottle away and tossed it back in the can. "Besides, Madison doesn't eat candy."

Aster dropped her head in her hands. She was acting crazy. Her desperate need for answers had altered her ability to think straight.

"I'm a mess," she said. "I'm losing my mind. I don't even know what to do anymore."

She lifted her gaze to find she'd spoken to an empty room.

"Ryan?" She peeked around the doorway and found him standing very still with his back turned toward her. Her heart sank. Great. She'd finally gone too far. And now he . . .

He glanced over his shoulder. His face pale, he said, "You were right. She was here."

Aster raced toward him, struggling to make out whatever it was he dangled from the tip of his index finger.

He dropped it onto the center of her palm, rendering Aster speechless when she gazed at Madison's diamond-encrusted Piaget watch.

"Where'd you find this?"

A smile tugged at his lips. "Inside the cookie jar." He ran

a hand across his chin. "Knowing Madison's eating habits, it seemed a bit odd she'd even own such a thing."

"What else is in there?"

Aster started to move toward it, when Ryan said, "Nothing. Only the watch. She wore it on the night she went missing."

"And you're sure this is hers?" Now she was the one doubting the evidence.

"Positive. It was one of the few things she actually cherished, aside from her dog and her house. Mostly everything she owned was given to her. But the watch she bought with her first real paycheck, and she was extremely proud of it. Go ahead, read the inscription."

Aster peered at the back of the case, where the letters *M.D.S.* were engraved. "MaryDella Slocum?" She turned toward Ryan.

"For someone so bent on hiding her past, she sure surrounded herself with a lot of reminders," he said.

Aster glanced between Ryan and the timepiece.

"C'mon," he said. "I say we search every last corner. Maybe she left us a clue on when she plans to return."

EIGHTEEN

YOU ARE GOODBYE

"You okay? You seem a little on edge."

Tommy gazed out the windshield. Edgy wasn't the half of it. He felt tense, confused, and rocked with uncertainty. Miles of freeway had whizzed by in a blur, and while Dahlia had asked what seemed to be a legit list of questions, something about the whole scenario was starting to feel really wrong.

"How much farther?" he asked, wondering, not for the first time, just where the heck she was leading him.

Tommy had read plenty of interviews where a bit of a drive was involved, but he'd never read one that dragged on for so long. It was starting to seem kind of creepy.

"Not much longer."

Tommy gripped the wheel and glanced in the rearview

mirror, wishing he could rewind all that asphalt until they were back at the record store. It was weird to think how a piece in *Rolling Stone* had always been the ultimate dream, but now that it was happening, he just wanted it to be over.

"Am I boring you?" Dahlia gave him a playful nudge, revealing hands that were surprisingly calloused and rough. Her nails were torn below the quick, and one of her pinkie fingers was wrapped with blue tape. What the hell had happened to her? "Do you want me to take over?"

"Thought you said it wasn't long." He shot her a sideways glance.

"It's not." She sank lower onto the seat and propped her injured ankle onto the dashboard, allowing Tommy a glimpse of white thigh that had him quickly turning away. "Sorry," she said, in a voice that seemed far more amused than conciliatory. "Not trying to make you uncomfortable. It helps with the swelling to keep it elevated."

"And yet, you just offered to drive." He sounded agitated but also saw no point in taking it back. After a few silent beats, he said, "Balance beam accident, huh?"

She tossed her hair over her shoulder and laughed. "Skydiving." She wagged a messed-up finger at him. "Just like I told you. But I guess you weren't listening."

She was playing him. It was obvious she was having fun at his expense. Though he wasn't quite ready to call her on it, that laugh of hers was hauntingly familiar.

He stopped at a light and took advantage of the moment to study her. She reminded him of a handful of girls he knew from working at the Vesper. That was probably all it was.

The car behind him honked, Dahlia idly brushed her hand against the inside of her thigh, and Tommy shook free of his daze and shot through the intersection like he was being pursued by something he couldn't quite name.

"Easy, cowboy." Again, she laughed, causing a chill to crawl across Tommy's skin. "Make a left up here. Followed by a sharp right. By the way, you hungry?"

He was, but for some reason he found himself shaking his head.

"Good. Because it's been months since I last went grocery shopping."

Grocery shopping? He looked at her. "Can I ask where we're going?"

"Sure." She inspected the ends of her hair. "You can always ask."

"But you're not going to answer?"

"And ruin the suspense?"

He focused on driving, turning, slowing, stopping, following all her instructions. The farther they wandered from the freeway, the creepier the whole scenario became. Sure it was still daylight, and Dahlia was skinny and injured and didn't seem to pose too much of a threat. But they were headed into an area Tommy wouldn't even call rural. Desolate was the word that best described it.

"Tell me, Tommy, does this remind you of home?" Dahlia made a sweeping gesture toward the windshield, indicating the countrified scene just beyond.

Tommy glanced between the dirt road and her, and in that instant, something clicked. Something so improbable, his first instinct was to deny it.

And yet . . .

He cleared his throat. "Not really," he said. "How about you? Does it remind you of home?"

She pulled her knees up to her chest, wrapped her arms around them, and arranged her features into an exaggerated frown. "Already told you, I grew up in LA. You really are a bad listener, aren't you?"

She scratched at the inside of her wrist, and Tommy caught himself sneaking a peek. If she'd just push her sleeve a bit higher, he'd know for sure if the unthinkable was happening.

A second later, she dragged the cuff down until it covered her knuckles and reached past her thumb. Tommy looked away, tapped his own thumbs against the steering wheel, and tried to decide how to proceed.

It wouldn't do any good to let on. It was better to see where they ended up and then maybe try to confront her with the startling truth he was growing more and more convinced of.

He snuck another look at her profile. Despite the wig, dark glasses, and heavy makeup—despite her California no-accent accent—he was left with no doubt that Madison Brooks was now sitting beside him.

"Hope your girlfriend's not the jealous type," she said, seemingly plucking the words out of nowhere.

Tommy thought briefly of Layla and said, "There's no girlfriend."

"Well, that's good. Then she won't get upset when you get home late." She grinned flirtatiously, just the barest curve of lip and a slight tilt of chin.

What the hell kind of game was she playing?

"That is," she added, "if you get home at all."

The way she said it, Tommy had no way of knowing if she meant ever—like if he ever got home at all—or for just that night.

Before he had a chance to respond, she said, "Make a tight right up ahead. Then follow the long dirt road all the way down. I'm taking you the back way."

"I've no doubt," Tommy murmured, committed to playing along.

NINETEEN

LADY GRINNING SOUL

Aster was so engrossed in searching through Madison's belongings that she failed to hear the sound of tires crunching over gravel as a car approached the trailer. Luckily, Ryan alerted her.

"Who is it?" She looked up in alarm as he bolted toward the window.

Ryan shrugged and whispered back. "I can't make out the driver."

Aster glanced around wildly. In such a small space, there was no good place to hide. Then again, there was also no good reason to hide. It was Madison. She was sure of it. The moment she'd been waiting for from the second she'd been charged with her murder had finally arrived.

Aster positioned herself just shy of the door. Ryan looked

uncertain, but Aster just nodded and kept her gaze firm. A car door closed, followed by the shuffle of footsteps. When the door latch lifted, Aster's pulse spiked with panic. They'd forgotten to lock the door! Would Madison get suspicious and run? It was a possibility Aster couldn't risk.

She sprang toward the door the same moment it opened from the outside and Heather Rollins strolled in.

"What the hell?" Heather rocked back on her heels as her arm shot out, grasping for something to steady herself.

"What're you doing here?" Ryan shouted, as Aster stood gasping beside him.

Heather righted herself, smoothed a hand over her long blond curls, and in an accusatory voice said, "Pretty sure I could ask the same thing of you two." She pushed past them and surveyed the messy space. Whistling under her breath, she said, "Was it ransacked when you got here, or is this your doing?"

"What do you want?" Aster folded her arms across her chest and glared.

Heather turned with a grin and wagged a finger between them. "Look at you with your matching tees. You two legit now?" Her brown eyes flashed. "Oh, relax," she said, reading Aster's enraged expression. "It's not like I'm gonna alert the press. Who you choose to hook up with is your business. Though I am curious . . ." She moved closer. "Does this mean you're no longer a virgin?" She set her gaze on

Aster, before switching to Ryan. "Or is she still making you wait for it?"

Aster was furious, ready to unleash the full extent of her fury, when Heather said, "Better get used to it. You're the one who decided to go on Trena's show and profess your purity to the world. I remember thinking just seconds after you said it that you'd live to regret it."

"What do you want?" Ryan slid a protective arm around Aster, but it did nothing to calm her. She was too wound up for that.

"Looking for Madison." She pursed her lips and looked around. "But apparently, she's not here."

"So you think she's alive, then?" Aster was annoyed, but she knew better than to let it get in the way. If Heather knew something, then Aster needed to try a little harder to befriend her.

"Of course she's alive." Heather rolled her eyes like it was a well-known fact, and not a question the whole world was debating.

"What makes you so sure?" Ryan watched as Heather wandered to the far end of the trailer, where she stood gazing at the collection of crystals.

She pinched a stone between her fingers and said, "Rose quartz." She held it up for better inspection. "Said to attract love and romance. Did she use this to cast her spell on you?"

Ryan's face went grim as Heather laughed, replaced the crystal, and sank down onto one of the cushions. Crossing her legs in a way that encouraged her dress to rise high on her thigh, she tossed her hair over her shoulder and said, "Then again, no love spell necessary, right? I mean, after all, she is Madison Brooks. And Madison gets what Madison wants. She's weatherproof, waterproof, scandalproof. Nothing ever sticks. Including her breakup with you." She nudged a finger at Ryan. "She made sure to manipulate it in a way that made her look good, while you two . . ." She shook her head and smirked. "Well, you looked like a couple of assholes, didn't you?"

Ryan frowned. Aster struggled to withhold her response.

"Anyway, despite all the evidence, I never believed she was dead. I also never believed you guys were guilty of anything other than being in the wrong place at the wrong time. And maybe, at least in Aster's case, a tiny bit of tragic naïveté. And then yesterday, when Paul called—"

Aster jumped in before she could finish. "You heard from Paul?"

Heather swiveled back and forth in the chair, making them wait. "He claims he wants Madison's dog. But if you ask me, it seems a bit sketchy."

"So what happened?" Ryan asked. "No one's been able to find him."

Heather inspected her nails. "And they still can't. I

waited for over an hour and he never showed." She looked around with a bored gaze. "One thing's for sure, if you find Paul, you find Madison."

"You make it sound easy," Aster said.

"Do I?" Heather looked amused. "You're the one who broke into his office. Pretty sure you know more about the mysterious Paul Banks than any of us."

Aster clamped her lips shut. She wasn't about to incriminate herself.

"Oh please, it's not like it's some big secret. The whole world knows you were there. Ballsy move on your part—didn't know a girl like you had it in you."

"A girl like me." Aster stiffened her stance. She didn't like where this was going, but she was braced for just about anything.

"Aw, see, now you've taken offense, and it's the last thing I meant. You have to understand, I didn't have many advantages in life. I worked my ass off to get where I am."

"So you assume my life has been a breeze because my family is rich?"

Heather scoffed. "Clearly not. It's just I was always fascinated by girls like you. As a kid, I was forced to work on a ranch, mucking out stalls and hauling around giant bales of hay. The girls who owned the horses always seemed so glossy and effortless, with their long shiny ponytails and their expensive britches and boots. They reminded me of the pedigreed horses they rode. Thoroughbred Girls, I used to call them. Anyway, I guess that's how I think of you too. You're a Thoroughbred Girl if I've ever seen one."

Aster was taken aback. She didn't quite know how to respond.

"No matter how many magazine covers, product endorsements, or decent roles I get, I'll never achieve that. I'll never know what it's like to feel so cushioned from the rougher edges of the world."

"And you think I'm cushioned?" Aster glared.

"Well, clearly not anymore. You want my honest opinion?" Heather's brown eyes fixed on Aster's. "I think there's a good chance you're about to face a jury of twelve people who also grew up hating the Thoroughbred Girls, and believe me, that won't end well for you. To make matters worse, your kind tends to lack the sort of survival skills girls like Madison and me learned by necessity."

Aster stood speechless.

Heather held her gaze, then said, "So, she was here, right?" She glanced between Aster and Ryan. "Madison was here."

Aster looked at Ryan. Ryan stayed silent.

"Oh, for God's sake," Heather said. "You're wearing her watch!"

Aster's gaze dropped to her wrist. She'd slipped it on just after they'd found it. She hadn't yet decided what to do with it.

"Madison had more Hermès bags and Louboutin heels than she could count, but she cherished that thing more than anything else. You're not going to try to keep it, are you?"

"Of course not!" Aster sounded offended, which she instantly regretted. It was better to stay neutral. Heather would consider any emotional reaction a victory, and Aster was unwilling to concede that to her.

"Then you better wipe it clean. Leaving any trace of your prints behind could really come back to bite you. Especially with so much evidence already stacked up against you."

Slowly, Heather rose and lazily tugged at the hem of her dress. "Well, thanks for the hospitality." She tossed a breezy wave over her shoulder as she brushed past them and made to leave.

"You're leaving?" Aster stared after her retreating form.

"No point in staying when she won't be returning."

"How can you be sure?"

Heather turned with a grin. "Because Madison won't stay in any one place for more than a day. I'm surprised she even came here, since it's registered in her name. Well, her real name. And now that we all know what that is, it won't be long before the LAPD and the press catch on. The fact that she was here just proves how desperate she is." Heather shook her head sadly. But Heather wasn't that good of an actress. It was clear she didn't feel the least bit sorry for her former friend. "It's weird to think she's been gone for so long but never made it past here. Maybe she really did just need a break, but then the whole thing kind of blew up and she didn't know where to turn." She twirled a random blond curl around her index finger. "It's kinda sad if you think about it. I mean, to be that well known and not have a single friend you can count on—other than Paul. All we can do is pray for her now." She focused on Aster. "I'm sure you already are, only for different reasons, of course." Heather reached for the door. "Anyway, gotta run. Shooting on the new show is set to begin." Looking at Ryan, she said, "I really did lobby for you, but they're trying to get Mateo Luna to sign. Pretty sure you know him."

"I took myself out of the running early on," Ryan said, his voice tight.

"Did you?" Heather looked amused. "My bad. Anyway, Mateo's a natural. A reluctant natural, which makes him even more perfect. Still, it's doubtful he'll do it. He's kind of a purist."

"So, you two a thing now?" Aster studied her. She hadn't liked her before. She liked her less now.

Heather laughed and stepped outside. "I never kiss and tell." She shot a pointed look Ryan's way. "You of all people should know that."

Aster watched Heather climb into her car and drive away. When she was gone, Aster turned to Ryan and said, "What the hell did that mean?"

A flash of pain crossed Ryan's face. "Nothing. You can't trust anything she says."

Aster wasn't sure she believed him, but they had bigger issues to deal with than the long list of girls Ryan may or may not have slept with. "Do you think we should've followed her?" she asked.

Ryan shook his head. "I doubt she knows anything. She's too narcissistic to waste much time on it. She'll keep herself just involved enough to be part of the story, but no more."

"You think she's right about Madison not returning?"

Ryan shrugged. "Makes sense."

"But then why would she leave the watch if she was supposedly so attached to it?"

"It was a sentimental attachment," he said. "But make no mistake, her only real attachment is Blue. Which gives me hope that she really is out there. Even so, if it came down to it, Madison wouldn't hesitate to walk away from him too."

Aster gazed in dismay at the mess that surrounded them. "I'm not sure what to do from here."

"You might want to start by checking your phone." He nodded toward the table, where her cell vibrated.

"It's Javen." She looked at Ryan. "He sent an address. Says Layla's headed there now."

"Another dead end?"

Aster sighed. "Guess we're about to find out."

TWENTY

SLOW DANCING IN A BURNING ROOM

Tommy was acting weird, and it was making Madison nervous.

She glanced in the vanity mirror, ensuring that her wig was still on, her makeup in place. She'd been careful to stick to her role and keep her arm covered. And yet not long after they'd exited the freeway, something had shifted between them, and she'd been unable to get him back on her side.

She remembered the previous times they'd met, back when he was a naive country boy who was in way over his head. He'd been so much easier to manipulate back then.

The summer had changed him. Now he seemed resentful, edgy, like he had somewhere better to be.

Was it because back then she'd been Madison

Brooks—the It Girl at the top of Ira's get list? She doubted it. Their kiss felt like something more had sparked between them—something more equal and intimate than the usual fan/celebrity hookup.

Did his change of heart have to do with Layla?

Was he really so devoted he wouldn't indulge in a little harmless flirtation?

And if so, what the hell did he see in her?

She guessed Layla was pretty enough. And God knows she was driven and ambitious in a way Madison might've found admirable if the circumstances had been different.

But the way Layla had gone after her on her blog had earned her a place on Madison's blacklist. Her most recent post ensured she'd remain there for good.

Madison looked out the window and sighed. Tommy was so keyed up, she worried he might try to drop her off and drive away before she even had a chance to put her plan into play.

"Stop," she said. "Stop right here."

Tommy motioned toward the windshield. "There's nothing here." His tone was a combination of jittery and annoyed.

"I know. Just—I want to say something before we arrive." She waited while Tommy reluctantly pressed his foot to the brake and slowly rolled to a stop. When he killed the engine, she said, "I'm sorry."

He removed his sunglasses and studied her face.

"If I got too flirty, or made you feel uncomfortable in any way, then I apologize."

The look she received in return was blank.

"I know you have a girlfriend and—"

"We've been over this." He gripped the wheel hard. She'd pushed him too far. "It's weird how you keep bringing it up."

Madison studied him. "I thought you and Layla Harrison . . ." She left it unfinished, but Tommy just stared out the windshield and clenched and unclenched his jaw.

"I'm tired of every nuance of my life being dished out for public consumption." His features sharpened, his lips flattened in fury.

"You wanted to be a star." Her words echoed between them. "It's part of the deal."

He turned to her, eyes burning. "I never wanted any of that. I never wanted people to dissect my choices—who I'm dating, what I'm wearing, what I drive, where I go, what I eat, drink. Everything I do is under a microscope, and if they don't like what they see, they don't hesitate to unleash their contempt in the comments section. It's total bullshit! My personal life is none of their business, and yet they act like they own me. All I wanted, all I truly ever wanted, was to make music that people enjoyed—that's it!"

Madison simmered in fury. Any residual guilt she

might've felt over stringing him along had just vanished. If there was one thing she hated more than anything, it was when people acted like victims of their own good fortune. The other thing was when people blamed outwardly instead of getting real with themselves.

"You sure about that?" Her voice was her own, no more pretending. "Because last I checked, you wanted fame and the fan base that comes with it. Only your dream didn't come packaged to your exact specifications, so now you think you have the right to complain to anyone who will listen. Well, too bad. The spotlight is shining on you, so what are you going to do about it? Are you going to run back to your hick town and let the locals use your return to defend their own sorry avoidance of whatever dreams they once had but never found the guts to pursue? 'Look at him,' they'll say. 'He soared so high he touched the sun, but in the end, he came running right back to us.' Will you play into their narrative? Performing sad songs at the local dive bar and pretending you're relieved to have escaped the evils of Hollywood—to be back among all the *real* people living *real* lives?" She rolled her eyes. "Give me a break, Tommy. I'm all too familiar with the sort of world you fled, and I'm here to tell you that Hollywood is far more raw and gritty and real than just about anywhere else. It's a place of soaring triumphs and devastating defeats. Where fortunes rise and fall on the whims of an increasingly fickle public that's impossible to please. Every choice is a risk and the stakes are tremendous, and yet every failure offers another shot at redemption. So you tell me, what's more real than that? From the moment you arrived here, you entered the game. And trust me, you're one of the lucky ones. It didn't take you very long to get known." The laugh that followed was harsh. And though she knew she should let up, she'd kept the sentiment bottled up for so long the words had to be spoken.

She'd been pretending to interview Tommy off and on for hours, and she was tired of the way he'd framed his life. Maybe that sort of regretful, wide-eyed, how-did-I-end-up-here bullshit story would work in print, but as it turned out, nothing he said would ever go any further than the inside of his car.

The irony wasn't entirely lost on her. For a person who specialized in deception, Madison was demanding 100 percent authenticity in return. Only then would she know she could trust him.

"You came here to be a star, right?"

Tommy glared, silently seething.

"And now you are. So own it, or leave. Your call."

"Kind of seems like the 'interview'"—he used air quotes around the word—"ended back in Calabasas."

"It was never an interview." Madison paused, letting the words sink in. The game was over. And though she had no idea what would follow, she knew it was time for her to get real too.

Tommy stared in astonishment. She'd just confirmed what he'd already been thinking, but now, from the looks of him, he was having a hard time processing it.

"What the fuck are you doing?" he asked, his voice low and menacing.

Still, Madison relaxed for the first time that day. Finally, they could start to move forward. She knew he wouldn't harm her. Tommy wasn't the type to ever raise a hand to a woman.

"Seriously! What the fuck?" He gazed around wildly. "I mean . . . *fuck!*" He slammed his fist hard on the wheel, repeating the word, as Madison watched quietly from the passenger seat. "Do you have any idea what you've put us through? I went to *jail* because of you! We all did! I got death threats. My tires were slashed. And you've been alive all this time?" He whirled on her. "What the fuck, Madison?"

He'd called her Madison, not MaryDella. She took it as a good sign.

A single tear slid down her face. Crying on cue had always come easily. But while her intent was to appear vulnerable in a way that would make Tommy calm down enough to talk, the flood that followed came of its own accord. Once it started, Madison found it impossible to stop.

It was the first time she'd cried in a really long time. It felt good to finally let it all out.

Tommy glanced from her messed-up ankle to her bandaged hand. "What the hell happened to you?" He reached for her arm and gently pushed up her sleeve, seeing the burn scar and the new one just above it, where her flesh was still tender and pink. He shook his head and sighed. It was the final confirmation he needed.

Next thing she knew, he drew her into his arms. Smoothing a hand down her back, he whispered a string of reassurances she longed to believe.

It was the second time she'd turned to him for solace. She hoped his support would extend a little further. She pulled away and dabbed at her cheeks with the cuff of her sleeve.

"Here." Tommy pressed a napkin he'd plucked from his cup holder to her cheek. "It's clean, I promise," he said, which made them both laugh.

With his other hand, he slid the sunglasses from her face and stared in confusion.

"Contacts," she whispered.

He gazed at her in wonder. "Down to every last detail."

"And yet, you still saw right through it." Her biggest fans hadn't even recognized her, and yet Tommy had.

"I might've kissed and told." He shot her a guilty look. "But I never forgot the moment you revealed the real you."

He held her gaze until her cheeks begin to heat. The rest of her body soon followed. "Where to now?" he asked, breaking the spell and returning them both back to reality and the decisions ahead.

"You're not going to turn me in?"

"No," he said, his voice firm. "Not before you've had a chance to explain."

It was the best scenario she could hope for. "Your mama raised you right," she told him. "You're one of the good ones."

Tommy laughed and engaged the ignition. "Someday, when this is all over, I'll tell her you said so."

TWENTY-ONE

KILLER QUEEN

Trena stood in the entry of Madison's trailer, not the least bit surprised to find it unlocked. First thing she'd spotted as she headed for the door were two sets of fresh tire tracks.

Inside, it looked messy, haphazard. Like someone had emptied all the cupboards and drawers, then shoved everything back in a hurry. Though it definitely belonged to Madison. Trena had done a quick bit of research on the property just to make sure Javen wasn't messing with her. Still, that didn't mean Madison had recently been there.

After checking out the bathroom and the bedroom alcove, she moved toward the area at the opposite end that was set up like a small den. Her gaze drifted from the stacks of cushions to the pile of art books, before coming to rest on Madison's diamond-encrusted gold Piaget watch sitting among a pile of crystals. Just like that, her hunch was confirmed: Madison Brooks was alive!

Despite the inflammatory stories she'd reported, Trena had never believed Madison was dead. Her provocative headlines had helped fuel her success, but the watch was the first real piece of proof she'd yet to come across.

The diamonds surrounding the bezel were dull and desperately in need of a cleaning. Even the band was scratched, which seemed odd, considering how Madison was known for being fastidious with her belongings.

Retrieving a pair of latex gloves from her bag, Trena hooked the timepiece with her finger and angled it toward the light. Trena had studied enough video footage and stills of Madison from the night of her breakup with Ryan to know it was the same watch she'd worn at the time. It was the only watch Madison was ever known to wear. And the engraved initials on the back of the case served to confirm it.

She dropped it into a plastic bag and considered how best to proceed. The only real question was whether or not to alert Detective Larsen.

On the one hand, she owed him. It was because of him that she'd been the first to break the Joshua Tree story.

Also, just because Madison was alive didn't mean she wasn't in danger.

And yet, the trailer showed no obvious signs of a struggle. Nothing to lead her to believe Madison was being held against her will.

No, something else was going on—something Trena couldn't quite put her finger on.

Her phone chimed with an incoming message. Not long after she'd started reporting on Madison's story, she'd set up a tip line. So far nothing solid had come of it, but as she peered at the screen, she had the unmistakable feeling that was about to change.

Someone had sent her a video. It had been filmed with an unsteady hand, but from what Trena could make out, it was taken at the impromptu memorial that Madison's fans had set up just outside Night for Night.

The usual street music of honking cars and sirens could be heard in the background, as the camera panned across the crowd gathered around the collection of items left in Madison's memory. The sound of laughter was soon eclipsed by a female voice saying, "What the hell are you doing?"

"Shhh . . . video in progress!" another voice said. And then in a mock-serious tone: "We're on Hollywood Boulevard outside Night for Night, where MaryDella Slocum was last seen." Uncontrollable laughter followed, prompting the video to swing wildly before someone else took over.

"And we sincerely hope she turns up dead, because that's what she deserves for lying to us all these years! RIP, bitch!"

Trena played the video again. And then again. On the third viewing she realized the words weren't important.

Whoever had shot the video hadn't intentionally set out to capture the skinny blond girl placing a single turquoise-and-gold hoop earring next to a stuffed teddy bear with angel wings. But as Trena watched it unfold yet again, she narrowed her focus to that girl, noting the way she stiffened and turned after hearing the words, "RIP, bitch!" The girl's face was hidden behind dark oversize sunglasses, though there was no mistaking it was *her*.

"Where are you now, Madison?" Trena whispered. "Where have you gone?"

She froze the frame to study the picture when another text arrived.

I have the earring. It's yours for a price.

Amateurs. Trena smirked. *A couple of dumb teens who could be bought off easily.* Without hesitation she replied.

I'll be in touch soon.

She dropped her phone in her bag and started to leave. Then, thinking better, she retrieved the watch from the plastic bag, placed it back where she'd found it, and put in a call to Larsen.

Let him have this one. If nothing else, he would owe her, and it was always better when he was in her debt.

Besides, thanks to the video, Trena was onto a much bigger lead.

TWENTY-TWO

LET'S HURT TONIGHT

Tommy pulled up to a surprisingly unassuming home and parked in the drive.

"What is this place?"

"A secret hideaway. Only now that you're here, I guess it's not such a secret anymore." Madison glanced over her shoulder and shot him a look he wasn't quite sure how to read.

He didn't want to flatter himself into thinking she was flirting, because it wasn't that, or at least not entirely, though her expression was unmistakably warm, bordering on intimate. Well, they'd shared a moment. He supposed it was an acknowledgment of that. Either way, he was done deciphering her every move. From this point forward, he planned to sit back and see what unfolded.

The house was remote, with no visible neighbors, which made sense for someone who guarded their privacy as much as Madison. Still, from the pictures he'd seen, the LA house was the stuff of fantasies. It seemed strange to want to escape from a place that represented everything she'd worked so hard to achieve.

Then again, Madison was a true star. Instead of griping over the price of fame, she'd accepted the inevitable and found a temporary escape from the pressure.

She swung the door wide, silenced the alarm, and invited him to follow. He blinked at his surroundings. The space was nothing like he'd expected, even though he hadn't known what to expect.

The ceilings were lined with thick beams, and the dark wood floors were occasionally interrupted by woven jute rugs. In the den, he found an ivory linen couch, a set of leather club chairs, and what looked to be an original fire-place made of hand-smoothed plaster. Through the French doors just beyond, he could make out a charming garden terrace filled with lanterns, a long table, and a hammock lilting in the breeze in the far corner.

"California ranch chic." Madison watched him survey the place. "What do you think?"

He turned with a start. While he'd been checking out the property, she'd removed her disguise, leaving her long dark hair tumbling over her shoulders as her violet eyes flashed on his. She was skinny and injured, and her makeup was heavy-handed, but at the moment, it was clear why Madison Brooks was the biggest star in the world. She radiated something that continued to thrive despite whatever had happened to her.

The look she gave him was so intense it set him off balance and left him wondering if she'd guessed at his thoughts. "I think it makes for a nice getaway," he finally said, forcing a crooked grin to his face.

She glanced around the space and nodded in agreement. "But now that you've seen it, I guess I have no choice but to sell it."

"You've never brought anyone here?" He understood the need to be alone, but it seemed strange not to share such a place.

"No one I wasn't one hundred percent sure I could trust."

He met her gaze. "So, no one then."

Motioning for him to sit, she went to grab a couple of beers.

Tommy wasn't sure he should drink. He was exhausted from the drive and hadn't the slightest clue what she had in mind. But when Madison emerged from the kitchen, handed him a bottle, and plopped onto the couch beside him, he figured a little blunting of the nerves might do him some good.

"Last time we shared a beer, things didn't turn out so

well for me." She tapped the bottle to her lip and stared thoughtfully.

"Same." He wiped the back of his hand across his mouth, then hesitated before placing the beer on the table.

"You've got old-school manners. I like that. But this is a coaster-free zone, so . . ." She placed her own beer directly on the table and gestured for him to do so as well.

She was trying to make him feel comfortable, and while Tommy appreciated the gesture, he was hoping to move on to the discussion they needed to have.

"So." She shifted her body toward him. "What now?"

Tommy eased back against the cushions. "Way I see it, it's my turn to interview you."

She leaned her head back and stared up at the ceiling. Then, without warning, she rose to her feet and extended a hand he was slow to take.

"What's this? What's going on?"

"Only one way to find out." She wiggled her brows.

Grasping her hand in his, he followed her down a hall to a large room at the end.

"I think you're going to like this." She grinned as she swung the door open.

Tommy stood on the threshold. One thing was sure: Madison never failed to surprise him.

"It's a combination training room slash rage room." She

slipped inside. "Have you ever seen one?"

Tommy shook his head and ran his gaze around the space. The floor was covered in wall-to-wall rubber that gave slightly under his step. Three of the walls appeared to be heavily padded, while the fourth consisted of badly dented drywall. In a far corner hung a large punching bag, along with an assortment of boxing gloves, paddles, and bats. A shelf stacked with cheap porcelain plates completed the theme.

"This is my favorite way to de-stress. Much better and far more effective than more illicit activities."

Tommy shifted uncertainly. How much built-up anger did a person have to possess to even need such a place?

"You should try it." She shot him a knowing look.

Tommy waved a hand. "That's okay," he said. "I'm good."

She peered at him so intently he cringed. "I'm guessing you accepted the beer not just out of politeness but to also take off some of the edge from what's turning out to be kind of a messed-up day."

He shrugged. She might be right, but he was under no obligation to admit it.

"Are you actually going to pretend you're not angry at me for hijacking your *Rolling Stone* interview?"

He turned on her.

"The interview was real. I simply got lucky and decided to take advantage of an opportunity that was presented to me."

His mind raced to catch up with her words. "I stood up *Rolling Stone* magazine?"

She handed him a bat and took a step back.

He gripped the handle and glared. "You sure you want to give me this right after admitting that?"

She lifted her shoulders. "People always have the capacity to surprise."

Their eyes met.

"Go ahead," she urged. "Show me how mad I've made you."

Tommy pressed his lips together and tightened his grip. He really was mad. Actually he was angry in a way words could never express. Once she'd confirmed her true identity, he assumed the interview was faked too. Discovering it wasn't left him enraged, and there was no telling how Malina might react.

His shoulders tensed. From the corner of his eye he glimpsed Madison's face. She looked pale, fragile, tragic, and vulnerable. But in her gaze, he caught a glimmer of unmistakable excitement.

Facing the padded wall, he swung the bat so hard a loud *whack* reverberated throughout the room. His biceps juddered in response, and his pulse raced as a rush of endorphins coursed through him. He longed to do it again, but with Madison watching, he lowered the bat to his side. "This is fun and all, but we need to talk. You have a lot to explain."

"I do," she agreed. "But not until you've worked through your anger. C'mon," she chided. "I know you can do better than that. What're you so afraid of, Tommy? This isn't just a rage room. It's a safe room."

Tommy hesitated, torn between looking foolish and smacking the hell out of that wall until he felt better. He closed his eyes, squared his shoulders, and widened his stance. The first swing had felt good, the second even better.

He swung again. And again. He swung for Detective Larsen, the paparazzi, for the faceless douche who'd slashed his car tires. He swung for every hater who'd sent a death threat. He swung for Trena Moretti, who dragged his name through the mud in a bid for higher ratings. He even swung for Layla because he liked her, and she drove him crazy in ways both good and bad. And because deep down inside, he knew they'd probably blow up before they could even try to make it work. He swung for Ira Redman, his piece-of-shit father. And he kept on swinging until he'd swung so many times he could no longer remember what he was swinging for or how he even got there.

Exhausted, he dropped the bat to the ground and turned to face Madison. His face sheened with sweat, his shoulder throbbed in a raging dull ache. Still, he felt more alive than he had in ages.

Madison pushed away from the wall and slowly walked toward him. "You have no idea how beautiful that was." Her eyes glimmered. "One of the most authentic displays I've seen in a while." She moved so close there was merely a hand's width between them. "How do you feel?"

Tommy's gaze rested on hers. "Good," he said, his voice hoarse as he fought to steady his breath.

"Good, like spent? Like you let it all out? Or is there a part of you that still wants to throttle me?"

He nodded toward the row of paddles. "What are those for?"

Madison's violet eyes flashed, and her grin grew wider. "I thought you'd never ask."

TWENTY-THREE

HEY, JEALOUSY

Layla spotted Tommy's car in the drive and stared dumbfounded at the sight.

What the hell was Tommy Phillips doing at Madison Brooks's secret address?

Just how long had he known Madison was alive?

She parked at the end of the road and sent Aster a text.

Change of plan. Meet me at the end of the street. You'll see why when you get here.

So far, they'd communicated solely via Javen, but Layla was too keyed up to go through the motions. For all she knew, Tommy and Madison were responsible for the numerous threats she'd received. Hell, they'd probably been working together all along.

She glared at the rearview mirror. It took every ounce of her will to keep from breaking down the front door and pummeling them both until they resembled one of the cartoon cats on the notes she'd been sent.

Despite everything she'd been through—public humiliation, death threats, jail time—Layla finally knew what it was like to be so consumed by rage she literally couldn't see straight. What had once seemed like some dumb cliché of flaring nostrils, racing heart, shaking hands, seeing red, and an absolute inability to think clearly had become her current reality.

She'd trusted Tommy. She'd made herself vulnerable to him. And the whole time, he'd been stringing her along in whatever sick game the two of them were playing.

She fingered the door handle. Checked the time on her phone. Where the hell were Aster and Ryan? If they didn't show in the next five minutes, then she was going in on her own.

She pressed her forehead against the steering wheel and forced her breath to come. To think she'd traded Mateo for Tommy . . . what a colossal mistake that had been.

She'd always figured Mateo was too nice for her, that he deserved someone better, less cynical. Mateo was content living a quiet life, filled with simple pleasures. The contrast between his vision and Layla's had left her feeling restless, antsy, and craving a bigger experience.

At the time, Tommy seemed more her speed. He had big dreams and the ambition to feed them.

Being confronted with the truth was a humbling experience. Clearly she'd misjudged both guys.

When his little sister fell ill and his mom lost her job, Mateo didn't hesitate to do what it took to ease his mom's financial burdens and cover Valentina's medical bills. The swift and noble nature of his actions had left her both awed and ashamed for ever having doubted him.

And this was where Tommy's ambition had led him. She glared into the rearview mirror again.

She'd been such a fool, and now it was too late to reverse. Mateo's star was on the rise. He was dating Heather Rollins, of all people—a girl he'd once professed to dislike. From what she'd seen at Ira's tequila launch party, Mateo had since changed his mind.

Once this was all behind her, she vowed to walk away and never look back. Aside from Mateo, she'd never been good at maintaining romantic relationships. Maybe she really was more like her mom than she cared to admit. Rumor had it her mom's latest marriage was on the rocks and headed in the same direction as her first one, to Layla's dad.

Layla glanced at her phone and looked all around. Still no sign of Aster and Ryan. Well, screw it. The five-minute allowance had been arbitrary at best.

Tired of waiting. Going in.

The text swooshed into the ether as Layla bolted from the car and ran as fast as her legs would carry her.

TWENTY-FOUR

MY OH MY

"Stop the car!" Aster shouted, staring in dismay at the sight of Layla racing down the street.

Ryan slammed the brakes as Aster sprang from her seat and leaped in front of her. "Whatever you're planning on doing, *don't!*" She grasped hold of Layla's arm.

Layla struggled against her, but once Ryan joined them, she quietly surrendered.

"I know you're upset," Aster forced herself to keep calm, hoping it would convince Layla to calm down too. "But everything we need is finally within reach. So you have to put your personal feelings aside and let me handle this, since I'm the one with the most on the line."

"You're right." Layla's shoulders slumped forward as the fight seeped out of her. "It's just—" Leaving the rest unspoken, she closed her eyes and covered her face with her hands.

"Let's not jump to any conclusions." Ryan slipped an arm around Layla. At the sight of it, Aster grew tense. There was no telling how Layla would respond. She was unpredictable at best, volatile at worst. "Let's give them a chance to explain," he said.

Layla dabbed at her face and lifted her gaze. "Yes, let's give them that chance, shall we?" Her mind made up, she tucked her hair behind her ears and motioned for Aster and Ryan to lead the way. She'd cycled from rage to grief to bitter determination so quickly it left Aster uneasy.

They paused before the front door. "If we ring the bell, we'll tip them off." Aster spoke in a whisper.

"You're not seriously thinking of breaking a window like you did in Joshua Tree." Layla stared, horrified.

"I will if I have to." Aster frowned. "But I'm thinking we should slip around back. It's hot as hell out. Maybe they've opened a window or something."

"Pretty sure Madison can afford an air conditioner," Layla quipped.

"Yeah, well, she's not really Madison, though, is she? She's MaryDella Slocum. So I'm guessing she's a fan of fresh air and wide-open spaces. It would explain why she chose to buy a secret house in the middle of nowhere."

"She used to crank the air and leave all the windows

open," Ryan said. "I told her she was single-handedly destroying the environment, but she said she hated feeling confined."

"So, what're we waiting for?" Layla nodded toward the side gate.

To Aster's relief, Layla let her take the lead, though there was no telling how she might react once they were inside and found Tommy and Madison together. Aster just hoped they wouldn't catch them doing something embarrassing. Then again, the more compromised they were, the better it was for her.

With Ryan's help, they scaled the gate and crept across the terrace to the french doors that opened to a nicely appointed den. Inside, she found two beers sweating on the coffee table, but no sign of Tommy or Madison.

Moving deeper into the room, they froze at the sound of dull, rhythmic pounding coming from the far end of the hall.

"Feels good, doesn't it?"

Aster swayed unsteadily. Even though she'd been expecting it, hearing Madison's voice was like a jolt to the heart. After all this time, she finally had proof of the one thing she'd known all along: Madison Brooks was alive.

"Fuck yeah," Tommy grunted, followed by a whoop that made Aster flush in embarrassment.

The pounding continued. And though her heart broke

for Layla, Aster shot her a look that warned her not to do anything rash. Then, slipping her cell from her pocket, she prompted the camera app and rushed forward toward the open door, ready to capture a scene that would make Aster's striptease video seem positively PG in comparison.

She watched through the screen as Madison whirled on her and cried, "What the hell?" Turning on Tommy, she said, "Did you call them?"

Tommy stood before them, shirtless, sweaty, and seemingly caught in the act of something Aster couldn't make sense of. His gaze bounced between Aster and Ryan. By the time it landed on Layla, his face had drained of all color.

Aster took note of the paddle Tommy gripped, along with the padded walls, rubber floors, and strange array of equipment, unable to comprehend whatever sort of messed-up role-playing fantasy they were engaged in. Clearly it was some kind of fetish room, though it wasn't like it mattered. Not when Madison Brooks was living, breathing, and standing right there before them.

After weeks of heartache, Aster's life had changed in an instant. The burden of proof had been lifted. She no longer had a reason to fear her own future.

Fueled by a summer's worth of pent-up rage, Aster advanced on Madison, ready to make her suffer for all the pain she'd inflicted. Her fingers catching at Madison's skinny arm, she started to drag her closer when Tommy intervened in an effort to protect Madison. It was a move that was not lost on Aster, nor on Layla, for that matter.

"It's not what you think!" he cried, but it was too late for that.

"What the hell, Tommy?" she spat, refusing to let go of Madison's arm until Ryan gently pried her fingers from Madison's flesh.

"Pretty sure we need her alive," Ryan said, drawing Aster close to his side.

Tommy raised his hands in surrender. Realizing he was still holding the paddle, he dropped it to the ground and tried again. "It's not what you think." His gaze darted wildly. "Just—just give us a chance to explain."

"*Us?*" Aster fought to free herself from Ryan's hold. Sure they needed Madison alive, but Tommy, not so much. "So you're admitting to being an *us*?"

"Not what I meant, just—please. Can everyone just relax?" Tommy was pleading. He looked horrified, terrified. Well, too bad.

"Sure," Aster said, voice edged with sarcasm. "As soon as I send this video to Detective Larsen so he can drop all the charges against me and clear my name of a crime I didn't commit, I'll be happy to relax and watch as you two"—she wagged a finger between them—"are exposed for the frauds that you are. Seems like a fair trade to me."

Aster scrolled through her contacts, leaving no doubt she was willing to make good on her word.

"Don't." Madison spoke for the first time since they'd burst into the room. Reading Aster's scathing look, she added, "Please. Don't."

Aster held Madison's gaze and lifted the phone to her ear.

"They can't know I'm alive. No one can."

"No one but Tommy?" Layla spoke up. Aster was surprised she'd managed to remain quiet so long.

"Layla—" Tommy started, but Aster stopped him before he could start.

"You sort out your love life on your own time." Aster glared. "I have better things to do at the moment."

"Do it," Ryan said, egging her on. "Post it to Instagram too. The sooner the world knows, the better." He gave her an encouraging look.

In her cheap clothes and heavy-handed makeup, Madison appeared small and frail, battered and beaten—the exact opposite of her usual highly curated look. But Aster was too jacked up to focus on Madison's drastic appearance or how she might've gotten that way. Her fingers were shaking so badly she found it difficult to press the right prompts on the keypad.

"Listen," Madison pleaded. "I get why you're angry. But if you can just spare me five minutes, I can explain.

After all, what's five more minutes after everything you've already been through?"

For the first time since she'd been caught, Madison sounded appropriately desperate. It had sure taken long enough.

"I know you don't like me," she continued. "And I know you blame me for every bad thing that's happened to you. But you've got it all wrong. Calling Larsen will just put me in more danger than I'm already in."

"And I'm supposed to care because . . . ?" Aster smirked.

Madison paused. "Because I guarantee it will put you in more danger too."

Aster rolled her eyes. "Sounds like a line from one of your movies. You're going to have to do a lot better than that if you want me to believe you." She arced an arm wide. "I couldn't care less about whatever you do in your kink room. Though I'm sure the tabloids will love the footage I send them."

Madison squinted in confusion.

"Is this how Madison got to you?" Aster regarded Tommy closely. "Is this how she seduced you and persuaded you to keep all her secrets?" Aster was furious, but fought to keep her anger subdued. "I can't believe you sat right alongside us, pretending to be one of us, when you were in on it all along."

Tommy shook his head and mumbled something about

how Aster had it all wrong. But Aster wasn't interested in Tommy's excuses. Not when the truth was unfolding right in front of her.

"We just came from your trailer." With Tommy sufficiently shamed, Aster switched her focus to Madison.

"Breaking and entering. Twice in one day." Madison folded her arms across her chest.

Aster seized the chance to gloat. "Broke inside your LA house too, just so you know."

Madison's face was impassive, her look cool. And that was when Aster realized she'd given her exactly what she wanted. Five minutes had passed and Aster had completely lost sight of calling Larsen.

"I'd really like to share my side of the story." Madison's voice was quiet and controlled.

"What could it hurt?" Tommy broke in. "If you decide you don't like what you hear, then you can go ahead and call Larsen."

Aster took her time to consider. She had all the evidence she needed standing right there before her, so maybe Tommy was right. What could it possibly hurt?

She was on the verge of agreeing, when Layla said, "You can't be serious? Why should we trust either of them?"

"I went to jail!" Tommy shot back. "Or have you already forgotten?"

"Of course you let yourself get caught," Layla snapped.

"After all, it's the perfect cover."

"All we're asking for is a chance to explain."

"*We.* Nice." Layla rolled her eyes, as Tommy sighed and closed his.

"I think Madison deserves a chance to explain," he said.

"Shocking you'd feel that way," Layla seethed.

For a handful of seconds, Aster felt badly for Layla. Clearly, her feelings were hurt. Or maybe it was just her pride, it was impossible to tell. But Layla's argument was getting them nowhere, and Aster was tired of listening.

"Enough!" Aster cried. Turning to Madison, she said, "You have five minutes to make me believe you."

Madison held Aster's gaze. "If you betray me, or decide to blog about any of this"—she shot a pointed look at Layla—"I will sue you for slander."

"It's not slander if it's true," Layla bit.

Aster groaned. Layla never knew when to quit.

"It'll be my word against yours." Madison glared, leaving no doubt she meant every word. "Who do you think they'll believe?"

Layla fell silent.

"Also," Madison said, "I need you to refrain from calling Larsen. For my own safety, I have to insist."

"And what about my safety? What about the upcoming trial, and all the haters and trolls sending me death threats?" Aster glared.

"All I'm asking for is a little more time. I promise I won't let this get to trial."

Aster forced a sarcastic grin. "Tell me, just how much are your promises worth these days?"

"It's all I've got." Madison shrugged. "Clearly, you're the one in the driver's seat. You decide where this goes."

Aster retrieved her phone and aimed it at Madison. Instinctively, Madison lifted a hand to cover her face as though Aster was some particularly aggressive paparazzo.

"Think of this as insurance," Aster said, snapping a series of pics. "A picture is worth a thousand words. And, in this case, I'll use it to ensure you don't go back on yours. So, if you could please just lower your arm and say cheese, I can get the money shot, and you can tell us your story."

"Fine," Madison said, dropping her arm to her side. "But for the record, this is a rage room, *not* a sex room. When we're done, I'll be happy to let you use it. Seems like it might do you some good."

TWENTY-FIVE

CANDLE IN THE WIND

Madison was used to being stared at, but this was entirely different. She'd just gotten everyone seated in the den, and now they were looking at her, waiting for the show to begin.

It was the most nerve-racking performance she could ever imagine. Her entire future rested on her ability to sway them into believing everything she said. Judging by the skeptical looks on their faces, it wouldn't be easy.

They were searching for the sort of truth no one had yet been able to uncover. Madison was prepared to tell them a story based on some semblance of facts, though every word would need to be chosen with care. One false move and Aster would call Larsen before Madison could stop her.

Still, she had no intention of sharing her real life story with anyone, ever.

She settled onto one of the club chairs, pulled a gray crocheted throw over her lap, and propped her ankle onto the coffee table. Partly because keeping it elevated really did help lessen the swelling, but mostly because the visual reminder of the physical toll she'd paid might veer them toward kindness.

It'd been so long since she'd last seen them in person, and though they looked more or less the same, clearly the summer had changed them.

With her long, glossy dark hair, smooth olive complexion, vibrant brown eyes, and the uncanny way she had of elevating a simple pair of jeans and a T-shirt into a runway-ready look, Aster was as stunning as ever. Though strangely, she also seemed *happy*.

Happy wasn't a word that easily applied to a girl like Aster. Snooty, privileged, self-satisfied—those were the words that fit. Happy was a yellow smiley face, a red Mylar balloon floating high in the sky. Happy was a triple-scoop waffle cone dipped in chocolate and covered with sprinkles. And tonight, Aster seemed like the happiest girl alive.

It wasn't just the relief of having the evidence needed to prove her innocence—it was also because of Ryan and the way he stayed glued to her side. The two of them moved in unspoken tandem, an intimate choreography known only to them.

Unlike Aster, Layla was the opposite of happy. Which wasn't surprising considering Madison's experience of their previous run-ins. Still, a good chunk of the drive that had once been Layla's most defining characteristic had since been replaced with a palpable uncertainty that left her looking haunted and lost.

And Tommy, well, Madison had spent the day observing him. But now, after having been falsely accused by his friends, who obviously didn't trust him, he was clearly the most uncomfortable person in the room.

Breaking the silence, she pulled at the fringed edge of the throw and said, "I don't know who took me, though I have my suspicions." She paused, noting the way they all edged a bit forward. Good. She had their full attention. "I left Tommy after receiving a text I thought was from Paul. I went to Night for Night expecting to see him, but Paul was late, or so I thought. I went up to the terrace, and I guess I got distracted, because the next thing I knew, a hand was clasped over my mouth, and then . . ." She shrugged. "I don't remember anything until I woke up hours later in an entirely different location."

"Do you remember anything leading up to that?" Aster pressed. "Any sort of sign, no matter how small?"

Madison stared into the distance. "I heard footsteps. And I caught a whiff of a scent I recognized." She looked at Ryan. "Same one you always wear." Ryan started, and Madison lifted a hand. "Relax. I know it wasn't you."

"Okay, so, the footsteps—heavy, light, anything in particular that stood out?"

Madison closed her eyes, letting them think she was summoning the memory, when really she was just trying to cement her own strategy. She shook her head. "All I know is I woke up alone in a strange room. I don't know where. I never saw anyone else the whole time I was there. The lights were programmed to go on and off, and they fed me three times a day through a slot in the door. The walls were covered with an image of me as a kid, along with multiple strips of mirror."

"So, clearly they'd been planning it for a while. But how did they know when to act? Who besides you two"—Aster gestured between Madison and Ryan—"knew you were going to break up and set the whole thing in motion?"

"Paul." Madison studied her nails. "But he didn't do it."

"I thought you suspected him." Tommy turned on her.

"I do suspect him—of withholding evidence and lying to me. But he didn't abduct me."

"Were you ever in Joshua Tree?" Aster asked.

"There were two locations. I have no idea where the first one was. The second was Death Valley. That's where

I escaped and Paul found me."

"Paul found you." Aster stared. "In the middle of Death Valley. Doesn't that seem a little too coincidental?"

Madison withdrew into silence. She needed to show them this sort of questioning would get them nowhere.

"What are you hiding?" Layla asked.

Of course Layla was the one to force the conversation to a more substantive place. If Madison wasn't so wary of Layla, she might be impressed. As it was, she said, "I'm not hiding anything."

"Sure you are." Layla crossed her legs and settled in. "Save your sad story for your memoirs or a very special edition of *In-Depth with Trena Moretti*. Right now, you need to cut the crap and give us a reason to trust you. In case you haven't noticed, you're outnumbered. You don't decide how this ends, we do. The sooner you understand that, the better for everyone."

Madison inhaled a steadying breath. She couldn't afford to let Layla bait her. "What exactly is it you want to know?"

Layla was quick to reply. "Did you kill your parents?"

Someone gasped. Madison guessed it was Aster, and though she felt equally jolted by the question, she was too self-possessed to show it. Funny how in the ten years since her parents had died, no one had ever bothered to ask. Then again, Paul had been right there when it happened, and he'd set up an airtight alibi that cleared her of suspicion. And yet, just like that, Layla's question had transported Madison right back to that horrible night.

The sound of gunshots roared in her head.

Her vision blurred at the sight of blood-spattered walls.

Paul had stood by and watched as Madison's parents, Henry and WillaJean Slocum, tried to sell her to their drug supplier in exchange for forgiving their debt. Even at eight years old, Madison knew they were serious.

Her father pushed her toward their supplier as though she was something other than human—a commodity to be bartered or sold.

At first, the man laughed and nearly pushed her right back.

But once he'd caught a glimpse of her deep violet eyes, he reconsidered. His mouth twisted cruelly, his gaze hardened on hers, and life as she knew it was forever altered.

One moment she was a helpless, terrified eight-year-old girl, and the next she'd made a dive for the gun on the coffee table, aimed it straight at her parents, and shot them both dead.

Her small hands shook as she spun on her heel and pulled the trigger again, effectively wiping that sick grin off the supplier's face as a bullet tore into his gut and he crumpled to the ground.

Paul was the only one left, and as Madison leveled the

barrel on him, he raised both hands and in a soft voice said, "Don't shoot. I'm a cop."

Madison wavered. He was nothing like the others who used to hang around. Sure he was big, hardened, and scary in his own way, but in those dull, milky eyes she'd caught a flash of something she'd never seen in her parents.

This strange, beige, nondescript man actually cared about what happened to her.

"I know you're in pain," he told her. "I know how scared you must be. But I need you to give me the gun." He extended a hand, but Madison knew better than to fall for that trap. "It's okay," he'd said, somehow managing to stay calm. "I understand. Just hold tight and don't do anything rash. I'm just going to reach into my pocket and show you . . ."

A moment later he'd flashed her his badge, and Madison found herself howling and shaking in the shelter of his arms.

Paul was undercover and just days away from arresting her parents and their supplier and sending them all to jail for a very long time. But now he was faced with an entirely new dilemma. He explained how easy it would be to tell the truth, since Madison was too young to be held accountable for her actions. But Paul had also been around long enough to know how a crime like that could manage to stick.

He'd seen something special in her—the kind of spark most people lacked. In a bid to give her the sort of life she deserved, he staged the scene to appear as though the supplier had shot her parents and Paul had then shot the supplier.

She'd never forget the feel of her father's fingers digging into her arm just before he gave her away. The bruises he left marked the spot where she eventually pressed a piece of burning wood to her flesh. The resulting wound lent authenticity to the alibi, while serving as a visual reminder of why she'd chosen her path.

The memory faded as Madison met Layla's gaze. She'd stayed silent too long, and now anything she said would be met with skepticism. Still, in the end, it would always be Madison's word against the truth, and she would do what-ever it took to ensure that the truth never leaked.

"I didn't kill my parents," she said. The energy in the room was so charged it seemed to crackle between them. "Though I also won't lie and pretend that I miss them. I'm glad they're gone." She allowed the words some space to settle before she continued. "They were negligent, careless, reckless, and completely unfit. They sold drugs in order to pay for the drugs they took. Only they had a bad habit of not paying their debts, which is what got them into the sort of trouble that ultimately ended their lives. They also had a bad habit of forgetting to buy things like soap, and toothpaste, and food. Some of my earliest memories are of me digging through our neighbors' trash for scraps to eat. Stories like that aren't known for ending happily, and yet mine did. The day my parents died, I got a second chance at a much better life, and I'll always be grateful for that." It was more than she'd ever revealed to anyone, and after living with it in her head for so long but never daring to put a voice to it, the words felt strange and foreign on her tongue.

Everyone fell into a sort of stunned silence—everyone but her harshest critic: Layla, of course.

"I feel like you've mistaken this for a game of two truths and a lie." She wasn't the least bit affected by Madison's story. "Question is, which is which?"

Tommy shot her a sharp look, and the look Layla flashed in return assured Madison that whatever they'd once shared was now doomed.

"Think what you will." Madison inspected her nails. "But why would I tell you all that when I've worked so hard to sell a very different, much more wholesome version of myself?"

"Who set the fire?" Layla was relentless.

Paul. Paul set the fire. He risked his job, his reputation, and his life in order to protect me.

It would be so easy to finally confess and unburden herself. But so many years of her and Paul jealously guarding each other's secrets precluded her from spilling them now.

She couldn't imagine ever stating those words out loud. She hoped she'd never have to.

"Was it you?"

Madison shook free of her thoughts and focused on Layla.

"Was it Paul?"

Madison may or may not have blinked, but otherwise she remained very still.

"Or perhaps it was Gerald Rawlins?"

Madison froze. Layla had just spoken the name of the man she and Paul had framed for killing her parents.

Layla folded her arms across her chest and smirked. "Maybe you should start over, from the beginning. And this time, tell us the real story."

TWENTY-SIX

THIS IS WHAT YOU CAME FOR

Tommy could not believe the mess he found himself in. Madison had tricked him, his friends had all turned against him, but the worst part was the way Layla ignored him.

Layla was feisty and prone to occasional verbal sniping—two things Tommy had always liked about her. But he'd also seen another side that was tender, sexy, and loving in a way he never saw coming. She was the most passionate girl he'd ever known, and yet he couldn't help but wonder if he should maybe let her go without putting up too much of a fight.

He truly did like her, but sometimes he worried they were like some dumb reality TV couple—the kind who convinced themselves they were soul mates when their lives were filled with roses, champagne, and Jacuzzis, only to discover they could barely stand each other once the viewers and cameras turned elsewhere.

Real relationships required the kind of work the reality shows tended to skip. And Tommy was no longer sure he had it in him to keep trying.

At some point, Madison had stopped speaking. And Tommy had been so lost in his thoughts that he struggled to catch up to where she might've left off.

"You're seriously trying to pretend you didn't know he survived and that he was in jail all this time?"

Tommy watched Madison squirm. Nothing obvious, but he'd been studying her all day, and the way she pulled the throw higher onto her lap was a sure sign Layla had hit a sore spot.

Still, Tommy felt sorry for her. Madison was bruised, battered, and exhausted, yet she put on such a good show of having it all together no matter the circumstance, it was easy to forget she was just an eighteen-year-old girl who'd spent the bulk of the summer fighting for survival.

"As far as I knew, he died in the fire. Last I saw, he was unconscious and the house was in flames. Not long after, I was taken to the hospital, and then Paul had me stay with his mom until my name was changed and my adoption arranged. Paul did everything he could to protect me, and I guess that includes lying about what happened to the shooter. You have no idea how shocking this is. It makes me question everything I thought I once knew. And while I'm definitely upset to learn I've been in danger all this time, I wouldn't have had half my success if it wasn't for Paul. It's because of him the shooter was never able to find me. Or at least not until now."

"Well, the shooter's not the one who found you," Layla spat. "The shooter is dead. He died in jail last year."

Madison stifled a yawn. It seemed a strange way to react in the face of such news, but Tommy guessed her fatigue was getting the best of her. Or maybe she was faking. It was impossible to tell what was really going on with her.

"Do you think you would've gone missing if it weren't for the contest?"

Tommy looked at Aster, startled by the question.

"I mean . . ." Aster paused to collect her thoughts. "Do you think it was somehow connected or linked? Or do you think we're just all wildly unlucky victims of unfortunate timing?"

"How could it be linked?" Tommy tried to make sense of it.

"Unless Ira was involved." Ryan voiced the thought they were all thinking.

"You think Ira Redman kidnapped me?" Madison was more curious than incredulous. "You think there's a connection between him and Gerald Rawlins?"

Aster shifted uncomfortably. "Listen," she said, her voice quiet, as though afraid of being overheard. "I feel like a traitor even saying it, especially after all that Ira's done for me, but sometimes I wonder, you know? I mean, Ira's been there from the start, and I can't just stick my head in the sand and refuse to see something because it's inconvenient and makes me uncomfortable."

"And I don't think you should let it go," Tommy said. "Looking back, that whole night seems perfectly choreographed to set you up for the crime, and Ira played a big part in that."

"But why me?" Aster's look was pleading.

"Why *you*?" Madison balked. "You sure you don't mean why *me*?" She jabbed a thumb toward her chest.

"I meant why did he set me up? Why not Ryan, Tommy, Layla, or any of the other competitors? Why did Ira target me as the one to mess with?"

Tommy had a few suspicions, but he chose not to voice them.

"Whatever." Aster sighed. "It's done. I may never know the answer to that one." She waved a hand in front of her face.

"Say Ira is behind it." Madison spoke as though testing a theory she wasn't even remotely convinced of. "What would he possibly get out of it? Pretty sure he knows me well enough to know I plan to prosecute whoever did this to the full extent of the law. And as far as I know, Ira has no connection to my past."

"He gets a boatload of free PR," Ryan said. "You can't believe what's gone on since you've been away."

Madison fell quiet, her expression contemplative.

"But let's say Ira is behind it," Ryan said. "How exactly did he arrange all of that? I mean, he must've had help. Even Ira can't be in more than one place at a time. He would've needed at least one accomplice, maybe more."

"Starting with the girl at the apartment," Tommy said.

"Who the hell was she?" Aster pulled her knees to her chest and wrapped her arms around them. "From the back, she looked just like you." She nodded toward Madison.

"I assure you, it wasn't me. I was hanging at the Vesper with Tommy."

Tommy was dumb enough to glance at Layla. What he saw left him convinced that any hope of reconciling had just died a quick, easy death.

"Okay, so someone who, from the back anyway, looks like Madison, lured me to an apartment more or less around the same time you disappear. Then a few days later your blood very conveniently shows up on the Night for Night terrace as well as on the dress I was dumb enough to leave behind in that stupid apartment."

"What's up with the blood?" Layla asked.

Madison was quick to defend herself. "I had my blood

stored, and it's not nearly as crazy as it may sound. Presidents do it all the time."

"Yeah, except you're not exactly the leader of the free world, are you?" Layla sneered.

Madison was undeterred. "Billionaires, CEOs of Fortune 500 companies, and many A-list celebrities have done the same thing. I wouldn't be surprised if Ira has too. Over a period of time, someone collects your blood and stores it in a safe place. It's not as uncommon as you think."

"But why?" Tommy asked. "What's the point?"

"Normally, it's to use in a medical emergency. For me, it was mainly in case I ever needed to disappear in a hurry."

"Which you did," Layla was quick to point out. "And your blood was splattered all over the same terrace you were taken from."

"So I've been told." Madison held Layla's gaze until she was the first to look away.

"So, who had access to the blood?" Ryan asked.

"Paul and me. That's all I know of."

"And James? What sort of deal do you have with him?" Ryan studied her in a way that made Madison squirm.

"Nothing." She tried to dismiss the thought. Then, realizing she wouldn't get away with that, she said, "He used to do some light spying. Petty stuff." She glanced between Aster and Ryan. "He's the one who told me about you two."

Ryan looked away in embarrassment. The room grew

quiet as they all retreated into their individual thoughts.

"Listen," Madison said. "If I hadn't been the one taken, I'd be in a complete state of awe. The whole thing is kind of genius, if you think about it. It's a complicated series of events. And trust me, Paul is capable of all of that and more. Ira too."

"Does Paul know Ira?" Aster asked.

Ryan nudged her arm. "Everyone knows Ira."

"But does Paul work for Ira? You know, as a fixer, or whatever it is Paul does."

"No idea." Madison shrugged. "I'm his most important client, but not his only client. Either of them are capable of pulling that off, but neither of them could've done it alone."

"The girl, whoever she was, had to be in on it," Aster said. "That was a real live girl, not the Ghost in a wig. Also, we found your car waiting for us just outside Ira's tequila launch party. The GPS led us right to Paul's office, presumably so we could find the blood-collecting kit."

"I doubt that was legit," Madison said. "Paul would never leave a blood-collecting kit randomly lying around for someone to find."

"It was in a filing cabinet," Ryan corrected.

"That makes even less sense. What else did you find?"

"An empty file with your name on it."

Layla piped up, "The contents were sent to me."

"Let me guess: It was full of diary entries and whatever

else you posted on your blog or saw fit to give to Trena Moretti?" She glared at Layla, but Layla refused to confirm or deny. "Clearly someone planted the blood kit and empty file folder," Madison said. "What would Paul want with my diary entries?"

"I thought you suspected Paul?" Aster's tone was softer than Tommy expected.

Madison shook her head. "Now I realize he was trying to protect me from knowing the truth. But I panicked and ran, and he's probably freaking out trying to find me."

"It's equally possible he's trying to hunt you down so he can harm you," Tommy said, prompting Madison to send him a searching look that was not lost on Layla, who made a point of sighing and rolling her eyes.

Before it could go any further, Aster broke in. "If Paul is behind it, I don't think he'd want us to see any of those documents, much less the blood kit. Ira, on the other hand, could've easily made all that happen."

Tommy kept quiet. His head was spinning with theories.

"Look—" Ryan bumped Aster's shoulder with his. "I don't know if Ira's behind it or not. What I do know is that scandal is sexy. And this particular scandal is tailor made for a celebrity-obsessed public who never tires of rehashing the grisly details. There isn't a person left on the planet who hasn't heard of Jewel, the Vesper, or Night for Night, which is now one of the top five tourist destinations in town.

It's pretty much the best thing that ever happened to Ira. Though it's definitely the worst thing that's ever happened to us." Ryan's voice rang of anger, and the color rose to his face. He was getting seriously heated. Tommy could relate.

"So . . ." Aster shifted toward him. "Let's assume Ira *is* behind this." She frowned. "I mean, what now? What am I supposed to do? I've pretty much given him control of my life! Do I find a way to disconnect? Or do I hang in there with the hope that it's entirely possible that the reason he's gone out of his way to help is because he knows the charges won't stick? Like, maybe at the very last second he's planning a big reveal that'll prove my innocence. And then, in addition to building his business, he can be a hero for believing in me when everyone else turned away. God, that sounds cynical." She sank her head in her hands and rubbed at her face.

"Cynical and entirely possible." Ryan sighed.

"But would he really go that far just for an epic PR play?" Aster smoothed her hair behind her ears, her expression thoughtful as she considered the idea.

On the surface, it sounded crazy and woefully farfetched.

In reality, Tommy knew Ira was capable of all that and more.

Still, he said, "But why would he kidnap Madison? I mean, it's one thing to be an amoral businessman. It's another to actually abduct someone and hold them captive for weeks on end. That takes planning, patience, deliberation, resources."

"All of which Ira has in abundance," Madison said.

"So if Ira *is* behind it, do you think he planned to trot you in front of the courtroom at the last minute so my case would be dismissed? You think that's his big reveal?" Aster stared at Madison as though she had the answer. When Madison failed to reply, Aster frowned and slumped low in her seat. "I know, it sounds insane—like the worst sort of magical thinking. But at this point, it's all I've got. Ira controls my whole life! And the worst part is, I went along with it."

They all fell quiet, until Layla said, "While I'm not saying Ira isn't behind it, I'm not sure how he's connected to Madison's past. And clearly, whatever's going on here, it's connected to the night her parents died. We need a better strategy."

"I wasn't aware you had a strategy." Madison frowned.

"Last time we came up with a plan, it didn't turn out so well," Tommy said.

"Meaning . . ." Layla narrowed in on him, and Tommy couldn't help but cringe.

"Meaning we ended up charged with a crime we didn't commit! What do you think he means?" Aster rolled her eyes and shook her head.

Yep, the band was back together again.

"Well, we can't just sit back and do nothing." Layla refused to give in. "Or actually, I guess we can. One phone call to Larsen and we can all walk away and be done with it. Let the LAPD unravel this mess."

Madison looked terrified. Layla looked like she was about to make good on her word, and Tommy had no idea whether or not she was bluffing but knew he had to stop it from happening.

"No one's suggesting that." The second it was out, Tommy knew it was the final death knell of whatever he had with Layla, but it was the right thing to do. Madison was scared, and whoever had harmed her the first time was still out there. He couldn't live with himself if he didn't at least try to help. "But whatever we do from here, we have to be smart. I can't take another night in jail, curled up in the fetal position on the top bunk, breathing through my mouth in order to avoid all the foul smells. Or maybe that was just me." It was a lame attempt to add a little levity, and he instantly regretted it.

"No competing over which of us had the nastiest cell," Aster said. "Because I win. Hands down, I win. I won the first time I was locked up."

"Jeez, you're competitive." Layla rolled her eyes, but the smile that followed smoothed away all the snark.

Madison glared. "You guys are ridiculous. Seriously. Do

you even hear yourselves? So sorry you spent a few nights in jail. A smelly bunk sounds like a luxury compared to what I went through."

Unable to put words to what he was feeling, Tommy rose from his seat and headed out to the terrace in search of fresh air and a break from the tension. He'd rejoin them soon enough, but he needed a quiet moment to decide what to do about the fact that his dad was looking guiltier by the moment.

If it turned out Ira was responsible, what then? What did it mean for Tommy and all the plans he'd made?

"Hey—you okay?"

Tommy turned. "Are you?" He watched Layla's cheeks flush a lovely shade of rose as she forced her gaze to meet his.

"I'm sorry," she said.

Tommy shrugged, unsure where this was going. Though when she tucked her hair behind her ear in the way she did when she was about to be really earnest, he knew he needed to take her seriously.

"I jumped to conclusions, and . . ." She stared down at her shoes. "I guess I kind of lost it." He started to speak, but before he could get to the words, she stopped him. "But it's not you. It's—it's just that everything has changed and not necessarily for the better, and sometimes I just want to rewind, you know? I miss riding my motorcycle. I miss the person I thought I was at the beginning of the summer. I . . ."

She fluttered a hand before her face and scrunched her nose in a way so adorable he had to fight the urge to grab her and kiss her and never let go.

"You know what?" Her blue-gray eyes met his. "That's a lie. Truth is—it was about you."

Tommy forced himself not to speak. He knew how much a moment like this cost a girl like Layla, who equated vulnerability with weakness.

"I messed up the night I kissed you and didn't tell Mateo."

"You messed up because you kissed me, or because you didn't tell Mateo?" He inched closer. He'd been drawn to her from the beginning, and though so much had changed since then, his attraction to her had never once wavered.

Without hesitation she said, "I messed up because I *wanted* to kiss you and I *liked* kissing you, and that's the moment I should've known it was over with Mateo and I should've come clean and told him as much. I don't fall easily. And I'm certainly not the type who's attracted to every cute boy I see."

Tommy was flattered, but he knew better than to let on. "And now?" His voice was hoarse. He'd already talked himself out of being with her. But now, he wasn't sure what she was offering, and he had no firm idea how to respond.

"Madison is lovely." She tilted her chin toward the den. "Even when she's battered and bruised and traumatized, she's the most beautiful girl in the room."

Tommy knew better than to comment. If Layla was baiting him, he was too smart to bite.

"Funny how she turned to you for help."

Tommy shifted his weight between his feet. He was beginning to feel like a bug under her lens. "I can't explain that," he said.

"I can. It's because she trusts you."

Layla regarded him as though she could see right through his flesh to the beating heart below. Did she realize in that moment it was beating just a bit faster for her?

"You two have a connection. Anyone can see it."

"And what about us? What about our connection?" He forced the words from his lips. He might not like the answer, but he needed to know where they stood.

Layla's cheeks lifted in a smile. "You're pretty easy to connect with. Easier than me."

Any other girl, he would've let the statement go, sure he was being forced into a compliment he might be reluctant to give. But Layla wasn't that kind of girl, and no matter where this went, he wanted her to know she meant a great deal to him. "I've seen you—the real you. The sharp-edged side you share with the world, and the softer one you save just for private. And if you decide you never want to share that softer side with me again, I want you to know I feel lucky to have known it for the short time I did."

Without a word, she lifted a hand to his cheek and traced the line of his jaw with her fingertip. Tommy leaned into her touch, sure they would kiss. It was what he ached for most in the world.

Just as quickly, she pulled away. "I know why you came here," she said.

At first he thought she meant to Madison's hideaway, but something about the look in her eyes told him she meant something else entirely.

"I know why you moved to California."

His eyes widened. His body went still. Just like *that*, his secret was out.

His first instinct was to deny it, but then he remembered who he was talking to. "Who else knows?" He cast a nervous glance toward the house, but Layla was quick to assure him that no one else knew of his connection to Ira.

"Are you going to confront him?"

Tommy swiped a hand through his hair. It felt really weird to discuss it out loud.

"Yes." He nodded. Followed by: "Maybe." He scratched at his cheek. "I haven't decided." He sighed. "It changes daily."

"Do you really think he's behind this?"

Tommy screwed up his face and squinted at the fence surrounding the yard. "I wouldn't put it past him," he said, returning his focus to her.

"So what's the plan?"

Tommy sank his hands into his pockets. "I guess I'm going to find out once and for all, so I can get on with my life."

Layla regarded him thoughtfully. "You know you don't have to go this alone. Surprising as it seems, you've managed to make a friend or two since you arrived in LA."

A slow grin lit Tommy's face as he remembered the first time they'd met, when she'd said just the opposite. "Then I'll consider that a victory, considering how you warned me friends were in short supply."

Layla's eyes flashed. "I seem to remember it differently. You spoke the words. I merely implied you were right. As it turns out, we were both wrong."

When she laughed, Tommy had the unmistakable feeling that everything would be okay. Not just between them, but overall.

He watched as she started to head back inside. "And what happens next?" he called.

She paused and looked over her shoulder. "We put our heads together and work out a plan."

"And after that?" The question was loaded, but he had

no doubt she knew what he meant.

"I guess we just have to wait and see how this particular story ends."

He waited a bit before he joined her. He was just crossing the room, about to reclaim his seat, when everyone's phone began to simultaneously chime.

Tommy peered at his screen, then looked at Layla, Aster, and Ryan, wondering if they'd received the same message.

"It's a breaking news alert." Layla's voice was tipped with panic.

"Larsen went to your trailer." Aster stared at Madison. "He found your watch."

Madison narrowed her gaze. "But I hid it."

"Not very well." Ryan frowned.

"I left it out in plain view," Aster said. "I was angry, and I wanted you to know we were onto you in case you returned." Turning to Ryan, Aster said, "Do you think Heather called him?"

"Heather?" Madison became visibly alarmed. "Heather was there? Why didn't you mention this earlier?"

"I didn't think it was a big deal." Aster shrugged. "I mean, you guys were friends, right?"

Ignoring the question, Madison said, "Tell me everything—leave nothing out."

Aster paused as though carefully choosing her words. "She talked about how much she missed you, then she flirted with Ryan, called me a Thoroughbred Girl—which she meant as an insult—"

"A what?" Layla leaned closer.

Aster groaned. "She's got some chip on her shoulder from when she grew up on a ranch or something."

"Heather didn't grow up on a ranch." Madison's face darkened. "She's from coastal Florida."

"Well, she told some story about working on a ranch and how she hated the rich girls who boarded their horses there, or something like that." Aster leaned her head against Ryan's shoulder.

"Did she mention the name of the ranch?"

Aster looked up at Ryan, and he shook his head. "Not sure it matters," he said. "If Larsen found the trailer, it's just a matter of time before he finds this place too. I think we should leave. The sooner the better."

"But what about her?" Aster stared pointedly at Madison. "She's my ticket to freedom. We can't just let her out of our sight."

"I think she should stay with Tommy," Layla said, surprising pretty much everyone in the room, but no one more than Tommy.

After the moment they'd shared outside, it was the last thing he expected.

"There's no other option," she explained. "I live with

my dad and Aster's at the W, which Ira owns. . . ."

"Actually," Aster said, "I've been staying with Ryan."

Tommy awkwardly cleared his throat. "Guess that leaves me then." He looked at Madison, regretting how he'd just made her sound like some sort of disappointing consolation prize. "I have plenty of room, but you're going to have to continue wearing the disguise."

Madison hesitated. Then, looking at Layla, she said, "Thanks."

Layla nodded curtly and headed for the door. Tommy was about to follow when everyone's phone chimed again.

"What now?" Madison peered over Tommy's shoulder to read.

Five little liars walking out the door
One ran off and then there were four

Four little liars looking for the key
One got scared and then there were three

Three little liars searching for a clue
One got caught and then there were two

Two little liars fighting for a gun
One shot the other and then there was one

One little liar convinced she finally won
Her fans turned against her and then there were none

"They know I'm alive—that I'm here, with you!" Madison clutched hard at Tommy's arm. He'd never seen her so spooked. Not knowing what else to do, he slid an arm around her waist and rushed her outside to his car.

TWENTY-SEVEN

SLEEPING WILD

Trena Moretti blinked her eyes open and listened to the soft muffled snore drifting from the man beside her. His back was turned, offering an impressive view of well-defined shoulders and dark, gleaming skin. Softly, so as not to wake him, she trailed a finger down the length of his spine and sighed. She had no business being there. She'd broken her own rule with barely a thought. Still, there was no denying James was a beautiful sight to behold.

She rolled onto her back and stared at the ceiling, reviewing the night in her head. On the drive home from Ojai, James had sent her a text asking if she wanted to go out for a bite. Originally she'd planned to meet with @LuckyHearts16—the person who'd sent her the video of Madison leaving her earring at the memorial. Not wanting to look overeager, she delayed the meeting and accepted James's offer instead.

But now, with the morning sun slipping through the crack between the curtains, she was no longer sure she'd made the right choice.

It had started innocently enough, with the two of them sharing a pizza at Pizzeria Mozza, where she'd effectively broken her strict no-carb rule. A couple of glasses of wine later, Trena found herself inviting him back to her place and doing the sort of things that, despite the lingering shadow of regret, still managed to bring a smile to her face.

Quietly, she swung her feet to the floor and was about to stand, when James rolled over, grasped her by the wrist, and pulled her back to him.

"You sure you want to do that?" His dark eyes were heavy with sleep, but something about his tone struck her as vaguely menacing.

"You mean take a shower and get on with my day?" She kept her tone playful and light, but when she tried to pull away again, he held tight.

Was he playing? Or should she be worried? With James, it was never easy to determine.

She shot him an uncertain look, unable to relax until he released his grip.

"Sorry." He propped an arm under his head and drew a slow, leisurely gaze down the length of her body. "Can't blame a guy for wanting a repeat. Especially when he's lucky enough to wake up next to you."

She frowned and pushed away.

"What'd I do now?"

It was a good question. One she wasn't entirely sure how to answer. "What're you doing here?" She faced him.

He cocked his head and sharpened his gaze.

"I mean, what exactly are you doing here—with me?"

He tried for a grin but only made it halfway. "Is this the relationship talk? The 'what are we doing, where are we going, what does it all mean' talk?"

Something about his exaggerated grimace made her laugh and ease up. "No, nothing like that. It's just—we seem a bit incongruous, don't you think?"

"Because I'm just a bouncer and you're an important news lady?"

She studied him for a long moment. "But you're not just a bouncer, are you?"

It was a question she'd been meaning to ask but kept putting off. Now that it was out there, she became acutely aware of the sheer awkwardness of waiting for his reply while she stood naked before him.

"What're you getting at?" His posture was that of a man at ease, but the way his jaw tensed gave him away.

"What exactly do you do for Ira? What exactly did you do for Madison, for that matter?"

To her surprise, in one swift movement, he was up, out of bed, and pulling on his pants. "So that's what this is about?" He buttoned his jeans and tugged on his shirt.

Trena stayed silent. She recognized a trap when she saw one.

"This was never really about you being into me. I'm just another potential source."

"That's not—" She didn't bother to finish. The accusation was only partially true, but still true.

He straightened the front of his shirt and went in search of his shoes. Was he hurt? It seemed impossible, and yet the tinge of regret on his face left her unsure.

"That's not how it works," she said, her voice quiet.

"What's that?" He moved closer, till they were mere inches apart.

"That's not . . . you weren't . . ." *Shit.* There was something about him that was just so annoyingly irresistible. And when he laid those dark eyes on hers, she could no longer remember why she ever thought resisting him was a good idea.

Closing the space between them, he clinched her hard at the waist and kissed her so thoroughly it left her breathless, longing for more.

Without warning, he withdrew, placed a hand on each of her shoulders, and said, "I'm into you. If you feel the same, we can see where it leads. If not, then it's probably better for both of us to walk away."

She swallowed hard. She couldn't date him. It was impossible, ridiculous to even consider. And not because he was a bouncer and she was an *important news lady* as he'd said, but because she couldn't afford the distraction. Now that she knew Madison was alive and out there, somewhere, she needed to focus all her attention on solving that case.

James was complicated, unknowable, and possibly dangerous. Trena had just gotten rid of a fiancé with similar qualities. Last thing she needed was to take on another. It was time to break the pattern, not continue to build on it.

She reached for a silk robe draped over a chair and pulled it snugly around her. It was all the answer he needed.

Slipping his feet into his shoes, he said, "No hard feelings." The look that followed was deeper and more reflective than she'd expected from him.

Maybe he really was into her.

Maybe she was using Madison as an excuse to not get her heart broken again.

Maybe she was making a colossal mistake.

She returned the look, wondering if it was too late to take it all back.

"A word of caution," he said, breaking the spell. "Be careful where you tread."

She followed him to the door. He couldn't leave like that—she had no idea what he meant.

"Your girl's not all that she seems."

"Which girl—who're you talking about? I need you to explain."

He was halfway out the door when he said, "Thought I already did."

At first, she wasn't sure what he was referring to. But then she remembered the night at the studio, when she'd received the text with Madison's birth certificate. She could've sworn she'd heard the telltale swoosh of someone sending a message just seconds before she'd received it. Had James sent it?

She yanked the sash of her robe, pulling it tighter, and raced for the elevator bank. "Was it you?"

James regarded her as though he had no idea what she was talking about.

The doors began to slide shut, so she thrust her hand between them to keep them from closing. "That text—the birth certificate—was it you? Are you the one who sent it?"

Their gazes held. Trena watched the corner of his lips twitch as he uncurled her fingers from the doors and let them slide shut.

TWENTY-EIGHT

LOVE LIES BLEEDING

Mateo Luna stood in the entry of Valentina's hospital room, gaping at the incomprehensible scene unfolding before him.

On one side of his little sister's bed—dressed in a body-skimming, pink strapless sundress—was Heather Rollins. On the other side—wearing one of her signature shapeless housedresses—was his mother. The startling sight left Mateo feeling like he'd wandered into an alternate universe.

"There you are!" Heather's brown eyes flashed. She gave a little wave of her hand, as though she'd been waiting for him.

As though they'd discussed this ahead of time.

As though she had any right to be there hanging with his family without his consent.

Mateo froze, trying to make sense of how this could've happened.

"I'm sorry," Heather gushed. "I know I should've waited for you, but I couldn't hold it in any longer. I just had to share the good news!"

Mateo made an uncertain approach. He had no idea what Heather was referring to, though one thing was clear: the meeting wasn't nearly as disastrous as he'd imagined it would be. While they couldn't have been more different on the outside, there was no denying his mom and Heather looked perfectly happy to be sharing each other's company.

When his gaze met Valentina's, he forced an encouraging grin. While he'd grown used to the jolt of seeing her looking so pale and weak, nothing could've prepared him for the heartbreak of seeing that her hair had been shorn all the way down to her scalp. The once shiny, wavy dark mane she'd been so proud of was now replaced with an array of glimmering stars and moons—an entire constellation of gold and silver temporary tattoos.

"What's the good news?" he asked. Leaning in to kiss his sister's cheek, he noticed the purple butterfly tattoo that matched the one Heather wore on her face.

"She's being moved!" His mom's voice rose with excitement.

"I hope you're not mad." Heather shot him a tentative glance. "But I know it's what you've been wanting, so I pulled a few strings and got your sister transferred to a hospital that specializes in childhood cancer. She'll get the best care possible, and she'll be back at school in no time." From over the sheet, she playfully tweaked Valentina's big toe, and Mateo was chagrined to watch his little sister laugh delightedly in response.

How was it possible for something to feel so wrong and yet clearly make everyone so happy?

"Why would Mateo be mad?" His mother frowned. "This is what we've wanted all along."

Mateo stood silently, unsure how to respond. When Heather had mentioned she wanted to meet his mom, he hadn't taken her seriously. He guessed this was Heather's way of taking matters into her own hands. Sure he felt manipulated, but in light of the relief on his mother's face and the hope and adoration on Valentina's, how could he possibly complain?

Realizing his mother was still waiting, he forced a neutral expression and said, "I'm not mad."

"You sure?" Heather cocked her head to the side and twisted a random blond curl around her index finger.

"Nothing but the best for my princess." Mateo brushed the back of his hand across Valentina's cheek.

"So, the rumors are true then?" Valentina narrowed her gaze. "You two really are a couple?"

Mateo cringed under the glare of his little sister's

laser-eyed stare. One moment she was a sickly little girl fighting for her life, and the next she was a savvy preteen obsessed with tabloid magazines. "You really need to get more age-appropriate reading material."

Valentina was about to respond when the nurse entered the room and declared visiting hours were over.

"Your family is great," Heather said, as they headed for the elevator bank.

Mateo gave a distracted nod. He felt simultaneously annoyed with her and indebted to her, and he wasn't sure what to do about it.

"But despite your game face, I can tell you're mad."

"I'm not mad," he repeated, but the words came too quickly to be believed.

"Well, I've seen your happy face, and that's definitely not it."

The elevator doors slid open, and he waited for the car to empty before he and Heather slipped in. "Maybe a bit frustrated." He punched the L button and paused as the car began its descent. "Also, confused."

"About what?" Heather began to pout. Then, reading his expression, she pulled her bottom lip back into place.

"Everything." Mateo moved into the lobby and stopped under a large skylight. With the sun shining down from overhead, leaving Heather haloed with light, Mateo was sure he'd never seen her looking more beautiful. But nothing was ever quite what it seemed, including her. Especially her.

"The word 'everything' makes for a pretty big umbrella, don't you think?"

Mateo shifted uncertainly. He'd never been any good at this sort of thing. Funny to think how he'd dated Layla for two years—a girl with no fear of confrontation—and yet, he couldn't remember a single time when she'd made him feel as uncomfortable as Heather currently did. Not even at the very end of their relationship had he felt so much unease. Layla spoke her mind freely, and Mateo had appreciated her honesty.

Heather was just the opposite—rarely, if ever, authentic. Mateo always walked away from their encounters feeling like he'd been used to further her agenda. It was the way he felt now. And yet, because of her, Valentina would gain access to the very best doctors. He had no right to protest.

"I thought you'd be happy about the transfer. I thought that's what you wanted. So when Ira mentioned he had a connection to the board of directors—"

"Ira?" Mateo's voice hardened, his gaze locked on hers. It was the worst thing she could've said, and the look of regret that washed over her face told him she knew it.

She lifted a hand as though she could somehow stop what she'd started, but it was too late for that. "Listen," she said. "I know how you feel about him, but you can't deny—"

Mateo turned on his heel and pushed through the glass doors that led outside. "You asked Ira for *help*?" He stopped and faced her. He didn't know what upset him more—that Heather would betray him like that, or that Ira had succeeded in helping Valentina in a way Mateo couldn't. "I can't believe you did that." He ran a hand through his hair. He couldn't bring himself to look at her. "You know how I feel about him."

"So you are mad."

"I'm not mad, I'm just—" *Indebted to Ira Redman!* He couldn't bring himself to put a voice to it. "Why do you have a picture of Layla and Tommy kissing?" It came from out of nowhere, and yet, once it was out, he found he didn't regret it.

"Did you go through my belongings?" She spoke with an edge that surprised him. If anything, he'd expected her to play defense. Then again, everyone had a shadow side they kept under wraps. Maybe Mateo had just glimpsed hers.

Technically, in his search for paper and a pen he had gone through a few of her things, but he wasn't *snooping*. He wasn't hunting for anything incriminating, and it had nothing to do with whatever she was implying. If he hadn't found the sexy pic, he would've written the good-bye note and been done with it.

But then maybe Valentina wouldn't be getting the transfer she so desperately needed.

He met Heather's gaze. "No, I . . ." The words faded. There was no good way to explain. "Just tell me, are you the one who sent it?"

Without hesitation she said, "What if I did? Would that be so terrible?"

Again, her answer caught him off guard. He'd expected her to deflect, or possibly even lie. His mind reeled back to the first time they'd met. She'd acted aggressively flirty despite his insistence that he'd been looking for Layla. At the time, he hadn't paid it much notice. In retrospect, maybe he should have. Whether or not it was terrible was more complex than she wanted to pretend.

"Why would you do that? Do you have any idea how hurtful that was?"

"More hurtful than living a lie?" Heather's features were hard, her voice indignant. "I thought you deserved to know the truth. I thought you deserved better than that. And yeah, I admit, I liked you. I still do."

Mateo sighed and closed his eyes, wishing he could block out the world and everything in it. When he opened them again, Heather was still standing before him, looking so impossibly beautiful, he felt a twinge of regret for what would come next. "Thanks for your help with Valentina. I'm sorry if I seemed ungrateful. I have a lot on my mind, and you took me by surprise."

She gave a quick nod. "You don't have to explain."

Without warning, she leaned in and pressed her lips softly to his. Her kiss was warm. Lush. Hinting at the promise of all she had to offer.

Mateo leaned into the moment. Willfully ignoring the warning bells sounding in his head, he clasped her tightly against him. *What could it hurt to just . . .*

Before he could finish the thought, he withdrew.

"It's okay." Her voice was choked and tight as she fought to blink away the flash of pain in her gaze. "Turns out, you were right to be suspicious. Ira's willingness to help wasn't entirely altruistic."

Mateo stilled. He did not like where this was going.

"Trena's devoting an entire episode to Ira's 'meteoric rise.'" She hooked air quotes around the phrase and rolled her eyes. "His words, not mine. Anyway, I convinced him I could get you to take part if he made a few calls on Valentina's behalf."

Mateo was seething but did his best not to show it.

"I'll explain to Ira. I'll—" She started to reach for his arm, but reading the look on his face, she dropped her hand to her side. "Don't worry. I'm sure she'll still get the transfer. Ira's a shark, but he's not Satan. He really does have a heart."

"You sure about that?" Of all the things he wanted to say, that didn't come anywhere near the top of the list. But it was the only thing he wouldn't live to regret.

"I'll fix it. Promise."

"When are they filming?" he asked.

"At RED, tomorrow night." She scrunched her brow as though it pained her. "But seriously, you don't have to come. I told you I'd fix it and I will. Say what you want about me, but I always keep my word."

Mateo was too angry to respond. If he didn't show, he ran the risk of Ira seeking revenge by blocking Valentina's transfer. If he did go, he'd get sucked further into the sort of Hollywood hype he abhorred. He had no choice but to go through with it, and it left him angry in a way he'd never felt before. There went another piece of his soul. Who said Ira wasn't Satan?

"I know I crossed some boundaries, and I probably came on a little too strong and too fast. I just hope we can stay friends?"

Mateo couldn't even imagine such a thing. But she was waiting for his reassurance, so the least he could do was nod in agreement. Surely she'd realize the promise was empty.

"I know this'll probably sound silly," she said. "But I have a thing about being the first to walk away. So—" She was halfway to the parking structure when she said, "For what it's worth, I really did like you. For the short time we were together, I could forget everything and just feel happy for a change."

Mateo watched her go, wondering what she'd meant. It

was a strange thing to say for a girl as famous and success-ful as her.

Once she was gone, he typed a message to Layla.

Just solved the mystery of the anonymous text ➜ Heather Rollins.

His index finger hovered above the send arrow, but he hit delete instead.

Summer was nearly over. A new season was about to begin. And still there wasn't a day that went by that he didn't think about Layla a minimum of three times. But now that he'd ended things with Heather, it was clearly time to move forward, not back. The sooner he stopped finding excuses to be in touch with Layla, the sooner he could forge a new life without her.

One by one, he watched the words vanish. Then he slipped his phone into his pocket and headed back to his family.

TWENTY-NINE

GIRLS ON FILM

Tommy stood before the side door of the Vesper, jiggling the key in his palm as he continued to volley the pros, cons, and possible risks back and forth in his head.

Ira had given him the code, which meant Tommy was free to come and go as he pleased. In fact, since Tommy fully intended to check out the progress being made on the VIP room, he figured he was acting well within the confines of his job description. There was nothing for Ira to get upset about.

And yet, none of that would matter if Ira caught him breaking into his office. Tommy didn't even want to think about how Ira might choose to handle such a breach.

He tightened his fist, causing the hard edge of the key

card to cut into his palm. It would be a shame not to use one of the few tools he'd been given to help nudge the investigation along.

Without another thought, he tapped the card against the reader and slipped inside. Once the door closed behind him, the alarm began shrieking.

He punched a sequence of numbers onto the keypad. If Ira had changed the security code, Tommy was screwed.

With each individual tap, the buttons let out a chirp. By the time Tommy completed the sequence, the shrieking stopped and he audibly exhaled.

"So far so good," he whispered out loud. He wasn't in the habit of talking to himself, though in that particular case it helped lessen the tension.

He moved toward the stairs leading to Ira's office and the VIP room beyond. When his foot hit the bottom step, he heard music drifting from one of the second-floor rooms. He wasn't alone like he'd thought.

On any other day, someone blasting music wouldn't be cause for alarm.

But on any other day, Tommy never would've attempted what he was planning to do.

The Vesper was closed until nine, and Layla had assured Tommy her dad was spending the day with a woman he'd recently started seeing. Was it possible H.D. had decided to bring her by the club to impress her with his work in progress?

Tommy shot a wary look toward the top of the stairs. He didn't know which was worse—catching Layla's dad getting intimate with his new girlfriend or having Ira catch him breaking into his office and immediately seeing right through any excuse Tommy tried to sell him.

Whoever was up there had purposely locked themselves inside. Yet they'd also blasted the music so loud it drowned out the alarm. It was entirely possible they still thought they were alone.

Tommy continued up the stairs. At the top of the landing he noticed the door to the VIP room was slightly ajar. If he edged up close enough, he might be able to get a glimpse inside. But that also put him at risk of being seen.

The song switched to the Who's "Won't Get Fooled Again," which was exactly the kind of music H.D. listened to when he worked. In the background, Tommy could just make out a series of dull thumping sounds that . . . if it really was Layla's dad and his new girlfriend . . .

Then again, it was just as likely the mural was ready and Ira had hired a crew to move the furniture back into place. It all made perfect sense, except—why would they have alarmed the place?

There were a thousand different ways this could blow up

in his face, but despite having every reason to leave and few to stay, he made for Ira's office anyway.

He tried the card on the door, but not surprisingly, it didn't work.

Luckily, it didn't need to. The door was unlocked.

Ira's office being left unlocked could only mean one thing—Ira was in the VIP room.

It was as good an excuse as any for Tommy to bolt while he could. Under the circumstances, no one could blame him for playing it safe.

The music and thumping continued, and against his better judgment, Tommy pushed the door open and quickly slipped inside.

With its dark walls and notable lack of windows, it was the drabbest of all Ira's offices. Unlike the ones he kept at Jewel and Night for Night, it hadn't received the usual ego makeover. There wasn't a single framed magazine cover or newspaper article.

Still, this was where Tommy had seen the picture of the cartoon cat, and he was determined to bring it back to his friends, along with any other incriminating piece of evidence he might find.

He pulled on a pair of latex gloves and got to work. The desk was covered in neat stacks of papers that left Tommy wishing he'd brought along help. But they'd all agreed to work separately so they could cover more ground, chase different leads, and not risk the wrath of whoever was watching. Still, it would've been nice to have company. Tackling the corner nearest the door, Tommy went to work. He moved quickly, methodically. He couldn't afford to get sidetracked by anything not directly connected to the case.

The plan was to photograph anything even vaguely incriminating, then return it to where he'd found it. His guess was that the desk only appeared disorganized. Knowing Ira, nothing was random. He'd definitely notice if something was misplaced.

So far, it was mostly purchase orders and bills—the everyday bureaucracy of running a string of successful nightclubs. Or at least that was what he thought, until he came across a heavy file titled *Unrivaled Finalists*.

The first document was a list of their names and contact information, along with a photo of each of them. The date listed at the top left corner was the same date the interviews had taken place.

Had Ira already chosen the finalists before the contest even began?

And if so, did that mean he'd been setting them up from day one?

His fingers trembled with rage. It was one thing to think the worst of his dad. It was another to prove he'd been right all along.

Tommy had always assumed Layla made the cut because

of her blog. As a club promoter, her numbers were poor. But her posts about Madison's disappearance amounted to free publicity for Ira. He'd given her insider access to the Madison scandal, and in return Layla didn't hesitate to write about it.

Aster was easy. She was beautiful, snooty, spoiled, rich, and willing to do just about anything in pursuit of her dreams. In other words, she was just the sort of girl the whole world would be all too willing to root against.

But that still left Tommy. Up until the moment Ira had offered him the job, Tommy was convinced he'd blown the interview. But with every favor Ira granted, Tommy was sure there was another, darker motivation behind it. Ira never acted from kindness.

He raced through the pages, surprised to find they focused more on the competitors than the contest. While plenty of employers were known to run background checks, the info Ira had collected went much further than that. Ira had kept them under surveillance from the day of their interviews, and he'd collected the photos to prove it.

There was a pic of Tommy and Layla standing outside a restaurant on Abbot Kinney Boulevard. Tommy recognized it from the day he'd asked her to meet him at Lemonade. He'd been looking to form an alliance, hoping to pool their talents and work together. Only he'd flubbed the pitch and had ended up alienating her.

He dug deeper. Flipping past a photo of Aster and Ryan

embracing in the Night for Night parking lot, he unearthed a separate file buried beneath it, with Madison's name printed on the front.

Inside was a picture of Madison as a young girl. She was barefoot and bedraggled, dragging an old doll by her side. Along the top someone had written in all caps: *MARYDELLA, WV, age 8*.

It was the same picture someone had sent Layla—the same one that had covered the walls of Madison's cell.

Farther in, Tommy found a newspaper article about the fire. Just beneath was another childhood photo of Madison. Only this time her hair was neatly combed, her dress was pressed and clean, and she sat smiling beside a plain, nondescript woman Tommy was sure he'd never seen, and yet something about her seemed vaguely familiar.

He flipped it over. On the back someone had written *MaryDella & Eileen*. Eileen was Paul Banks's mother.

Why would Ira even have such a picture?

After photographing both sides, Tommy was about to dig deeper when he noticed footsteps sounding in the hall.

"What're you doing?" The voice belonged to a girl. Probably one of Ira's hot assistants—there was no shortage of them.

"I need to check something," Ira said. "It'll only take a minute."

The doorknob rattled, sending Tommy into a panic as

he quickly abandoned the folder, swiped at the light switch, and raced for the small supply closet. Contorting his body to fit, he managed to ease the door shut just as the office door swung open.

Inside the closet it was hot and dark, and there was barely enough room to hold him. Something sharp wedged into the middle of his back, forcing Tommy to take short, shallow breaths in an attempt to keep the noise to a minimum, though he was sure the frantic pounding of his heart would give him away. The only thing standing between him and Ira was a thin piece of wood and a knob with no lock.

"What do you think you're doing?" Ira sounded hurried, if not wholly annoyed.

"Sitting in your chair, seeing what it's like to be you."

"Yeah, and what do you think?" Ira seemed distracted. The girl was flirting, but he'd clearly lost interest.

"I think it would be a lot more fun if you came over here and joined me."

Tommy closed his eyes and cringed, hoping Ira would deny her request.

"How about I take your picture instead?"

"Again?" The girl tried to sound burdened, but it was clear she loved the attention.

"Like you ever tire of it."

She let out a low, throaty laugh. "You mean, like *this* . . . or maybe even *this* . . ."

After a series of muffled thumps (*what the hell are they doing out there?*) Ira said, "You ready?"

"Always."

Tommy listened as the door clicked shut, the lock engaged, and the outside room descended into silence. Determined to wait a bit longer to make sure no one returned, he slipped a hand into his pocket in search of his phone, only to find it was gone.

He reached into his other pocket. Then both front pockets. It was nowhere to be found.

Closing his eyes, he did a mental retracing of his steps. He'd taken a couple of pics of the photo . . . then he'd heard footsteps . . . shut the light . . . raced for the closet . . .

The file—he'd closed the cover and left his cell phone inside!

Tommy sprang from his hiding place and bolted for Ira's desk. The file was gone, but Tommy's phone sat prominently in its place. A quick check showed that Ira had deleted the photo of Madison and Eileen and replaced it with one of the girl. Her hair was long and blond, her lips parted and pink, as the tip of her tongue slid suggestively over her teeth. And though he'd purposely angled the shot in a way that obscured her eyes, an impressive cleavage was on full display.

Ira was taunting him. Letting Tommy know he hadn't gotten away with anything. Hell, he'd probably known he was there all along. In an instant, Tommy's biggest concern shifted from the fear of getting caught to the fear of why Ira had chosen to let him get away with it.

Next thing he knew, the alarm sounded through the building. Ira must've set it, purposely locking him in. Tommy had only a handful of seconds to make it outside before it rang straight through to security.

Would he find Ira waiting, ready to bust him for trespassing, breaking and entering, or whatever trumped-up charge he'd hold against him?

Anything was possible, but Tommy had no choice but to see it through to the end.

He flew down the stairs, raced past the bar, and burst outside just seconds before the alarm sounded its flat, ominous tone. Anyone still inside wouldn't be able to hide for very long.

He took another peek at the picture of the blond girl. Without the eyes, she was impossible to identify. Then again, it didn't really matter. There was no shortage of hot blondes in LA, and clearly it was more about Ira mocking him than anything else.

Tommy paused before the security camera long enough to flash it the middle-finger salute. Then he made his way across the empty parking lot, unable to shake the unmistakable feeling of being watched from afar.

THIRTY

CALIFORNIA DREAMING

Layla stood before the coffeemaker, waiting for the brew cycle to finish. She could've picked up the pot at any point and filled her cup, but the longer she could delay the long walk of shame back to her cubicle, the better.

She'd psyched herself up during the commute by repeating the mantra that her first day back at work wouldn't be nearly as bad as she feared. From the moment she entered the Unrivaled corporate headquarters and saw the way everyone openly turned and stared, she knew she'd been right all along—it wasn't nearly as bad as she'd feared, it was far worse than she'd ever imagined.

Quitting isn't an option. Another mantra she silently chanted as she moved from her desk, where she'd dropped her bag, to the break room, where she was currently hiding.

Quitting isn't an option. Yet another lie she told herself. Truth was, she could give notice at any time. And once that was accomplished, she could pick up the phone, call Larsen, and tell him to head over to Tommy's swanky apartment, where Madison was hiding.

In less time than it would take for a pot of coffee to fill, Layla could effectively clear her name, quit the soul-sucking job, and get on with her life.

And yet, as simple as it seemed on the surface, deep down she knew she'd never go through with it. She'd given her word, and she'd never been one to renege on a promise.

"You're back."

At the sound of Ira's voice, Layla stiffened. Then slowly, methodically, she filled her cup and prepared to face him.

"I didn't expect to see you so soon. I told H.D. you should take as much time as you need."

Layla forced a tight grin and nervously reached for a stir stick, mostly to burn off the nervous energy Ira never failed to invoke.

Ira loomed in the doorway, looking as tall, dark, and handsome as any other Hollywood leading man. But between the slant of his gaze and Layla's suspicions, his appearance veered much closer to villain than hero.

"I'm not really one for taking it easy," she said. "Never have been."

"I can relate." Ira met her grin with one that, on the

surface anyway, seemed more or less genuine. "But as it turns out, I'm glad you're back. I have a new venture I'd very much like you to be a part of."

Layla stuck to a neutral expression and braced for whatever came next. Ira was always promoting his brand, which in turn promoted himself. His entire empire was in service of raising his profile, securing his position of power, and adding to his already considerable wealth. His string of nightclubs had cemented his image as the nightlife czar of LA, and now, with his recently launched tequila label, his brand had been elevated to the sort of global audience Layla suspected he'd always dreamed of.

Still, as much as she made fun of him in her head, she had to admit it was a business model that did deserve a certain amount of respect. Ira had come from humble beginnings, and in a relatively short time he'd managed to make a huge name for himself. If it had been anyone else, Layla would be flattered by his interest. But where Ira was concerned, everything he did was best viewed through a scrim of suspicion.

"It's about RED."

Layla started. She'd been so lost in her thoughts that at first she could've sworn he'd said *code red*, which seemed a perfect fit for how she currently felt at being trapped alone in the break room with him.

"I've had countless offers to franchise the clubs, and

while I'm not interested in relinquishing control, I am giving serious consideration to additional locations. Right now, I'm looking at the possibility of adding a Vesper in New York City, a Jewel in Chicago, a Night for Night in Miami, possibly Vegas as well. And that's just the beginning. Of course, it's all still in the talking and scouting stages, but when it comes to RED, I want it to be different. Something truly special."

He paused as though waiting for her to react. Layla merely nodded for him to continue. When his left eye twitched the tiniest bit, she took it as a signal that her lack of enthusiasm had annoyed him.

"I think of RED as the crown of the Unrivaled empire. It marks the culmination of nearly two decades of work. Nineteen years ago I landed in this city and went straight to work."

"So you're not from here." She wasn't sure why she said it, and from the irritated flattening of his lips, he did not appreciate the interruption. But now that it was out there, he had no real choice but to acknowledge the statement.

"No." His reply was curt. A second later, in a more jovial tone, he added, "Considering all the magazine articles and interviews I've done, I would've assumed you'd know that by now. Are you telling me you showed up at the interview without researching my backstory?"

Backstory. It was such a weird, Hollywood way to

phrase it. It left Layla wondering if Ira's *backstory* might turn out to be as fictional as Madison's.

"I'm sorry," she said. "I guess I'd forgotten. You're from Oklahoma, right?" She forced her gaze to remain steady. She had researched his *backstory*, and thanks to Trena, she now knew he'd purposely omitted the time he'd spent there. What she couldn't figure out was if he deemed it unimportant and therefore unworthy of a mention, or if he'd intentionally left it out for other, more nefarious reasons. This might be her chance to find out.

Ira squinted. "No," he said. "I'm not."

Layla frowned, as though she wasn't quite willing to give up on the idea. "Huh." She took a sip of her coffee and studied him from over the rim of her mug. "Could've sworn you did a short stint at the university there." She swallowed hard and wondered why she didn't just shut the hell up. Instead, she did the opposite, and continued to dig the hole he'd most likely use to bury her in. "Don't mind me." She took another small sip. "With everything that's been going on, my mind's turned to mush. Tommy's from Oklahoma, not you." She paused for a beat, searching Ira's face for any hint of a reaction, but Ira remained as impassive and unreadable as ever. "Anyway, what were you saying about RED being the . . . ?"

Ira stared without blinking, then went on to say, "RED is no ordinary nightclub—it's an experience, an event. I've poured a great deal of money into it, more than any of my other clubs combined. It's going to be highly unique. The first of its kind."

Layla tried to look as though she was following, but so far it felt like a hard sell for a place she had no plans to frequent. She wished he'd just get to the point.

"There's nothing else like it . . . ," he continued.

She fought hard not to roll her eyes. *First of its kind! Nothing else like it!* And the most recent accolade: *It defies description!* To her ears, it all added up to nothing more than a bunch of nonsensical hype.

"I envision it as a sort of performance space."

Layla frowned. "You mean like for weddings and stuff? Like you plan to rent it out?" Did Ira want her to be a wedding planner? Because she couldn't think of a job she'd be worse suited for.

His gaze darkened. He preferred to be the one talking. "Performance space in the most literal sense."

She continued sipping her coffee and fought to smile with her eyes, though she doubted her ability to feign such a look.

"The space is all white—like an empty canvas, a blank slate in which to design your own night and write your own ending."

Layla continued to fake interest, but Ira was veering toward the surreal. It was beginning to feel more like the late-night ramblings of a stoner after too many bong hits than a conversation with a world-famous tycoon. The way the fluorescent lights overhead illuminated the pale yellow walls of the employee break room seemed to reinforce the bizarre, dreamlike feel.

"Picture a series of long hallways with multiple doors to choose from. Some of the rooms will offer a mostly auditory experience, while others will be more visually driven, where you're entering a performance in progress—maybe as a participant, maybe just an observer—to be determined. The idea is for the experience to be so seamless that the line between fiction and reality is blurred." He paused, clearly demanding a response from her.

"Wow. That sounds . . ." Layla stalled. She had a hard time imagining any of it, much less attaching a label to his vision. "Ambitious." She nodded firmly. It was the best she could offer under such scrutiny.

Ira's gaze drifted. "It is. And that's where you come in." He leveled his focus on her. "I'm planning a soft opening of sorts. We're still building out the space, so it's not yet ready for the public. But Trena Moretti has agreed to devote an entire show to me and the business I've built, and we've decided to include some of the before shots of RED. I'd like you to be a part of that."

On the outside, Layla nodded uncertainly. Inside, she wondered what she could possibly add.

"What I'm offering is the chance of a lifetime. I'm asking you to join a small, exclusive group hand-selected by me to represent what I hope will become the crown jewel of my brand. All I ask from you is to keep an open mind. You never know what you're capable of until you're put to the test. Also, dress appropriately. You will be filmed."

Layla froze. The part about being *put to the test* was similar to what Trena had said at Lake Shrine. And while there was nothing unusual about the statement itself, it did strike her as odd to hear the same advice twice in the course of a week.

"So, when is this happening?"

"Tomorrow night, seven sharp. Are we in agreement?"

What she wanted to say was, *No, we are definitely not!* Then flee as fast and far as her legs would carry her. She'd known Ira since the start of the summer and it was probably the longest conversation they'd ever had, and it gave her the creeps.

Instead, she forced what she hoped was an amiable expression and said, "I'd be honored."

"Great," he said, already turning away. "Tomorrow night then. And don't mention this to anyone. You know how upset people get when they don't make the list."

THIRTY-ONE

I TOOK A PILL IN IBIZA

Madison Brooks was restless. Aimlessly roaming the expanse of Tommy's apartment, she rifled through his extensive vinyl collection and picked up random framed photos before setting them back down again with barely so much as a glance. She felt edgy. Fidgety. Once again she was counting the minutes until she could make her escape.

So far, Tommy had been nothing but generous, and to Madison's chagrin, a perfect gentleman. He'd made up a room for her, given her free run of the place, and had even stocked his fridge according to the long, detailed list she gave him. It was the most luxury she'd enjoyed in a very long while, and yet, she still felt as trapped as she had when she'd been locked up in the cinder-block cell.

It was surprising how easily she'd been able to sway them

all to her side. At the time, she thought for sure Ryan, Aster, and Layla would cut her off halfway through her story and put a call in to Larsen. Somehow, against all odds, she'd managed to convince them to delay alerting the authorities just a little bit longer. Which was why she felt so bad about her plan to betray them.

She paused by the breakfast bar and ran a finger across the stack of newspapers and magazines Tommy had left for her to read. *People* was on top, and yet again, Madison's face stared back from the cover. She recognized the picture as a still from one of her movies, where she'd played a small-town grifter. The way her mouth pulled tight and her gaze narrowed and veered off to the side was a perfect match for the headline, which promised a deeper look at a star no one really knew.

Funny to think how she'd vanished from sight, only to find her image more prominent than ever. There was even talk of an Oscar nom, a Golden Globe too. Ira wasn't the only one getting a major PR bump. Madison's abduction had sent her star meter soaring to the sort of stratospheric heights even a lead role in a critically acclaimed blockbuster could never accomplish. Not everyone was willing to sit in a darkened theater and watch a two-hour movie unfold, but most everyone liked to keep up on the sordid details of the latest tragedy in the making, and Madison planned to milk it for all it was worth.

For those who made their living in the public eye, attention was currency. The day the fans stopped talking was the day they stopped caring. Like a forced retirement, the end of celebrity gossip was the beginning of obscurity.

Still, she'd have to find a way to reframe the diary entries. Since the first one had been posted, a new one appeared every day. The incendiary content had inflamed news outlets the world over, but Layla was too afraid of the threatening notes to do anything to stop the carnage. As soon as Madison came out of hiding, she'd deny every word. She just hoped it wouldn't be too late. The reveals had left her fans feeling deeply betrayed. The longer the mess was allowed to drag on, the more their rage would cement until there was no turning back.

She paused before the full-length mirror. A few healthy meals and a decent night's sleep in a comfortable bed had gone a long way toward adding a bit of color back to her cheeks. Her cuts and bruises were still visible but beginning to fade. And while her ankle was still an issue, the pain was lessening, which made it easier to accommodate.

The hem of Tommy's old Led Zeppelin T-shirt curled at the top of her thighs. She knew it was his favorite and hoped he wouldn't mind that she'd borrowed it. Funny to think how just a few miles away she had a fantasy closet filled with the most coveted designer offerings, while here it was a choice between the cheap denim miniskirt she'd arrived in, a souvenir T-shirt featuring her face, or what-ever she could cull from Tommy's closet.

She fluffed her hair around her shoulders and frowned. She'd aimed for pretty but accessible, sexy yet friendly. While she hadn't exactly nailed the look, she did exude a sort of haunting frailty that might convince Tommy she was in need of his comfort . . . in whatever form that might take.

Her plan was awful. But she refused to believe it made her an awful person. It was like the old saying went: desperate people do desperate things. At the moment, Madison Brooks felt like the most desperate girl in the world.

She made for the kitchen, where she unearthed a bottle of Unrivaled tequila from one of the cupboards and carried it into the den with two shot glasses in tow. Then, before she could talk herself out of it, she retrieved the bottle of pain pills she'd taken from the safe at Paul's hideaway and placed two tabs in the bottom of Tommy's glass.

With more regret than he'd ever likely believe, she poured the tequila and watched as the pills began to dissolve and bleed seamlessly into the liquid.

Satisfied, she arranged herself among the couch cushions. Tommy would be back soon, and she wanted him to catch her looking beautiful, alluring, and inviting in a way he'd be unable to resist.

She'd just reached for the cashmere throw to prop under

her ankle, when the doorbell rang and Madison cast a worried look toward the entry.

Had Tommy misplaced his key?

A series of quick, insistent taps was followed by a voice softly calling, "Hey, open up—it's Aster."

Annoyed, Madison dutifully pushed away from the couch and peered through the peephole. Sure enough, Aster waited in the hall, wearing a pair of faded old jeans, a gray V-neck tee, a baseball cap, and oversize sunnies. She hugged a large canvas bag to her chest.

Madison swung the door open and ushered her inside.

"Ryan's waiting downstairs," Aster said in response to the way Madison peered past her shoulder before closing the door.

Madison nodded, secretly relieved by the words. She had no idea what Aster wanted, but if Ryan was waiting, then she wouldn't stay long.

Aster moved into the den and surveyed the scene. Her gaze lighting on the bottle of tequila and the two full shot glasses placed right beside it, she swung toward Madison with a knowing look. "Drinking alone is a really bad sign. You know that, right?"

"What do you want?" Madison made no attempt to play nice.

"I could ask you the same," Aster fired back.

Madison lifted her chin and kept her manner firm. "Me?

I'm just hiding out, lying low, and playing by the rules you all set."

"Give me one good reason why I shouldn't call Detective Larsen right now."

"Same list of reasons we already discussed."

Aster steeled her gaze. "I don't know what you're up to with"—she gestured toward the shot glasses—"whatever that's supposed to be. But don't drag Tommy into your schemes. He's gone out of his way to help you. The least you can do is respect the risk he's taking and not use him to relieve your boredom or loneliness or whatever story you've told yourself that makes it okay for you to seduce someone you don't actually give a shit about."

Madison's anger flared, but it would do no good to show it. "Well, look at you with the moral outrage." She laughed. "Wasn't so long ago you had no guilt about stealing my boyfriend."

"You can't steal a person who isn't open to leaving."

Madison smirked. "And to think you were once my biggest fan. According to your former friend Safi, you kept an entire file filled with pictures of me."

"And then I met you and realized everything about you is a lie." Aster's eyes blazed, and her tone was defiant. "The only one you've ever cared about is you. I can shut you down with a single phone call. So you better tread carefully where Tommy's concerned."

Aster was looking for a fight, but Madison refused to indulge her. Tommy would be home soon, and she couldn't afford another hitch in her plan. "Is there another reason you're here?" She gestured toward the canvas bag Aster clutched in her arms.

"Layla thought you might need some clothes." Aster sneered at Madison's getup and dumped the sack on a nearby chair. "Clearly she was right."

Madison plucked the first item from the top. It was a pale pink T-shirt featuring a fading photo of a kitten. "Wow, thanks," she said. "Did you pick this out yourself?"

"That's from Layla's ironic T-shirt phase. But not to worry, I managed to dig up an ugly sundress or two. Turns out your usual stylist is busy dressing Heather Rollins. Besides, you're in disguise, remember?"

Madison returned the T-shirt to the pile. On the one hand, it was a nice gesture. On the other, Aster's obvious glee at handing her a bag of their ugliest discards made it hard to be grateful.

Aster had just reached the door when she said, "Listen, Tommy's an adult and he makes his own choices. But while you might be able to fool him, just know I see past your shiny surface to the devious, manipulative, selfish person you are."

"And yet, you're still willing to help."

Aster sighed. "That says less about you, and more about

me. Don't make me regret my good deed."

With Aster gone, Madison resumed her position on the couch. A few minutes later, when Tommy walked in, she felt her heart skip a beat when his gaze went in search of her.

Her reaction caught her off guard. Was it the result of the excitement of finally putting her plan into place? Or did she actually like him more than she allowed herself to admit?

"How'd it go?" She forced a welcoming grin.

"What was Aster doing here?" Tommy dropped his key fob and phone onto the table and stood before her. "I saw her leaving. She seemed upset."

"She brought me some clothes." She tugged at the hem of the T-shirt, drawing Tommy's attention to her bare legs. "Guess she doesn't approve of my outfit." She lifted her gaze to meet his. "What do you think?" She bent one leg and kept the other extended, hinting at a classic pinup pose without being too obvious.

Tommy's eyes grazed the length of her, causing her pulse to quicken, her skin to heat. But just when she was sure she had him, a conflicted look washed over his face. Maybe this wouldn't be quite so easy.

"You look tense." She swung her legs around and patted the cushion beside her. "And as it just so happens, I have the perfect remedy right here." Her violet eyes flashed with promise, as she offered him the shot glass.

Reflexively, he moved toward her. Her smile brightened; her plan was a go.

A second later, he withdrew and said, "This is a really bad idea."

Madison fought to hide her disappointment. She needed him to drink it. Her immediate future depended on it. "I don't understand."

He swiped a hand through his hair and gazed toward the terrace, contemplating the view for a sobering moment. "You. Staying here." He shook his head and faced her. "All of it."

"But everyone agreed," she reminded him. "Besides, I have nowhere else to go. . . ." She watched in relief as he sighed deeply and sank onto the cushion beside her. "You want to talk about what's really bothering you?"

He shot her a baleful look.

"You want to make out?"

His eyes widened with shock, and then he let out a laugh. Leaning his head against the cushions, he said, "I always feel so off center around you."

Madison felt herself relax. This, she could handle. "I know, and I wish you didn't, but I'm used to it. It's the whole mega celebrity thing. Sometimes I hate how it makes people act so weird and nervous and unnatural around me. Other times, it comes in handy. It's like an invisible shield keeping people at bay."

"Is that what you like—keeping people at bay?"

"It's a matter of survival. But now, in times like this, it kinda sucks."

Wordlessly, he stared at her.

"Do you ever think about the night we kissed?"

Tommy gazed up at the ceiling. "The night you went missing, you mean? Yeah, I live with it every second of every day. It dictates my whole life."

"I mean before that. Back when it was just the two of us, sitting in the Vesper, drinking a beer and talking." She studied his profile, willing him to look at her, to see what she was offering. "It was one of the most normal moments I'd experienced in a really long time. And it's weird, because I'd just gone through this super-dramatic public breakup and—"

"A breakup you staged." Tommy cast a sharp look her way.

"Still, for that brief time we were together, I was happy. And when you kissed me—"

"You kissed me."

She cocked her head and grinned flirtatiously. "Did I?"

"I never would've made the first move. Not with you."

"Why not?" She sank her teeth into her bottom lip.

"Uh—because you're Madison Brooks and I was secretly freaking out just from being near you."

She closed her eyes and shook her head. When she opened them again, she said, "Can I tell you something?"

He looked at her.

"It really wasn't so secret."

To her relief, he laughed.

"But when we kissed, all of that seemed to disappear until it was just you, me, and whatever song was playing in the background. I can't even remember, can you?"

"'Melt with You,' Modern English." Tommy grinned sheepishly. "I remember every moment."

She had him. The moment he admitted to remembering the song (the right song, as it turned out, she remembered too), and she watched his gaze grow heavy at the memory, she knew it was time to put her plan into action.

"I thought about it a lot when I was held captive." She leaned toward him, handed him the shot glass, and tapped her own against it. "To nice memories." She raised the glass to her lips, making sure he tossed his back first before she followed suit. "It's better than I thought it would be." She rubbed her lips together as she continued to study him. "I had no idea Ira knew his way around tequila."

"Not much he doesn't know his way around." Tommy refilled their glasses and tossed back another. Madison demurred. She couldn't afford to lose control of the situation.

"Speaking of . . . did you find anything?" She watched

him closely, but he shook his head no. "I wish there was some way I could help. I feel so useless hiding out here all day by myself. Not to mention how lonely I get . . ." She reached toward him and traced a series of slow circles along the inside of his arm. "I want you to know how much I appreciate everything you've done for me. I know you're taking a big risk just by agreeing to look after me."

"You don't owe me anything."

"According to Aster, I do."

"Did she say something?" Tommy pressed.

"She was just being protective. Doesn't want to see you get hurt. But why would I do that when I'm completely indebted to you?"

She raised her glass, but instead of drinking from it, she wet her lips and said, "I heard your song. 'Violet Eyes.'"

Tommy closed his eyes and sighed. Madison could sense the battle waging inside him. He was torn between wanting her and wanting to do the right thing, but she couldn't allow his conscience to win.

"No one's ever done anything like that for me."

It was unclear who made the first move, but the next thing she knew she was in Tommy's arms as he pressed his lips urgently against hers.

Madison leaned into the kiss. Her tongue swirling in tandem with his, she twined her fingers in his hair and anchored a leg over his hip. It felt good to be back in his arms, with her body pushing hard against his. What a shame there was no time to see it all the way to the finish. Still, that didn't mean she couldn't enjoy it for as long as it lasted.

She dipped her hand low and was delighted by how quickly he responded to her touch. Good. He was right where she wanted him. All that was left now was . . .

"Tommy?" Her voice barely a whisper, she grinned as she pulled the T-shirt over her head and revealed herself to him.

Tommy squinted, struggling to focus.

"Do you love me, Tommy?" She tilted her head and studied him closely.

He blinked several times. Tried to form words he was unable to voice.

She dropped the T-shirt to the ground, and arched her breasts toward him, practically begging for his touch. "Do you think I'm lovely, Tommy?"

He lifted a hand as though it were leaden and fell face-first into her arms.

"I'm so sorry," she whispered, brushing his hair from his face as she settled him gently against the cushions and arranged his body into the recovery position in case he got sick. "You're going to be just fine. Get some rest now.

You've earned it. I only hope someday you'll be able to forgive me." She tucked the throw around his body and kissed his lips tenderly.

After jotting a quick note, she changed into one of Aster's ugly sundresses, pocketed the key to Tommy's car, grabbed her bag and her gun, and stepped into the hall, shutting the apartment door securely behind her.

THIRTY-TWO

ALL MY DEAD DRUNK FRIENDS

Layla stood outside Tommy's door and pressed hard on the buzzer. He wasn't answering his phone, wasn't responding to texts, but according to Aster, he was in there and possibly in need of help.

Being on Tommy's permanent guest list allowed easy access to his front door, but it did nothing to get her inside. Only a key card could do that, and it wasn't like Tommy had ever given her one.

She watched as a member of the cleaning crew entered an apartment down the hall. Maybe they would help her get in? Then again, it was just as likely Aster was wrong. Sure she'd gone to great lengths to describe the scene Madison had set, but last Layla checked, Tommy was an adult who could decide for himself who he did and didn't want to sleep with.

Layla had pushed Madison on him for precisely that reason—a sort of test to see if there was still something between them. If she and Tommy were ever going to make it work, Layla needed to know he was really and truly over whatever he and Madison once shared.

If it turned out he was still into her, well, it wouldn't be easy, but at least Layla would know where she stood. She'd always been more comfortable dealing with the truth. As a journalist, facts were her friends. She took the same approach to her personal life.

She was halfway to the elevator, when she found herself sneaking a peek inside the open apartment and giving a little wave. "Hi, um . . ." She forced a friendly grin and forged ahead. "My friend lives a few doors down, and he's not answering. I was wondering if you could maybe let me in?"

Well before she could get to the end, the woman was already shaking her head.

"I know it's against the rules," Layla said, unwilling to surrender so easily. "But I thought maybe just this once you could—"

"You're Layla Harrison." The woman placed a hand on her hip as Layla tried not to cringe under her scrutiny. "And you're asking me to help you break into Tommy Phillips's apartment?"

"No!" Layla flashed her palms in defense. "No—not at all! Not even close. You see, Tommy's inside—he's in there right now. But I think he's sick, which is why he's not answering the door. I just want to check and make sure he's okay. It's totally legit. I swear. If it turns out he's not there, you can kick me out. It's all good."

"Is this about the girl?"

Layla squinted, unsure what she meant.

"Because I tell you right now, this is no way to handle it. You're in enough trouble already, don't you think?"

Layla was horrified, but did her best to keep her face blank.

"I should call TMZ."

At the sound of that, Layla started backing away. "Not necessary," she said. "Forget this ever happened. Sorry to have bothered you."

She could feel the woman's piercing gaze as she retraced her steps. Stopping before Tommy's door, she rang the buzzer again, then composed a text to Aster explaining how it was none of their business. If Tommy decided to hook up with Madison, that was his choice. Layla was choosing to move on before she could embarrass herself any more than she already had.

She was about to hit send, when the door swung open and Tommy swayed unsteadily before her.

"Tommy? *Omigod!*" Layla scrambled toward him,

catching him by the arm before he could topple over.

His eyes were glassy, his face pale, and there was a trail of what looked to be vomit running down the front of his T-shirt. She started to veer him toward the couch, but there was more vomit on the floor, so she steered him toward the bedroom instead.

"Are you okay?" She settled him onto the mattress and pulled his soiled T-shirt over his head. "How many fingers am I holding up?"

He squinted but couldn't quite focus. "I think she drugged me." His chin bobbed against his chest.

"Shit—just—" Layla glanced around wildly. She had no idea what to do. Racing for his bathroom, she grabbed a clean hand towel, ran some cold water over it, and pressed it against his forehead and cheeks. "What did you drink— what did she give you?"

"Tequila. Couple shots. I think she . . . she set me . . ." He tried to form words, but all he could manage was an incoherent mumble.

"She set you up. I know. Don't talk, just—" She looked at him. "Or maybe you should talk? I don't know—*crap!*"

Panicked, she reached for her phone, about to call 911, when she remembered Aster's warning and texted Mateo instead. He was the only one she knew, aside from her dad, who had experience with these things.

What do you do when someone ODs?

She hit send, then waited impatiently. A few seconds later, he replied.

Call 911.

What else?

Are they conscious?

She looked at Tommy and typed:

Yes.

Call 911.

It's complicated—it's Tommy.

I'll be right there.

You don't have to.

On my way.

In the meantime?

Stay with him—not far.

She eased Tommy back against the pillows and checked his pulse. She didn't know if it was slower than usual or faster than usual. She was mainly relieved to confirm that he had one.

"You okay?" she asked.

His head bobbed in a way she took as a yes. Then she watched as he curled into a fetal position and hugged himself at the waist. The sight of him looking so vulnerable left her struggling between wanting to protect him, and wanting to find Madison and make her pay for doing this to him.

"Don't move," she instructed, quickly realizing the

ridiculousness of the statement. He was in no shape to wander. It was amazing he'd made it to the front door to let her in. "I'll be right back!" She raced for the den to try to get a handle on what Madison might've given him.

It was just as Aster described: a bottle of Unrivaled tequila, two shot glasses, and Tommy's favorite Led Zeppelin T-shirt balled up on the floor. She frowned, trying to imagine what might've occurred for it to find its way from Madison's body to the ground. Hating herself for even thinking that way, she forced herself to look past it to the note left on the table, tucked under his phone.

Tommy—

I'm so sorry for what I've done. You've been nothing but kind from the start, and I owe you in ways I'll never be able to repay. I hope someday I'll have the chance to explain, but mostly I hope you'll find it in your heart to not hate me—even though I've now given you every reason to turn against me.

Just so you know, you ingested two hydrocodone pills along with two shots of tequila. I didn't try to kill you and you didn't OD. At the very worst, you'll fall asleep and wake up with a raging headache and a heart that's hardened toward me.

M.

Layla had just finished reading the note when she heard Mateo at the front door.

"Where is he?" He rushed to her side.

"It's okay. He's okay. Or at least he will be. I think he just needs to sleep it off."

She handed him the note, then reached for Tommy's phone.

"Wait—this is from Madison? She was here?" Mateo stared in what could only be described as disbelief.

"She was." Layla sighed. "But not anymore." She motioned him into the bedroom, where she perched on the mattress and pressed the wet towel to Tommy's forehead. "Are we doing the right thing?" She looked at Mateo. "Should we take him to the hospital?"

Mateo paced the length of the room. Ignoring her question, he said, "I can't believe this! After everything you went through—getting arrested, jail time, the tabloids—and you've actually been hiding her all along?"

"No," she murmured. "Not all along." She checked Tommy's pulse again. He seemed fine. Or at least she hoped that was the case.

"Why haven't you told anyone? Why isn't this breaking news?"

Mateo was incredulous, and while she didn't blame him, she also knew the explanation she was about to give would sound completely ridiculous to anyone who hadn't been there when they'd found her. "Because Tommy, Aster, Ryan, and I unanimously agreed not to tell anyone. We're the only ones who know. We truly thought we were helping her. Clearly, she played us."

"I don't get it," Mateo said. "Why would you agree to help her?"

"It's a really long story." Layla sighed, in no mood for a retelling. "And it's hardly worth getting into at this point."

"Don't be mad at her," Tommy mumbled as he struggled to sit. "It's not her fault."

"I'm not mad," Mateo shot back. "Just—" He shook his head. "Never mind. You okay? You want some water or something?"

Tommy shook his head. Looking at Layla, he said, "What'd she give me?"

Mateo handed over the note.

Tommy scanned it, then tossed it aside. "I feel like an ass."

"Don't," Layla said. She thought of the crumpled T-shirt. Madison had set him up, pretended to seduce him, then fled—oldest trick in the book. Though she wasn't about to tell him that and make him feel worse. "Why don't you sleep it off? We'll stay with you, if you want."

Tommy shook his head. "No, I'm not . . ." He acted like he was about to get up, but Layla pressed a hand to his shoulder to stop him.

"Oh, no. You're not going anywhere. For one thing,

I'm pretty sure she took your car. That's probably why she drugged you, to get the keys. For another, you're under the influence. So you can either sleep it off or chill, but you're not leaving until it's worked its way through your system."

"Yes, Mom." Reluctantly, he sank back against the pillows, but the look he gave her was grateful.

"Did you find anything at Ira's?" Layla perched beside him as Mateo took a chair just opposite.

Tommy's lids drifted shut in a way that made Layla think he was falling asleep. When he opened them again, he said, "Check my phone."

Layla handed it to him, watching as he input the passcode, then showed her the screen.

"Why are you showing me this?" She took the phone, struggling to make sense of why Tommy would show her a picture of a topless girl. Was he trying to emotionally torture her? If so, it was working. If that was what he was into, she could never compete. More importantly, she shouldn't have to.

"I messed up," Tommy said, rubbing his knuckles against his tired eyes. "He knew I was there. The pic is Ira's way of screwing with me."

"I don't get it." She looked at Tommy.

"There's nothing to get."

Layla was about to return the phone when Mateo said, "Can I see that?"

She smirked. "At your own risk. It's R rated." She started to laugh, but the look on Mateo's face cut her short.

She watched as he stared at the image. When he lifted his gaze, he said, "You sure Ira took this?"

Tommy nodded. "Positive."

"But why would Ira give you a picture of Heather Rollins?" Mateo glanced between Tommy and Layla.

"Wait—what?" Layla grasped at the phone to take another look. "You sure?" She studied Mateo.

His face flushed in embarrassment. "The broken-heart tattoo on her finger gives it away."

"Lots of people have those." Layla needed to be absolutely sure and not jump to conclusions.

"Trust me." Mateo cringed. "I recognize the rest too."

Layla dropped her gaze. Now she felt embarrassed for both of them.

"So, what's going on?" Tommy inched up the headboard. "Are you saying Heather Rollins is with Ira? Because I thought she was with you."

Mateo swiftly averted his gaze, and Layla couldn't help but feel bad on his behalf. He hated gossip, loathed drama, but now, despite his best efforts to avoid all of that, he found himself right at the center. "They know each other. That's all I can confirm. As for Heather and me, we had a thing, but it's over."

"But why would Ira do that?" Layla glanced between

Mateo and Tommy. "Give you this picture, I mean?"

"To taunt me, mess with me." Tommy scowled. "Let me know he knew I was there."

"But why wouldn't he just expose you?" she pressed. "Why would he be so discreet?"

Tommy covered his face with his hands, allowing the silence to stretch between them. When he finally looked at them, he confided about the video surveillance at Night for Night, and how the pictures had recently resurfaced despite Ira's promise. "He's evil," he said. "He likes to screw with people."

It was clear how much it hurt him to say it. Layla and her mom were estranged, but she'd never believed her mom was purposely plotting against her. She couldn't imagine feeling that way about a parent.

"What if we've been reading this all wrong?" she said, unsure if she was trying to make him feel better, or if she was truly onto something. "What if Ira hasn't been out to get us at all? What if he's not behind any of it? What if it's Heather?"

"That's crazy." Mateo was quick to refute it. *Maybe a little too quick?*

"But is it?" Layla looked at Tommy, who merely shrugged in reply. "Thing is," she said, unwilling to abandon the idea now forming in her mind, "Heather was obsessed with Madison. She kept loads of pictures of her on her phone, which always struck me as odd."

"She admired Madison," Mateo said. "And they were friends. She explained to me once how she used to study her like an opponent before a big match—"

"And that didn't strike you as weird?"

"Hollywood is weird. It's also really competitive. Heather's constant scrutiny of Madison was about trying to best her—not ruin her."

Layla took her time to consider. While it wasn't too difficult to bend her theory in a way that fit, obviously Mateo knew Heather better than any of them. Besides, what possible motive could Heather have for doing all that? Never mind the fact that she seemed too self-involved to have the sort of patience required to pull off such a stunt.

Heavy with regret, she realized they were right back where they'd started. "So what now?" she asked.

She hadn't expected an answer, which was why she was surprised when Tommy said, "After I force myself to vomit, I'm going to take a shower, then track down Madison once and for all. Care to join me?"

"I'll brew some coffee," Layla said, as Mateo followed her into the kitchen.

THIRTY-THREE

UPTOWN FUNK

Trena Moretti followed the Road to Hollywood as she made her way through the Hollywood & Highland shopping center. Funny how she'd made plenty of previous visits but had never taken the time to read the individual stories.

The mosaic trail was a collection of tales of how the famous and not so famous came to Hollywood to fulfill their dream of working in the industry. Some of the stories were funny, some were heartbreaking, and others—like the one about a famous director telling an actress she was too fat to work in the United States—were downright maddening. Trena was so engrossed in reading them she'd followed the trail all the way to the tiled chaise lounge that overlooked the Hollywood sign before she realized she was late for her meeting.

Luckily, Starbucks was nearby, so she wandered over and waited for the person who went by the name @LuckyHearts16 to find her. A large pair of dark sunglasses covered her face, but Trena was confident her wild bronze-tinged curls were easily recognizable.

It wasn't long before someone called her name and Trena looked up to find a pretty young girl, probably in her mid-teens, striding toward her. She was tall, skinny to the point of gawky. In her denim shorts and black tank top, her pale, gangly limbs appeared especially vulnerable under the harsh glare of the sun. At first sight, the girl seemed an awkward arrangement of angles and bones. But as she drew near, Trena had no doubt she'd soon blossom into a formidable beauty.

"You're Trena Moretti, right?" The girl smiled nervously.

"And you are?"

The girl fidgeted, shifting her weight from one well-worn Converse to the other. "Just—let's leave it at Lucky-Hearts16, or maybe Lucky for short."

Trena nodded agreeably.

"So, where should we do this?" The girl looked around. She seemed agitated, on edge. Trena took it as a good sign. It gave her the upper hand.

"Why don't we just grab one of these chairs?" Trena smiled gently, wanting the girl to know there was nothing to fear.

Funny how they were always so different in person. In her texts, the girl had been brazen, bordering on rude, in her eagerness to meet. But now she acted skittish, almost meek. Celebrity often had that effect. People would throw endless amounts of shade online, but once they were face-to-face, all they wanted was a little acknowledgment and a selfie to share with their friends.

"Sorry I'm so nervous." The girl swept her long brown hair over her shoulder. "It's just . . . I'm a really big fan."

"And Madison?" Trena crossed her legs and rested her hands on her lap. "Were you a fan of hers too?"

The girl lifted her shoulders and quirked her mouth to the side. "I was. But after reading those diary entries, I realized she's just a big liar. How do you get used to it?" She blinked from under a thick fringe of chestnut-colored bangs.

The question left Trena confused, wondering if the girl was asking how she got used to people lying, or how she got used to being a liar.

Reading Trena's expression, the girl leaned forward and whispered, "Being famous, I mean. Having everyone watch you all the time. Isn't it weird?"

Trena leaned against the backrest and stifled a laugh. This coming from the most over-photographed, over-documented generation the world had yet seen. "I ignore it." She pretended as though she hadn't been the least bit aware of the whispering, head turning, and scrutiny happening all around her. A few beats later she said, "So, Lucky—you have something for me?"

The girl slouched low in her seat and shot a furtive look all around.

"Relax." Trena leaned forward and placed a reassuring hand on the girl's arm. "It's not like we're conducting a drug deal."

The girl let out a short, startling laugh that immediately sent her cheeks flaming. Taking a few controlled breaths to collect herself, she said, "Okay, here's the thing: You watched the video, right?"

Trena was losing patience. "I think that's why we're both here."

"Right. So, anyway, do you think she did it?"

Trena was taken aback. She had no idea what the girl was getting at. "Do I think who did what?" She spoke the words slowly.

"The girl! In the video!" Lucky leaned closer and lowered her voice so much that Trena strained to hear. "Do you think she did it? Do you think she killed Madison? I mean, she had the earring and all, so . . . it's possible, right?"

Trena was stunned. She'd thought for sure the girl had come to the same conclusion as she had—that the blond in the video was Madison in disguise. Quickly, she rerouted all the responses she'd planned.

"Thing is, I really don't want to get dragged into it, see? I mean, if she did do it, if she did kill Madison, well, I wasn't even supposed to be anywhere near Night for Night. I told my parents I was at the library studying for a history exam. But now, if I get pulled into court or something because of the video . . ." She shook her head and bit down on her lip as though she couldn't imagine anything worse than her parents discovering she'd lied to them.

Trena paused long enough to carefully frame a reply. What a gift this was turning out to be.

"I can keep your name out of it," Trena assured her. "I give you my word."

Lucky stared as though trying to determine if that was good enough for her.

"I see no reason for you to get involved," Trena continued. "As a journalist, it's my right to keep my sources anonymous."

It must've worked, because the girl slipped a hand inside her bag and retrieved a small object she pushed across the table toward Trena.

It was round, wrapped in tissue, but from what Trena could tell, it had all the familiar qualities of a hoop earring.

She looked at the girl, stunned to realize that despite what she'd written in her text, she wanted nothing in return other than her solemn promise to keep her secret safe from her parents.

"Thank you," Trena said. "This helps."

"I erased the account I sent the video from. You can't trace it back to me. Just so you know."

"Wouldn't dream of it. You have nothing to worry about. Again, you have my word."

A second later the girl stood. "Okay, well—good luck," she said, clearly eager to leave.

Trena knew she should've left it at that, but for some reason she said, "That's it? We're good here?" She was used to people always working an angle. The fact that this had gone down so easily seemed sort of suspicious.

The girl faced her with a frown. "Nobody knows about this but you. My friend never even noticed the girl in the background with the earring. And I never told her I went back to see if it was still there. So if the cops knock at my door, I'll know it's because of you. But you promised you'd keep me out of it, and that's all I'm looking for. So—yeah, we're good."

She shot Trena a tight grin and quickly moved away. Trena was just about to head into Starbucks to get a chai latte for the road, when Detective Larsen approached.

No such thing as a coincidence, she mumbled under her

breath. To Larsen, she said, "Walking the Road to Hollywood?"

He shot her a blank look.

She motioned toward the very ground where he stood.

Ignoring it, he looked at her and said, "Who was that? One of your sources?"

Trena drew her gaze toward his. "Seems a little young to be a source, don't you think?"

"That depends. What were you discussing?"

"Babysitting tips." Trena didn't so much as blink.

Larsen regarded her closely. "Coulda swore I saw her hand you something."

"Am I under surveillance?"

"Mind telling me what it was?"

"Sure, show me a search warrant and it's all yours." She knew Larsen liked to provoke, but she refused to play along. She turned on her heel, only to feel his fingers catching at her arm. Whirling on him in anger, she jerked free of his grip. "Pretty sure you don't want to do that," she said.

"Do what?" He flashed his palms and adopted an innocent expression.

"Get between me and my chai latte," she spat. "Never mind that unwanted advance."

"Advance?" He laughed. "That's how you're going to spin it?"

She folded her arms across her chest. It was entirely

possible that at this moment she actually hated this man more than she'd ever hated anyone. Including her lying, cheating ex-fiancé Marcus. "Clearly this is not a random meet-cute." She frowned. "So get to the point. What do you want?"

"I want to know how you knew about the trailer."

Trena tilted her head in a way that sent a spray of curls spilling across her forehead. "And here I thought you were going to deliver my thank-you card in person. You know, the one that says, 'Dear Ms. Moretti, thanks for doing my job for me.'" She was pushing it, but she was tired of the way he manipulated her into kowtowing to him.

"Question stands." He kept a straight face.

"I did my homework." She shrugged. "News flash—studying pays off."

"What'd you take from the trailer?"

"Pretty sure you found the watch. If I was going to take anything, don't you think it would've been that?"

"Just know I'm watching you." He pointed a stubby freckled finger at her.

"You and the rest of the nation, every Sunday, eight p.m. sharp." She forced her lips into a wide grin.

She wasn't sure how he'd respond, but the way he rested his gaze on hers left her more chilled than any words could.

"Enjoy your chai." He turned on his heel and went on his way. "Until we meet again," he called over his shoulder.

Trena stared after him. Once he'd disappeared, she poked through the tissue and peeked inside the small package Lucky had given her. Sure enough, it was a single gold-and-turquoise hoop earring, just like the one in the video. Just like the one Madison wore on the night she'd gone missing.

Of course, there was little hope of proving it actually belonged to Madison. So many people had touched it, it was doubtful any good prints could be lifted. Still, Trena considered it one more piece in the puzzle. Besides, she knew in her gut it belonged to Madison, just like she knew the girl caught on video was Madison in disguise.

She was out there . . . somewhere.

Trena popped the package back in her bag and headed into Starbucks. She was due for a walk-through at RED for the feature she'd promised Ira. While she wasn't exactly keen on the idea of promoting him, she knew that a favor granted was a favor banked. She just hoped it wouldn't backfire like it just had with Larsen.

THIRTY-FOUR

HEART OF GLASS

Madison drove Tommy's car to the coast, all the way to Santa Monica Beach, where she found a place to park and headed out toward the sand. She preferred Malibu, but it was too far a drive and she still had so many loose ends to attend to.

With her future looming uncertainly, she was desperately in need of some guidance. The calming rhythm of the waves with their continuous rush and retreat always helped to remind her just how small and insignificant she was in the big scheme of things.

In just eighteen years, Madison had managed to live two distinctly different lives. Like dramatic before and after shots, one bore little resemblance to the other, and yet, the past would not be defeated. Madison felt just as lost, alone, and unsure as she had a decade ago. She had a gun in her bag and she knew how to use it, but she no longer had Paul to shield her from the aftermath.

She walked along the shoreline, enjoying the feel of her toes sinking into the sand. The small pebbles slipped inside the bandage that covered her ankle, causing the grains to rub against her skin, abrading her flesh, but Madison paid it no notice. For all she knew, this could turn out to be the last time she enjoyed a pleasure so simple. She had a plan, sure, but there was no way of knowing if it would actually work.

Her first trip to the ocean, she was eight years old on her way to meet her new family in Connecticut. Paul's mom, Eileen, had taken her, and Paul had caught up with them during the latter part of the journey. Madison remembered the way they'd led her down to the water—how she'd shrieked and squealed in delight when the small swells raced up to cover her feet, before retreating and leaving a froth of bubbles behind.

She also remembered overhearing bits of their conversation when they thought she wasn't listening. How worried they'd been about her ability to adjust to her new, upper-crust world.

Or at least Eileen had been worried. She'd even waged a good argument to keep Madison behind in West Virginia, but Paul wouldn't hear of it. "She's not like us," he'd said.

"She'll be fine wherever she lands. Holding her back would only delay the inevitable."

At the time, Madison had taken his statement about her not being like them to mean she was special, maybe even superior.

But over the last few months she'd done enough reflecting to conclude Paul hadn't meant that at all. He'd been referring to the moment Madison had pressed the piece of burning wood to her flesh—how her tears weren't the result of losing her parents, but from the sheer joy of being released from that life.

Paul had watched her with a conflicted look of admiration and fear. When he'd referred to her as different, he didn't just mean she didn't feel things the same way other people did. Paul had gone so far as to question if she felt much of anything at all.

She knew why he'd think that, but she wasn't heartless, not even close. Sure she may have used people from time to time to get what she needed, but she felt terrible about what she'd done to Tommy. She felt even worse about having suspected Paul of plotting against her, especially after having discovered the truth.

She wasn't a sociopath. It wasn't that simple. In her professional life, she easily conveyed a wide range of emotions and was often lauded for her ability to summon whatever response a director required. In her personal life, it took a lot for her to trust anyone enough to feel empathy. Funny how the price of being famous was the same as living a lie—requiring her to keep everyone at arm's length, and never run the risk of exposing herself.

Despite what Tommy might think once he realized what she'd done, she knew in her heart she cared deeply for him. Still, driven by her own desperate need to save herself and the life she'd created, she'd crossed a line Tommy would never forgive, and it wasn't like she could blame him.

A small child ran past, flying a kite and laughing gleefully as he stared up at the sky. Madison dipped her toes deeper into the tide and watched as the water rushed over her ankles and soaked through her bandage.

It's time.

The words rang in her head as though they were whispered from across the ether. But Madison recognized the sound of her own inner voice telling her it was time to finally confront the person who'd kidnapped her.

It had taken a while to piece it together. But while Tommy had been breaking into the Vesper, Madison took advantage of his absence to use his laptop to follow a hunch. She'd spent the previous night investigating the lead, making sure she was right. Though her findings had surprised her, in retrospect she realized she should've known all along.

She waded in farther, allowing the waves to break against her shins and wet the hem of her dress before she slowly made her way back toward her car. Stopping to unwrap the now soggy dressing that covered her ankle, she paused near a trash can to dispose of it and send a quick text from her phone.

Sorry I ran. I know who's behind this. I'll explain when I see you.

Faster than expected, she received a reply.

Where & when. You decide. Just glad you're OK.

A moment later Madison replied:

Griffith Park—view of the Hollywood Sign.

After all, what could be more symbolic than a place that honored both kinds of stars?

She took a steadying breath and patted the side of her bag, seeking assurance her gun was still there. Then, with a quick tap of the key fob, she unlocked Tommy's car and settled in.

She'd just fastened her seat belt and was starting the engine, when she caught a trace of a sweet yet slightly cloying scent.

Startled, she turned just as someone rose up from the backseat and smashed a cloth hard against her face.

Her fingers tore at the rag, trying to rip it away. But the chloroform worked quickly, rendering her helpless against it.

Last thing she remembered was staring helplessly into the rearview mirror and meeting her attacker's gaze.

"You!" She struggled to speak but didn't get very far before the whole world faded away.

THIRTY-FIVE

WHITE ROOM

Aster and Ryan sat in a car across from RED and stared at the building. From the outside, it wasn't all that impressive. Aster wondered if the inside would be any better.

"Last time I was here, it was mostly sawdust and jackhammers." She glanced at Ryan. "Hard to believe it's opening already."

"A *soft* opening," Ryan said, reminding her of the language Ira had used when they were leaving her lawyer's office and Ira had invited them to stop by.

Aster's first instinct was to decline. But Ryan, sensing her hesitation, squeezed her fingers with his, prompting her to switch gears and say, "Sounds fun, what time?"

Ira seemed pleased and had given them firm instructions

to be there at six forty-five sharp. Not a moment later.

"Is it time yet?" She glanced between her watch and her phone.

"Almost. You ready?" Ryan looked at her.

"Is *no* a valid answer?"

She figured she must look as frightened and unsettled as she felt, because next thing she knew, Ryan cupped a hand to each of her cheeks and kissed her with such reverence, she veered dangerously close to a full-on ugly cry.

"It's going to be okay. *You're* going to be okay." He acted as though if he said it enough times with enough force, the universe would respond by granting his wish. Just yesterday she would've believed it, but now, with Madison on the run, she was no longer sure.

"If nothing else, you have uncontestable photographic proof she's alive. You couldn't have possibly killed her."

"Do you think Ira knows?"

Ryan squinted.

"I mean, the way he kept looking at me today when we were with the lawyers. I had trouble focusing on what they were saying, and I'm pretty sure he could tell."

"Seems normal to have a hard time focusing when you're worried about going to jail."

She paused to consider. "Still, I felt like he was onto me." She leaned her head back against the neck rest and stared through the sunroof. "I'm so conflicted. I don't know what to do. I feel like everyone's playing me, and yet I still kept Madison's secret. Do you think I should've said something while I had the chance? Or am I just being paranoid?"

"I think Ira has a way of unsettling people," Ryan said, his voice patient and kind. "It's his superpower and he knows it. It's the true secret behind his success." He let that sink in. "Madison will show up eventually. She can't stay hidden forever."

Aster wasn't sure she agreed. "Can't she?"

"Trust me," Ryan said. "She won't want to. She's addicted to the spotlight, and right now, she's more famous than ever." He reached across the console and gave her knee a reassuring squeeze. "So, you ready?"

Aster faced him. More than anything she wanted to reply: *Do I have a choice?* Or: *Hell no!* Or: *Please do not make me go in there!* But in order to prove to Ira he had no reason to suspect her of anything, she needed to get out of the car and join his stupid party or soft opening or whatever this was.

She flipped down the mirrored visor and checked her hair and makeup. She looked all right, she guessed. At the start of the summer she'd been obsessed with her looks; now, she barely gave it much thought.

"I'm all in." She slipped free of the car, watching as Ryan came around to meet her.

His lips eased into a grin as his gaze slowly took her in.

"When this is over . . . when all this is over . . ." He was standing so close she could feel the heat emanating between them. "I'm going to take you away somewhere amazing. And we're never once leaving our bed."

"Then it doesn't really matter where we'll be, does it?" she teased. "I mean, if we're just going to stay in bed the whole time."

He kissed her once, deeply, passionately. When he pulled away, he said, "Fine. We'll slip out for the occasional meal, but the rest of the time . . ."

He slung an arm around her waist and led her toward the entrance. James was working the door, which came as a surprise. If it was a soft opening that no one knew about, then why did Ira need James?

Then again, Ira never missed an opportunity to make a dramatic display, and it was hard to find a more impressive bouncer than James, who was so handsome Aster was sure he had a hundred better options than working for Ira.

James looked them over, nodded wordlessly, then opened the door and ushered them inside.

The room was dimly lit and done up entirely in white. The only color came from hidden projectors that first cast the space in spots of gray that left it looking shadowed and haunted, before transforming it to a deep, bloody red that made it look like a particularly grisly crime scene.

Ryan hesitated, trying to make sense of it. "I'll say one

thing, Ira sure knows how to make a dramatic impact."

"But where is everyone?" Aster whispered. Except for them, the room was empty. She turned to ask James, but the door was shut. "On a scale of one to ten, how worried should I be?"

One look at Ryan's troubled gaze provided the answer. Still, he tried to ease her alarm by saying, "I'm sure they're around here somewhere. Let's take a look. See what this place is all about."

Aster grasped his hand tightly in hers and walked alongside him to an area that consisted of a long white hallway flanked by a series of doors on either side.

"This reminds me of a hypnosis session I did once."

Aster glanced at him nervously.

"Whatever door you pick is supposed to reveal some hidden part of yourself that gives you better insight into how to conduct your life, or provide guidance, or something like that. It was a while ago."

"Well, it's freaking me out," Aster whispered. "Why would Ira build this? Who would actually pay to come here?"

"Plenty of people," Ryan laughed. "Anyway, we're here. What's the worst that can happen?" Seeing the look on her face, he said, "You're with me, and I'm not going anywhere. So, go ahead, pick a door, any door. Which one is calling to you?"

Aster gathered her courage and approached the second door on the left. But when she tried the knob, the door was locked. "Did that happen in your hypnosis session?" She frowned.

Ryan looked a bit shaken, but tried not to show it. "When at first you don't succeed . . ."

Aster screwed up her nerve and tried the door across from it. The knob turned, the door swung open. Tentatively, she stepped inside.

"I'm not sure I get it." She squinted at what appeared to be a big, white box of a room. "What is this supposed to be? What is this place?"

She turned to Ryan, but he was nowhere in sight.

"Ryan!" she cried, only to have her words echo right back as the door slammed shut, locking her inside.

THIRTY-SIX

WHERE HAVE ALL THE GOOD TIMES GONE

"Hello?" Layla stepped deeper inside the club and looked all around. The way her footsteps echoed on the white concrete floors gave her the chills. It wasn't like she'd expected a crowd, but the absolute emptiness of the place left her wondering just what exactly she'd agreed to.

In an instant, the colored lights switched off and a series of spotlights kicked in. She blinked against the sudden brightness and looked toward the far side of the room, where an image of a hand was projected onto a wall, pointing in the direction it presumably wanted her to go. Not knowing what else to do, she followed. Ira said he wanted RED to be an experience—the ultimate performance space—and so far, she had to admit she'd never experienced anything like it.

She found herself staring down a long hallway offering various doors to choose from. Ira had told her about this part as well, claiming some of them would be auditory, some visual, and all where you could choose your own ending.

At the end of the hall a pair of eyes stared back, seeming to beckon her closer. Once she'd reached a certain point, the eyes veered in the direction of the door on her right. So Layla grasped the knob and stepped inside.

The first thought that came to mind was how creepy it was.

The second was that she had no intention of staying.

She turned, eager to flee, when the door slammed shut and locked from the outside.

THIRTY-SEVEN

ANY OL' BARSTOOL

Tommy crossed the large, cavernous, all-white space and approached Ira sitting alone at the bar.

"What do you think?" Ira turned on his stool and swung an arm wide, gesturing toward his latest creation.

Tommy looked all around. "Well, it's really, really white."

Ira laughed and punched a few prompts on his iPad, first drenching the space in slanted gray shadows and lines before switching it to a deep bloody red that seemed to drip down the walls and spread across the floor.

"I think of it as a canvas," Ira said. "Those are just two of the landscapes I can create. It's seemingly limitless. Check this out." He tapped another prompt and the room glowed a deep, translucent blue. There were colorful coral reefs, sharks swimming by, like being under the sea, no tank or wet suit necessary. After a moment, he switched it back to red.

Tommy paused uncertainly. Ira had summoned him there just a few hours earlier, and Tommy still didn't know why.

"Sit. Have a drink," Ira said.

Tommy obeyed, watching as Ira grabbed the bottle of Unrivaled tequila, filled a couple of shot glasses bearing the word RED, and pushed one before him.

Tommy paused. His last encounter with tequila, just the day before, hadn't gone down so well. Still, Ira was waiting, so he braced for the worst, hoped for the best, and tossed back his drink. As soon as it was empty, Ira filled his glass again and looked at him expectantly. "I'm pacing myself," Tommy said, raising a hand in protest.

Ira laughed and drained his own glass.

Tommy tilted back on his stool. He felt nervous, anxious. The whole scene set him on edge, partly due to the strange heightened environment, and partly because he worried Ira was softening him up before he called him out on breaking into the Vesper. He wondered if he should mention it first— beat Ira to the punch. Since they both knew it happened, it seemed strange to not just get it out into the open.

"How are things going at Elixir? Malina treating you well?" Ira asked, before Tommy could put a voice to his thoughts.

Tommy debated whether to confess. Deciding Ira probably already knew, he said, "Been better."

Ira gave him a look that encouraged him to continue.

"I screwed up." He ran a hand through his hair and toyed with the rim of his shot glass. "She threatened to cancel the contract."

"Not sure she can do that," Ira said.

Tommy shrugged. "She thinks she can, and that's all that matters."

"Do you want me to speak to her on your behalf? Or set up a meet with a lawyer?"

Ira was acting like a dad, and it made Tommy uncomfortable. Why was Ira always trying to help him, or at least pretending to help him? Should he tell him? Finally speak the truth he'd been waiting to put into words?

Tommy wavered, on the verge of a full-blown confession, when instead he shook his head and said, "She has the grounds. And honestly, I'm not sure I'm cut out for all this."

"All what?" Ira's gaze was as sharp as his tone.

Tommy could sense an impending lecture, and he was pretty sure he wasn't cut out for that either. Last thing he wanted was to confide in Ira Redman, the very person responsible for getting him into this mess.

Malina was pissed about the botched *Rolling Stone* interview and had threatened not only to cancel his contract, but to kick him out of the apartment as well. He had an appointment to speak with her first thing in the morning. A week ago, he wouldn't have thought twice about keeping it. Now, he was no longer sure.

He remembered the way Madison had lectured him when she called him out for complaining about the haters and tabloids.

Maybe she was right.

Maybe he was ungrateful, or unwilling to take the bad with the good.

Maybe he was being naive.

Maybe he just didn't have it in him.

Maybe he really was spineless and scared and would always be more comfortable being a big fish in a minuscule pond, where admiration was assured and little was required in return.

All he knew was that the summer had forced him to face some harsh truths that left him questioning who he was, what he stood for, and just how far he was willing to go to accomplish his dreams.

He studied Ira sitting beside him. To most, Ira was a living legend. But Tommy could only guess at the sort of questionable things he might've done in order to rise so high. He wasn't sure he was willing to follow Ira's lead.

"I don't know how much longer I'm going to stick around." Tommy cleared his throat before adding, "I don't think I'm a good fit for this town."

Ira regarded him with a searing gaze. "We all tell ourselves a story, Tommy. We make up entire narratives about who we are and what we're capable of. We set limits on ourselves without ever being tested. It's natural, human, though it's also an excuse for playing small. You have a gift. I've seen it firsthand. Which is why I'd strongly caution you against scripting an ending that indulges your fears before you've had a chance to discover if they're even valid or real."

Tommy grew still. It wasn't the first time Ira had gone on a philosophical bent. Hell, he liked to pontificate more than anyone Tommy had ever met. What he didn't understand was why Ira could possibly give enough of a shit to put so much thought into warning him against the worst part of himself.

There was a strange intimacy to the moment. They were alone, with no immediate threat of distraction. It was, Tommy realized, the perfect opportunity to confront one of his biggest fears and tell Ira the other half of the dream that had fueled the move west. Ira had just praised him, so surely he wouldn't reject the idea of Tommy being his son.

It was all in play, just like he'd imagined. Tommy was famous, he had a record deal (well, at least for the moment), and enough money banked that he didn't actually need Ira's help. There was nothing Ira could give him that Tommy didn't already have.

Except a willingness to admit to being his father.

It was now or never. He'd rehearsed the speech so many times the words were easily summoned.

His hands splayed on the table before him, he inhaled long and deep. His mouth opened to speak, when he suddenly realized that while he did want to salvage the record deal and continue to pursue his dreams, he was done caring what Ira Redman thought of him. All that mattered now was what Tommy thought of himself.

He pushed the shot glass away. "I've got an early morning." He started to rise from his stool.

Ira's gaze narrowed and held fast to his. "I'd like if you could stick around just a bit longer. I've got something special planned that I'd hate for you to miss." He flashed Tommy a look that said the offer was nonnegotiable, and then he led him down a long hall to the last door on the left.

Tommy glanced nervously between Ira and the door.

"Why don't you wait in here?" Ira swung the door open and ushered Tommy inside yet another room done up all in white. "Make yourself comfortable." He gestured toward the long bench against the far wall. "The show will begin soon."

The next thing Tommy knew, Ira was gone, and the door locked behind him.

THIRTY-EIGHT

LA WOMAN

Trena gazed around the empty white space, surprised to find she was the only one there. At the very least, she'd expected to find Ira waiting, but as it was, no one was even working the door.

She moved toward the bar, where she saw two shot glasses sitting side by side, one full, one empty, and beside them a bottle of Unrivaled tequila.

If nothing else, it was a sign that at least someone had been there. She just didn't know if they still were.

The space was quiet, too quiet. And the way the light played against the stark white walls, splattering them with bright droplets of red, set her on edge.

"Welcome."

Trena turned to find Heather Rollins dressed in a body-skimming white dress.

"I hope we haven't kept you waiting too long."

Trena frowned. *We?* So far Heather was the only person she'd seen. And something about her arrival seemed oddly showy, even for Ira's standards.

"I'm here to see Ira." Trena played it firm, professional. She was there to do a walk-through, frame a couple of scenes, and get a feel for the place. She wasn't the least bit interested in Ira's theatrics. It was a waste of her time.

Heather grinned. "I know, and you will, soon enough. Meanwhile, he's asked me to show you around and explain his ideas."

Trena looked her over. Heather was camera ready and flawlessly groomed. Her white dress hugged every curve, and her blond hair was perfectly fluffed and curled. "So, let me guess—you serve as a sort of club ambassador?"

Heather laughed. "Sure. That works. But before we begin, can I get you a drink?" She nodded toward the bar, causing Trena to notice that other than the open bottle of tequila, the shelves were completely empty.

Trena returned her focus to Heather. "I never drink on assignment. I prefer we get started."

Heather led her away from the bar and down a short hall, where she stopped before a closed door. "First, a bit of a tour, and an explanation as to the sort of place Ira envisions."

Trena braced for the worst. Dealing with Ira was a never-ending power struggle. The show was called *In-Depth with Trena Moretti*, yet Ira assumed he could insert his views into the script and control that too.

"He's not interested in the same old run-of-the-mill profile piece." Heather glanced over her shoulder. "He wants something different, and I'm sure you do too."

Trena gave a noncommittal nod. So far they were on the same page. She had no interest in repeating the usual tired format. And yet, it struck her as odd that Ira would choose Heather Rollins to speak on his behalf. If anything, she would've expected Aster, or Layla, or one of his numerous assistants. Not some B-list TV star. Still, Trena's job at the moment was to look, listen, and learn. The time for judgment and conclusions would come later.

"He wants to tell a story."

"The story of Ira?"

Heather shook her luxurious mane of blond hair. "No, I don't mean a biography. Anyone who wants to know that can simply pick up a back issue of *Fortune* or *Vanity Fair*. Ira wants the focus to be not just on him, but on the world that surrounds him."

Trena stared wordlessly. She had no idea what Heather was getting at.

"His vision for RED was to build a space where one can

create their own narrative. The guest list will be extremely limited, very exclusive, and expertly curated. Unlike his other clubs, it's not about the number of bodies that walk through the door. It's about cultivating an interesting and eclectic group of adventurous people who are willing to check their egos in order to engage with each other in deeply experimental, new ways."

"It's starting to sound like a combination of Soho House and a private sex club."

"Not at all!" Heather's face was aghast. She'd completely missed the fact that Trena was joking.

Trena vowed to lighten up and go easy on her. After all, Heather was merely the mouthpiece, and she'd probably spent days memorizing the spiel. The least Trena could do was pretend to go along.

While she'd been lost in her thoughts, she realized Heather had taken the opportunity to study her. "How's it going with James?" she asked, brown eyes flashing.

"Excuse me?" Trena balked.

Heather shot her a knowing grin. "Can't say I blame you. James is hot as fuck and loyal to the core. You could do a lot worse, you know."

Trena stared in shock. Surely Heather had wandered wildly off script.

"Wondering if we can get back on topic," Trena said, her voice stiff.

Heather gave a casual shrug. "Sorry if I caught you off guard. Consider that part of checking your ego."

"Along with my right to privacy?"

Heather paused to consider. "In some cases, yes. But surely not all."

Trena was scrambling to make sense of the weirdness, when Heather motioned toward the sign on the door, which consisted of raised white letters that spelled WATCH. Opening the door, she ushered Trena inside.

Again, the room was done all in white. There were several rows of comfortable-looking white lounge chairs, all of them with individual video monitors.

"Ira's taken the idea of reality TV and kicked it up several notches," Heather said in response to Trena's reaction. "To quote the great prophet Andy Warhol," she said without the slightest hint of irony, "'In the future, everyone will be famous for fifteen minutes.' So why should the housewives and the Kardashians have all the fun?"

"You're going to film people?"

"Those who sign the consent form, yes. Those who prefer to watch can come here and indulge their inner voyeur."

Trena nodded like she was getting the hang of it, but she wasn't, or at least not entirely.

"So each room is a set?"

"Yes." Heather made a steeple with her hands, supporting her chin. "That's why everything is white, like a blank canvas. The participants decide the design." She dropped her hands to her hips and said, "So, what do you think?"

Trena rehearsed a few responses in her head. Rejecting them all, she said, "Are you the spokesperson just for tonight, or every night?"

Heather laughed. "Just tonight."

"And why have you agreed to do this? Surely it's taking time away from everything else you have going on?"

Heather met Trena's gaze and held it for longer than expected. "Because Ira asked me to help." Quickly switching gears, she added, "Anyway, for tonight, we thought it would be really cool if we let you guide the narrative."

"But I thought this was just a walk-through. I don't have my camera crew. I'm not sure what's going on here."

"Not to worry, you will." Heather grinned. Leading her out of the room and to the mouth of a long hallway marked with doors on each side, she said, "And trust me, you're in for a big surprise."

THIRTY-NINE

LOST AND FOUND

Madison lifted herself off the floor and looked all around. She felt woozy, uncertain. Nearly losing her footing, she needed a moment to stabilize before she could take in her surroundings.

Last time she'd found herself locked in a room, it was nothing like this. Nonetheless, the intent was the same. To isolate her from the rest of the world, then release all her shame.

Of course her purse was missing, leaving her unarmed. But she'd seen her attacker, which was a sort of ammunition all its own. Though considering the size and scale of the crime, it was doubtful the enemy had acted alone. There were more of them still out there, somewhere.

She wandered the perimeter, tapping her knuckles against walls that appeared solid and unmovable. If that turned out to be true, then she was completely at the mercy of her captor, with no real chance of escape.

This was not how it was supposed to go down. She'd made a plan, studied it from every angle, and convinced herself it was a good one. The mistake was keeping Paul in the dark. She'd texted him from the beach, planning to meet in person so she could tell him everything she'd learned. After, she figured she'd find a place to lay low while he did whatever necessary to ensure her safety. Then, with Paul by her side, she'd reenter the world. It was simple. Easy. Seemingly foolproof. And yet, once again, her captor was way ahead of her.

From seemingly out of nowhere, an image of herself was projected onto the wall. The name *MaryDella Slocum* was written above a picture of her at age eight, barefoot, dirty, and wearing a size-too-small dress. It was the same photo that had covered the walls of her earlier cell, and that, thanks to Layla's blog and Trena Moretti's show, had gone viral all over the world.

She stretched her gaze toward the ceiling and spotted a camera aimed right at her. She stepped to the left and then to the right, noting the way the camera followed her every move. Whether she was simply being observed or actually filmed, there was no way to tell. Realizing she wouldn't be getting out of there anytime soon, she settled onto a long white bench and watched the series of images play across the wall.

It was like a scrapbook of old memories, most of which she'd successfully wiped from her mind. There were old class pictures from junior high that seemed more or less benign, but there were also photos of her parents, looking haggard and grim, which felt more ominous in tone.

Paul had been right all along—this was purely an act of revenge. The goal was to take away everything she'd worked so hard to build by exposing her numerous lies to the world.

So far, they were well ahead, having managed to out-smart her at every turn. If Madison were ever to find her way out of that room, she'd find that the fans who'd once lauded her had turned so vehemently against her she might never succeed in winning them back.

A soft, lilting tune drifted through the speakers, as a voice that had obviously been disguised warmly addressed her. "Hello, Madison. So happy you decided to join us."

Madison turned toward the camera and stared back in defiance.

"In the interest of full disclosure, you're being filmed. I'm sure your many fans will enjoy watching this footage of you. Why don't you give a little wave and a quick hello? They've all been so worried about you."

Madison continued to stare. They could kidnap her, put

her in a box, destroy her reputation, and film her, but she wasn't some performing monkey. She would not obey their every demand.

"I know who you are," she said.

The voice laughed. "Indeed you do. Care to share it with the world?"

Madison started to put a voice to the name, then just as quickly decided against it. It was part of the trap, and if she had any hope of winning, she needed to play smarter than that. She'd underestimated them for too long, but no more. She assumed they were in possession of her gun, and there was nothing more dangerous than an armed person with nothing left to lose.

"Well then, let's get started, shall we? Just so you know, the gang's all here. At the moment you're separated by the walls that surround you. Only these walls aren't quite as permanent as they appear. If you're willing to play a little game, you have the chance of reuniting with your friends. But the rules demand you tell the truth. If you choose to lie, I'm afraid you'll be punished. Before we get started, let me introduce you to your host, Trena Moretti! Trena can see all of you, but you can only see the images I choose to share. So tell me, are you ready?"

Madison took a deep breath and nodded imperceptibly.

"Okay then. Trena Moretti—take it away!"

Madison watched as the picture on the wall shifted to an

image of Trena sitting in some sort of control room, looking distressed. She stared into the camera, then consulted the paper propped before her and said, "Madison—I'm so sorry that—"

Her mic was cut as the disguised voice broke in and said, "It's better for everyone if you stick to the script."

Trena squared her shoulders, looked into the camera, and said, "Madison, do you know why you're here?"

Madison nodded, then faced the camera. "I was abducted."

Trena looked at someone off screen, then returned to Madison. "There's a theory you planned your disappearance. Is that true?"

Madison stared at the camera, unsure how to answer. She had planned an elaborate disappearance, but then she got abducted before she could act on it. Still, it wouldn't do to give in so early. At least for now, she needed to stay defiant.

"No," she said. "I was abducted, and you know that because—"

Before she could finish, the voice shouted, "Wrong! Wrong answer, Madison."

The next thing she knew, the whole room went dark, as an earsplitting shriek emanated from the walls.

FORTY

RING OF FIRE

Aster was in full-blown panic mode. Her cell signal was dead, and as far as she could tell after relentlessly banging her fists against the walls, there was no way out of the space she was stuck in.

When the lights suddenly dimmed and Trena Moretti's face was projected onto the wall, Aster screamed, "Please, help me! Get me out of here—now!"

"She can't hear you."

Aster spun in circles, trying to determine where the voice was coming from.

"She can only hear what I want her to hear. Also, just so you know, you're being filmed. This is going out on a live feed. So you might want to pull yourself together and try to look a little more presentable. Your panicked face isn't nearly as pretty as your usual face."

For the first time since she'd entered the room, Aster noticed the camera in the upper right corner pointing at her.

"What do you want?"

She glanced between the wall and the camera.

"I want you to tell the truth."

"About what?"

"About whatever we ask. If you do, you'll be richly rewarded. If you don't . . . what's the opposite of richly rewarded? Poorly punished?"

"Where's Ryan?"

"Somewhere. Hard to say where exactly."

"What have you done with him?"

"All in good time. Now please, your attention on Trena. She has something to ask."

Aster turned toward Trena, who looked tense. If nothing else, it was a relief to know she had not volunteered for this—whatever this was. Clearly, it wasn't exactly the soft opening Trena had expected. Aster knew Ira would stop at nothing for free publicity, but this was way out of line, even for him.

"Trena, go ahead. Ask Aster the question on the script before you."

Trena consulted the page, then looked at the screen and said, "Are you still a virgin?"

Aster stared incredulously. "What kind of junior-high bullshit is this?"

"Language! You're being filmed, and there's a good chance your parents are watching, so—let's try that again. Answer the question, please."

Aster dropped her head in her hands. Her parents were watching? Great. After all the pain she'd put them through, it was about to get even worse.

She looked at Trena and said, "No. Not anymore."

Immediately, the bench where she sat began to warm, along with the rest of the room, which up until that point had been unbearably cold.

"Very good. See how this works? Who knows, another correct answer might connect you with Ryan. So, Trena, what say you?"

Trena took a deep breath, then looked at Aster. "This one's about your little brother, Javen."

Aster held her breath.

"Is he gay?"

Aster closed her eyes. This was insane. When she opened them again, she looked directly into the camera and said, "This is bullshit. I demand you open this door right now and let me out of here. Or so help me God I will—"

"You will *what* exactly?" The voice laughed. "Save your empty threats. I'm in charge. You're captive. I've shown you the way out. Now it's up to you whether or not you decide to take it by answering the question. Is your little brother, Javen, gay?"

Aster closed her eyes and lowered her chin to her chest.

"We're waiting. . . ."

Aster lifted her gaze, stared into the camera, and said, "No. No, he's not."

"Hmmmm . . . not sure that's a correct answer," the voice said. "Just to give your memory a nudge, I'm going to project two pictures onto the wall that only you can see. It's up to you to decide which secret goes out into the world."

Aster stared in dismay. One side of the wall featured a picture of Javen kissing a boy she recognized as his friend Dylan.

The other side showed a still from the video clip of Aster taking off her clothes and dancing seductively the night she went missing.

"You get to decide which one, but if you don't answer in the next five seconds, then they'll both be released."

Superimposed over the pictures was the image of a countdown clock. Aster watched in grief as the numbers counted down from five . . . four . . . three . . . She closed her eyes.

Please forgive me. . . .

She opened them again, and said, "Me. Share the one of me."

"You sure about that? Once it's out, there's no taking it

back, and I can guarantee it'll go viral."

Aster nodded. Her throat clogged with tears, she was unable to speak.

"As you wish . . ."

The next thing she knew, the lights turned back on and the wall went blank.

FORTY-ONE

HEARTLESS

Someone was on the other side of the wall, in the next room. She could hear the faint echo of a voice raised in anger. Despite their obvious panic, it gave Layla hope. She wasn't as alone as she felt.

"Hey, I'm here!" She shouted the words as loud as she could. "Can you hear me?"

Out of nowhere a voice said, "Not only can I hear you, but I can see you as well."

Layla spun around and searched for the source.

"Hello, Layla. I must say you look lovely tonight. Thanks for making the effort. You've come a long way from the girl who once wore knockoff shoes and rode a secondhand bike."

"What do you want? Who are you?"

"You were always the most impatient. The most straight-forward, and, I grudgingly admit, the smartest. But if you still don't know who I am, then I guess you're not as smart as I thought."

Layla frowned. The voice was disguised in a way that made it impossible to tell if it was male or female. But the word choice leaned toward female, especially the part about knockoff shoes. Only a girl would use that as an insult. Then again, Ira might do so as well.

"I want you to play a little game with me. Please direct your attention to the wall directly in front of you."

Layla did as instructed and was surprised to find Trena staring right back.

"Your host for tonight's show should be familiar. After all, you recently broke into her apartment, didn't you?"

Trena looked startled. Layla froze.

"Well, didn't you?"

"No." Layla shook her head.

"Aw, but I'm one hundred percent sure you did. Lying will not work in your favor, I can promise you that. So let's try again."

"I didn't break in," Layla said, unsure just how much to reveal. Considering she had no idea what this was about, she didn't know how far she could push it. "Someone let me in."

"Care to elaborate?"

She searched Trena's face for a sign of what was really going on. Her gaze was pained, and she moved her shoulder in a way that hinted she might be restrained.

"Still waiting . . . ," the voice said, exaggerating each word.

Trena gave a subtle nod, and Layla stared into the camera. "I convinced Javen to lure Trena out of her apartment so I could go through her files." Layla made an apologetic face, but Trena was under too much duress to notice, much less care.

"And why would you do that?"

"Because I suspected her of hiding evidence."

"And was she?"

Layla rubbed her lips together, buying a few seconds of time. "Yes," she said, figuring that whoever was asking the questions already knew the answers anyway.

"And what did you find?"

"The name of the man who went to jail for killing Madison's parents."

"I like how you phrased that. Just like a journalist—facts without judgment. So tell me, do you think this man killed Madison's parents?"

Layla sensed the answer they wanted, but she just wasn't sure what she believed.

"Let the record show that Layla shrugged. So, is it safe

to say you think Gerald Rawlins might be innocent of the crime?"

"I can't say for sure," Layla said. "I wasn't there."

"Aw, but you know who was there, don't you?"

Layla looked at Trena, who so far hadn't spoken a word. "Madison was there. Also Paul."

"Do you think it's possible that Madison did it? That Madison Brooks shot her own parents, and not Gerald Rawlins, even though he went to jail for the crime?"

The voice was disguised, but there was no doubt it was veering toward hysterical. Hoping to temper the mood, Layla took a deep breath and said, "Let's just say that under the right circumstances, I think anyone is capable of just about anything."

Layla locked eyes with Trena, the wall went blank, and next thing she knew, the wall had slid open a crack, allowing her access to the adjoining room.

FORTY-TWO

CARELESS WHISPER

The second Tommy saw Layla, he pulled her into his arms. "You okay?" he whispered, smoothing a hand over her hair. When she nodded, he said, "I know who's behind this. I know who it is."

He was about to tell her when a voice shot through the speakers and said, "Everyone loves a good love story. You two are sure to be a crowd favorite, but try to keep it G-rated, okay? People are watching."

Layla pulled away and dabbed at her eyes, then turned toward the wall bearing an image of Trena's face.

"Layla," Trena said, "you did a great job. But now I'm afraid it's Tommy's turn."

Tommy glanced worriedly at Layla, then turned back to Trena.

"Why did you move to LA?"

"Change of scene." He kept his voice unaffected and easy.

"What else?"

"To follow my dream."

"This is all very inspiring," the disguised voice cut in. "But allow me to remind you exactly what's at stake here."

On the wall, superimposed over Trena, was a picture of Tommy standing outside the Vesper the night Madison went missing.

He looked at the camera and said, "I don't give a crap about that. Madison's alive. You can't touch me now."

"You sure about that?"

"That Madison's alive? Absolutely. I can prove it."

"So you're admitting to withholding evidence? Because if Detective Larsen's not already watching, he will be soon enough."

Tommy shrugged. "Then all I have to do is wait until he gets here and puts an end to this bullshit."

"Wow, you're really sexy when you go all alpha like that." The voice laughed. "You know who it reminds me of?"

Tommy froze.

"From the look on your face, you do."

Tommy closed his eyes, mumbled under his breath. He'd already decided against telling Ira, and now he was being forced to do it in the worst way imaginable.

"Let's try this again. Why'd you move to LA, Tommy?"

He stared into the camera and clamped his lips shut, refusing to speak.

"Who's your daddy, Tommy? C'mon, you can tell us."

Layla nudged him. She was right, of course, but this wasn't the way he wanted it to happen.

"I came to LA to try to break into the music business."

"And . . ."

Tommy swiped a hand through his hair. Layla stood alongside him and gave his hand a squeeze. "And to meet my dad . . ." Tommy stalled. In the next breath, he said, "Ira Redman."

The lights flickered on and off, and the next thing they knew, another wall had slid open.

FORTY-THREE

SLEEP NOW IN THE FIRE

Aster glanced up from Ryan's arms to see Layla and Tommy standing in the doorway. "I'm ruined," she cried, tears streaming down her cheeks. "Even if I make it out of here, it's over for me. How will I ever hold my head up high, or face my family?"

Ryan pulled her closer as the voice crackled through the speakers. "Wow, this is really, truly touching. It warms my heart to see everyone reunited like this. In fact, I'm having so much fun watching y'all, let's check in on your other friend, shall we?"

An image of Madison blazed on the wall. She was curled up on the floor with her hands pressed tightly over her ears. Although the sound was muted, whatever she was listening to was clearly unbearable.

"You can help lessen her agony by answering one simple question."

Aster braced for the worst. If it was about her brother again, she wasn't sure she could help. Javen would always be her first priority, no matter what.

"Since we have all the couples gathered, I'm going to turn my focus to romance. As a reminder, if you choose to lie, Madison will pay. Take it away, Trena!"

Trena gazed dully at the camera and said, "Ryan, did you ever love Madison?"

Aster immediately dropped his hand. She didn't want him to feel any sort of pressure coming from her. This had nothing to do with them. Whoever was behind this was trying to upset his fans.

Without hesitation, he said, "No, not really."

"Did you ever cheat on Madison?"

This time he hesitated, but only for a handful of seconds, before he said, "Yes."

"How many times?"

He took a breath, rubbed a hand across his jaw. "A couple—few times."

"And was one of those times with Heather Rollins?"

Ryan closed his eyes and cursed under his breath. When he opened them again, he chanced a sideways glance at Aster, who urged him to go ahead. Staring directly into the camera, he said, "Yes."

"How many times did you cheat with Heather Rollins?"

Ryan shook his head. "I don't know. Once, twice maybe?" He shrugged. "It meant nothing, okay? Heather, if you're watching, or somehow behind this, it meant nothing!"

"Did you tell her she was hot, beautiful, irresistible? Did you tell her she had a rockin' bod and you liked screwing her more than you liked screwing Madison?"

"What the—?" Ryan looked pained. He glanced at Aster, his gaze pleading for forgiveness. "It was before you," he whispered.

"Yes, yes, it was before Aster," the voice cut in. "Just answer the question, please! Did you, or did you not, tell Heather Rollins that screwing Madison made you feel like a necrophiliac, because she was so cold and stiff it was like doing a dead person?"

Ryan emptied his lungs of air and said, "I never said that. I would never say a thing like that. I didn't hate Madison. I just wasn't in love with her. I don't know where you're getting this nonsense, but—"

"Relax." The voice laughed. "Let the record show I was having a bit of fun. Let it also show that you went after Heather a few times, so you must've liked that first taste more than you're willing to admit."

Furious, Ryan swung toward the camera. "Let it also show that I didn't go after her. She came after me. The only reason I went along was because Madison wasn't all that into me and I guess I felt lonely. The only reason Heather went after me was because she wanted to possess whatever Madison had."

The room grew silent, and Aster stared at the wall before her, watching as Trena's image was replaced with one of Madison rising to her feet in a daze as the wall slid open before them.

FORTY-FOUR

HEARTBREAKER

The entire time it took to drive from his photo shoot in downtown LA to RED in West Hollywood, Mateo Luna went over the long list of reasons why he should turn the car around and head home instead.

And yet, he still found himself parking on the street and standing before the big red double doors, which from all appearances seemed to be locked.

He ventured toward the sidewalk and squinted up and down the boulevard. He could've sworn Heather said the shoot was taking place that night, and that she and Ira would be there.

While he resented her bargaining on his behalf by trading his appearance at RED for his little sister getting better care, he'd since cooled down enough to realize he had no choice but to go through with his end of the deal.

He hated the idea of being in debt to Ira Redman, but at least by agreeing to take part in the shoot (no matter how grudgingly), they could each walk away and call it even. Or at least he hoped that was the case.

He tried the door. He was right; it was locked. And if anyone was in there, they weren't responding to his knocks.

Deciding to send Heather a text to let her know he'd changed his mind and that he was waiting outside, he settled onto a bench and typed:

Thought you said you were filming at RED tonight. I'm outside if you still want me to take part. I'll hang around a bit longer so LMK.

He waited for a response. He knew she was in there—he'd seen her car parked nearby. He'd seen Layla's car and Ryan's too, for that matter. And yet, they were inside while he was on the stoop, cooling his heels.

He frowned, checked his phone again, then got up and started to pace when he glanced across the street and saw Detective Larsen watching the building in an unmarked car.

What the—?

Mateo hadn't even finished the thought, when his phone vibrated with Heather's reply.

No reason to wait

It's already too late

Please don't you worry
Just go now & hurry
You've been nothing but sweet
I'm forever grateful we had the chance to meet
I'm going away for a very long while
Though I'll always think of you with a smile
Despite what you may hear
For me, you were the one true thing I held dear

Mateo's hands began to shake as he read the message again.

The rhyme reminded him of the ones Layla had been sent.

The picture Ira had taken with Tommy's phone wasn't meant to taunt him, but to warn him.

Finally, after all this time, the clues were falling into place in a way that made sense. Though the ominous tone of Heather's message didn't bode well for anyone locked inside with her.

He railed hard against the door. When it failed to so much as budge, he started toward the street, intent on alerting Larsen, when someone caught him by the back of the shirt and he turned to find Paul Banks standing behind him.

FORTY-FIVE

HERE'S WHERE THE STORY ENDS

Madison stood wearily before the glass wall, not the least bit surprised to see Heather Rollins holding her gun to Trena Moretti's head. Though she was surprised to find Heather acting alone. She'd been convinced Heather had help. Then again, considering the body found in Joshua Tree and the one Paul left behind in Death Valley, it was possible Heather was the only one left.

Somewhere in a corner behind Madison, Ryan, Aster, Layla, and Tommy were huddled together, but she paid them no notice. This wasn't about them. Never had been. They were merely pawns chosen by Ira and manipulated by Heather into her sick, twisted game.

When Aster had asked if any of this would've happened if it weren't for the contest, Madison hadn't known the

answer. Though she'd since figured out a few things leading her to conclude that while Ira and Heather were both
playing a game, the games they played weren't remotely the
same.

Heather had been after Madison from the first day they'd
met, which wasn't the date Madison had once thought.
Turns out, their connection stretched back a decade or
more.

"As you may have guessed, this won't end well." There
was no use for disguise. Heather spoke in her own voice
now.

"It doesn't seem likely," Madison agreed.

"I'll never forget how you looked at me in the car. You
weren't the least bit surprised to find me waiting in the
backseat. Tell me, just out of curiosity, what gave it away?"

"You're wearing my earring." Madison gestured toward
the single gold-and-turquoise hoop swaying from Heather's
left lobe.

"What else?"

"Your tattoo."

"Which one?" Heather grinned. "I've collected a few."

"The one on the inside of your arm—the shooting stars.
It's a symbol for Shooting Star Ranch, isn't it?"

For a handful of seconds, Heather looked shocked, but
just as quickly she recovered. "As you know, not all scars
fade." She raised her arm to display the intricate ink that

marked her flesh in a way that mimicked Madison's burn scar. "Go ahead, explain it to your friends and the fans at home watching this feed."

Madison glanced over her shoulder toward the others cowering in the corner, warning them with her eyes not to do anything heroic or stupid. Returning to Heather, she said, "Shooting Star Ranch is where they sent Heather to live after her dad, Gerald Rawlins, went to jail for killing my parents." From behind her, someone gasped. Madison suspected it was Aster. "You changed the spelling of your last name," Madison said. "But you are his daughter, aren't you?"

Heather nodded. The gun shook in her hand, setting Trena on edge. Trena was tied, gagged, and rendered completely defenseless.

"What I don't understand is why you'd risk everything for this."

"Watching you fail is worth it."

"But is it? Is it really?" Madison cocked her head and squinted.

"You don't even remember me, do you?"

Madison stared.

"I babysat you once. I'm only three years older, but I think we know how negligent your parents were. Though I can't say I blame them. Even back then you were a brat, so it's not the least bit surprising to see the sort of person you grew into."

"So, what now?" Madison made a gesture around the room and the forced situation they found themselves in.

"Now you confess," Heather said.

"Confess to what?" Madison feigned confusion.

"Pretty sure you know." Heather glared.

Madison stared blankly in return. Her goal was to drag this out for as long as possible. At some point, someone had to show up to help. If not, they were doomed.

"I need you to look into the camera and tell your fans how you shot your own parents along with my dad. Then you and Paul set the house on fire and walked away, leaving my dad behind to die. Only he didn't die like you planned, so Paul framed him for a double homicide and an arson he didn't commit and sent him away to jail, where he died just last year."

"He was a drug runner!" Madison spat.

"He was all I had," Heather said. "And while you went on to live your posh life with your fancy new name and family, I was left with nothing. They shipped me off to a life of menial labor until I could finally make my escape."

"Seems to me you should feel proud of how far you've come and everything you've accomplished. And yet, you're choosing to throw it all away."

"I'll admit, it wasn't supposed to end like this," Heather said. "I was supposed to enjoy my success while you spiraled down to the point of no return."

"Then you sadly underestimated me."

"I may have made a few miscalculations," Heather shot back. "But in the end, I'll get what I came for."

From behind her, Madison was aware of Ryan creeping forward. As subtly as she could, she shook her head and waved him away.

"Oh, for God's sake," Heather said. "Why don't you just go watch from the other room with Ira and James?"

Madison watched as Heather punched a few prompts onto an iPad, causing the door to slide open just enough for them to slip through.

"Go—now!" Heather shouted, waving her gun at them. "But not you!" She pointed the weapon at Madison as she watched the others disappear into the adjoining room.

Last thing Madison heard before the door slid shut was Aster's voice shouting, "*Omigod—Ira!*"

Once they were gone, Heather continued. "None of this would've happened if you hadn't become famous. I'd barely even thought about you until one day I was looking through a magazine and I saw some dumb bitch smiling back from the cover with these unmistakable violet-colored eyes. Despite the name change, I knew in that instant it was you. So I made it a point to track you down once I moved to LA. At first, all I really wanted was an apology for the horrible thing that you did. But you treated me like you treat everyone—like I was second rate. That's when I started making plans. And despite a few glitches, the fact that the whole world now knows the truth about you means it worked. Our conversation is being live streamed. People all over the world are tuned in. I like to think of it as the ultimate reality show."

"If that's true, then the cops are probably on their way."

Heather shrugged. "All I need now is for you to admit the truth. So just look into the camera and tell the world who really killed your parents."

Madison hesitated. While Heather had been talking, Paul had slipped into the room and was standing right behind her. She had no idea where he'd come from, but the look he gave her told her not to let on that she'd seen him.

Heather pressed the barrel of the gun to Trena's temple. "If you don't confess, I'll shoot. Pretty sure you don't want the whole world to know you're so selfish you'd actually let an innocent woman die."

"You say that so casually, like you've killed before. Does this mean the body in Joshua Tree was your doing?"

"You know how it is." Heather sighed. "At first you think you have a solid ally you can trust, but then they decide to get greedy and you're forced to teach them a lesson."

"A permanent lesson," Madison said.

"He's the one who snatched you from Night for Night. So don't pretend you give a shit about what happened to him. He knew my dad, so I thought he was on my side. But then he started blackmailing me. Demanding a ridiculous fee for his silence. He left me no choice. Besides, this is about *your* sins," Heather reminded her.

"Just to be clear," Madison said. "You're asking me to lie in order to save Trena's life?" Madison locked eyes with Trena. She hoped she wasn't making it worse. "Because I can do that. Hell, I'm an actress. I can make it convincing. The thing that worries me is it doesn't seem like you've thought this all the way through. Up until now you've managed to impress me by leaving a lot of unanswered questions, like: How'd you drug Aster? I mean, if Kevin O'Dell was arranging to abduct me, then you must've had additional help. Also, what about the guy in Death Valley? Just how many people were in on this?" Madison cared less about the answers and more about playing for time. Appealing to Heather's ego was the best way she could think of.

Heather looked annoyed. "It's not hard to find the right people if you know where to look. You have a long list of people who hate you, you know."

"Did Ira drug Aster?"

Heather rolled her eyes and shook her head. "Of course not. I did. Poor Ira. You guys were so quick to accuse him, when all he ever did was try to give you what you wanted. Ira is the most honest person I know. He's ruthless, yes, but he's hardly the demon you think. I met Aster in the bathroom. She was acting all jumpy and weird, so I tried to calm her and offered her a sip from a bottle of water that may or may not have been spiked. Then I put her in a car and met her at an apartment I'd rented so she could safely sleep it off. It all went smoothly, except for Layla. Her refusal to post the diary entries, even after I threatened her, really surprised me. I never expected her to protect you, considering what a bitch you were. Then again, you've never been very good to your friends. I should know. I used to be one. As for the rest, the guy who abducted you in Death Valley used to work for Paul. You fired him from your security detail for some minor offense. He never recovered. I'm guessing either you or Paul managed to kill him since he never stopped by for his check. For all I know, you shot him with this very gun, seeing as how I found it inside your purse." She waved the weapon before the camera.

While Heather was waving the gun, Paul sprang toward her. But Heather, spotting him from the corner of her eye, swung wildly toward him and ordered him to stand beside Trena.

"Enough!" Heather shouted. "Tell the truth now or someone dies!"

Paul looked at Madison and shook his head no.

But Madison knew Heather wasn't joking. She was so far gone she'd gladly kill them all.

"Tell them who did it!" Heather shouted, becoming

unhinged. Her hair was disheveled, her lipstick smeared, as thick black trails of mascara pooled under her eyes and ran down her cheeks. "Tell them it was you or Paul dies!"

Madison steeled herself and prepared to confess. She'd kept her secret all these years, but maybe, just maybe, her fans would forgive her. She was just a child when she'd shot them. She was scared and out of options. Paul had risked everything that night and all the ones that followed in order to protect her, and now the time had come to repay the favor. She couldn't imagine her life without him. The prospect seemed worse than facing a hostile world that knew her deepest, darkest truth.

Stepping forward, she looked directly into the camera. "I—" She started to speak just as Paul charged straight into the barrel of Heather's gun.

A terrible blast tore through the room, and Madison watched in horror as Paul reeled backward and Heather spun and fired another round through the glass wall that stood between them.

Instinctively, Madison ducked away from the hail of shattering glass as the bullet whizzed past her head and tore into the wall just behind her.

In a daze, she glanced over to where Paul lay. His gut was blown open, and a gush of blood pumped so profusely he'd bleed out in no time. It was over. Really truly over. Wearily, she lifted her gaze to watch Heather advance until she was standing directly before her, gun pointed at Madison's forehead.

"Please," Madison whispered. "Stop while you still can."

"Too late." Heather's voice was sad, her expression resigned. "Looks like it's over for all of us now."

From somewhere in the distance, Madison heard shouting, the sound of feet running. "They're coming," she said. "Put the gun down."

"They're coming for both of us." Heather's eyes blazed. "So go ahead, before it's too late—confess! It's not like it'll matter once we're both dead."

Madison stared at the lost girl before her, trying to get used to the idea that she really might die at Heather's hand. The possibility was frightening, but she was equally surprised to find how bad she felt for what had become of Heather's life.

Madison had used her rage to propel herself to great heights.

Heather had directed hers in a way that could only destroy her.

And now Paul was on the ground, the life force quickly seeping out of him.

Now that she'd lost everything, she could no longer see the point of the secret she'd kept all these years. She'd been a little girl when she'd pulled that trigger. Surely the world would've forgiven her?

Madison closed her eyes for a handful of seconds. The time had come to speak the truth, wash away her sins, and use what little time was left of her life to redeem herself and her lies.

When she opened them again, her gaze landed on Paul. She wouldn't let a decade of Paul's protection die in vain.

"I didn't do it." Her voice remained steady, leaving no room for doubt. "Your father killed my parents, and I'm sorry you ever convinced yourself otherwise."

"Liar!" Heather released the safety and pressed the barrel to Madison's forehead.

The metal was hard and hot, searing into her skin. Madison narrowed in on the tiny broken-heart tattoo on Heather's trigger finger, then shut her eyes against it and sent out a thousand prayers to whoever might still be willing to listen.

All she'd ever tried to do was save her own life. What could be so wrong about that?

Someone shouted in the distance, though their cries were soon masked by a deafening blast that burst through the room.

Madison's ears rang with the sound of gunfire, her nostrils filled with the scent of gunpowder, and she slammed hard against the floor as Heather rolled on top of her.

Blood streamed across her cheek and pooled into her hair.

Her head ached from the impact of hitting the concrete, though it took a moment to realize she hadn't been hit.

It was Heather's blood that washed over her.

Even with his gut torn open, Paul could still land a perfect shot in the side of a head.

Madison pushed Heather aside, scrambled to her feet, and grabbed hold of Paul. "Someone get help!" she shouted, spotting Mateo standing in the doorway, looking on in horror as Detective Larsen sped toward her. "Hurry!"

As Paul slipped toward the ground, Madison struggled to hold him until Larsen took over.

"Don't die!" she cried, cradling Paul's head as Larsen pressed his hands against the wound in an attempt to stop the bleeding. "Don't you dare leave me!" she sobbed, hardly able to speak through her tears.

Next thing she knew, a pair of hands grasped her by the shoulders and pulled her to her feet, allowing the necessary space for the emergency response team to take over.

Ira held her tightly as Madison watched Paul being pulled onto a stretcher and wheeled out of the room. "It's going to be okay." Ira spoke softly into her ear. "It's all over now."

SIX MONTHS LATER

FORTY-SIX

KIDS IN AMERICA

Spotlight magazine exclusive!

We here at Spotlight *were thrilled when Tommy Phillips agreed to take time out from his busy schedule to catch us up on his latest news! Read on to see what Tommy's been up to since that tragic night at RED.*

Spotlight: *Tommy, thank you for taking the time to talk with us. We know you've been lying low for the last several months, spending time in the studio, and recovering from what we can only imagine was a harrowing experience. How are you holding up?*

Tommy: *I'm doing okay. Not sure I'll ever be over it entirely; it's the sort of thing that's not easy to forget.*

Spotlight: *Understandable. Have you been in touch with the others—Aster, Layla, Ryan, and Madison?*

Tommy: *Sure. We've all remained friends.*

Spotlight: *Anything more you can tell us?*

Tommy: *I don't feel comfortable speaking for them. All I can say is that there was a lot of loss and everyone's doing their best to cope and move forward in the best way possible.*

Spotlight: *And what about your relationship with Ira Redman?*

Tommy: *What about it?*

Spotlight: *We were all shocked to learn he is your dad.*

Tommy: *There were a lot of shocking reveals that night. That was merely one of them.*

Spotlight: *What's it like being Ira Redman's son?*

Tommy: *No different from being anyone's son, I imagine. It's another relationship to navigate. What I'd really like to talk about is my music. I think my record label would prefer that as well.*

Spotlight: *Of course! Catch us up—tell us what to expect.*

Tommy: *Well, as you know, "Violet Eyes" hit number one on iTunes.*

Spotlight: *And stayed there for multiple weeks. If we're not mistaken, it's since maintained a solid position in the top ten. You must be so proud. When does the next single drop?*

Tommy: *Five more days until "Thoroughbred Girls" will be released, and of course there will be plenty more to follow. A world tour is also in the works, so keep an eye open for that.*

Spotlight: *We wouldn't miss it! And we can't wait for "Thoroughbred Girls"—any hint on what might've inspired it?*

Tommy: *It's a ballad about a sad, tragic girl who died too young.*

Spotlight: *Hmmm . . . sounds familiar. Guess we'll have to wait to decipher the lyrics and see if our hunch is right. Any truth to the dating rumors? We've been hearing whispers!*

Tommy: *I never discuss my love life.*

Spotlight: *We seem to remember a time when you were much more candid. Speaking of, Madison Brooks is up for an Academy Award. What do you think her chances are of winning?*

Tommy: *I have no doubt she'll get it.*

Spotlight: *Well, the competition is always tough, but we agree that she's got really good odds. Either way, your loyalty is admirable, to say the least. We know you have to run, but thanks so much for dropping by! And readers, make sure to download "Thoroughbred Girls," then check back here and we'll decode the lyrics together!*

FORTY-SEVEN

CITY OF STARS

Trena Moretti stood before the mirror as a swarm of assistants fussed at her makeup, gown, and hair.

The Oscars.

She was actually attending Hollywood's biggest, most glamorous event. As she took in the sight of her shimmering gown, she wondered if she'd ever get used to the constant stream of exclusive invitations flooding her mailbox.

Weeks after the tragedy at RED, she'd been awarded an Emmy for her reporting on *In-Depth*. Funny to think how not that long ago, she actually worried what might become of her career once the Madison case was solved. As it turned out, she'd be riding that wave well into the foreseeable future. Her nonfiction book proposal had gone to auction, with the highest bidder offering a healthy seven figures. And if there was one thing she knew, she could always count on Hollywood to offer up a new tragedy. It was just a matter of picking the right one on which to focus.

And, of course, maintaining a good relationship with Detective Larsen and Paul Banks was key. If Larsen hadn't been following her, and if Paul hadn't been tracking Madison from the moment she escaped, Trena might never have gotten out of RED alive.

It was Larsen's distrust that had placed him at the scene. But it was Mateo who'd alerted him that something weird was going on after receiving a disturbing text from Heather—a sort of rhyming good-bye that had left him alarmed.

"You look stunning."

Trena glanced into the mirror to see James standing behind her. He wore a custom tux, and she had to admit, despite her initial doubts about him, he cleaned up really well.

"Limo's waiting." He offered his arm.

Trena's makeup artist took one last pass at her lipstick, then stood back and watched in admiration as Trena headed for the door with James. "Any predictions?" the makeup artist called.

Trena paused and looked over her shoulder. "Madison. Always bet on Madison," she said. "That girl was born to win."

FORTY-EIGHT

LOVE'S PURE LIGHT

"Are you sure you have everything?"

Aster's mother stood in the doorway, wearing a worried expression.

"Pretty sure." Aster took one last look around her childhood room and realized she was ready. In fact, she felt really good about it.

"Then allow me to give you this." Her mother handed her a small black velvet box containing a beautiful gold-and-diamond hamsa pendant, much like the one Aster had lost at Paul's office the night of the fire. Only this one was nicer, and the diamonds were bigger. "For good luck," her mother said, helping to secure the clasp around Aster's neck.

It wasn't the first time she'd left home, but it was the

first time she'd left on good terms. And something about her mother's valiant attempt to keep her emotions in check made Aster want to give in to hers. Instead she held back her tears and bravely patted her mother's arm as they made their way into the hall and down the elaborate marble staircase.

Her mother loved her. Aster no longer had reason for doubt. Maybe she'd never show it in the demonstrative way Aster craved, but that just wasn't her style. Still, from the moment she'd walked out of RED, squinting against the glare of flashing lights and ogling crowds, only to find her parents, frantic with worry, Aster knew they still loved her, were still there for her, and had only wanted the best for her, even if their dreams didn't match hers.

After a few months spent recuperating at home, Aster had started attending classes during the winter quarter at UCLA. To everyone's surprise, she was leaning toward a law degree.

The most predictable, but still ironic, part of the scandal was the swarm of offers for acting jobs and modeling gigs, coming at a time when Aster was no longer interested. Like Heather predicted, her embarrassing video had gone viral, and Aster still hadn't grown used to that kind of exposure. Dating Ryan allowed her access to all the fun industry events, which at the moment was good enough for her. She was proud of his new hit TV show, but she was content with keeping Hollywood at a distance and focusing on her new role as a college freshman.

"Hey, you ready? I brought muscle in case we need it, and from the looks of it, you do." Javen gestured toward the backseat of Aster's car, piled high with her belongings.

Hugging her little brother, she grinned at his boyfriend, Dylan, then glanced nervously at her mom. It hadn't been easy for Javen to come out, but after everything Aster had put her parents through, the shock was mild in comparison.

A car honked, and Aster turned to watch Ryan waving as he headed up the long drive. Climbing out of the car, he went straight to Aster's mom, who, as usual, fawned all over him.

It was amusing to see how her mom transformed around Ryan. Normally, she was imperious and standoffish, like a cast-iron pan clad in Chanel. But Ryan had somehow managed to charm her, and more than once, Aster had caught her giggling in his presence.

"I figured I'd follow in my car. I have room for these guys." Ryan motioned toward Javen and Dylan.

Aster frowned. She wasn't ready to leave quite yet, but it wasn't like she could continue to drag it out. It was moving day, and later she was having everyone over for what she hoped would become the first of an annual Oscar-viewing party.

Still, she couldn't imagine leaving home without saying

good-bye to her dad. Her new apartment wasn't far, and she knew she'd visit often, and yet . . .

She sighed and headed for her car, figuring he was still tired from the flight home from Dubai and getting Nanny Mitra settled in her new home. Once she'd voiced her disapproval of the sort of people Aster and Javen had become, Aster's dad surprised them all by offering to fly her back home and move her into a beautiful building they owned. He loved his kids, no matter what. And if Nanny Mitra couldn't find it in her heart to do the same, then it was best if she lived somewhere else. It was a show of support Aster had never expected, and it left her feeling guilty for having spent so much time underestimating both of her parents.

Reluctantly, she slipped behind the wheel, waved good-bye to her mom, and slowly nosed her car down the long drive. When she heard someone calling her name, she slammed the brakes, jumped free of her car, and barreled straight into her father's arms.

"You weren't really going to leave without saying good-bye, were you?" he asked.

"Never," she said, whispering the words into the shoulder of his soft cashmere sweater. "Never again. I promise you that."

FORTY-NINE

GREEN GRASS AND HIGH TIDES

Layla settled onto the beach chair and pulled the towel closely around her. It was her favorite sort of Southern California day. The sun shone bright and hot, yet the air was brisk enough to bring a chill to her skin.

She squinted toward the ocean, watching as Mateo helped a child catch his first wave. The delighted look on the child's face when he managed to stand made Layla inordinately proud of the work Mateo was doing.

He was one of the good ones. One of the best she'd ever known, and probably ever would know.

As if sensing her thoughts, Mateo looked up in surprise to find she was there. He called to one of the instructors to take over, then made his approach. With his feet carving into the sand, he tugged the zipper of his wet suit and peeled it down low on his torso, easily proving he was still one of the most beautiful specimens Layla had ever seen.

She took a deep breath and forced herself to lift her gaze.

"I hear congrats are in order," he said as she tossed him a towel and watched as he rubbed it against his hair. It was a well-choreographed move they'd practiced countless times in the past. Only back then, Layla had given it little notice, or worse, felt resentful of the amount of time he spent in the water. The idea that it was most likely the last time they'd enact such a moment left her feeling bittersweet.

"I could say the same." She nodded toward an ocean full of kids who, thanks to the foundation Mateo had started to help at-risk kids, were learning to surf.

"It's pretty great, isn't it?" He beamed with pride, though Layla was quick to note that the pride was reserved entirely for his students. It was a complete lack of hubris that proved she'd been right all along. He really was too good for her.

"Still, it's not quite the same as a big book deal. And last I heard, a movie deal too?"

He looked genuinely impressed. But compared to what Mateo had built, she wasn't sure she deserved his praise. Writing what was hyped to become the hottest new teen thriller was one thing, saving lives was another.

"Are you going to write the screenplay?"

"They agreed to let me take a stab at it," she said. "But

most likely they'll fire me at some point and turn it over to someone with more experience." Mateo looked as though he was about to disagree, but Layla stopped him and said, "That's how it usually works, and I'm fine with it. I figure I'll learn a lot in the process."

"And school?" His deep brown gaze rested on hers.

"School is still happening. Not sure if I'll go for a journalism degree, but I have time to decide."

"So how is it in New York? Are you happy?"

Was she happy? She gazed at Mateo and thought of all she had lost the moment she decided to leave. Then she nodded and said, "Honestly, I love it." Her enthusiasm for the city was undeniable. "But sometimes I miss it here. You know, mellow moments like this—hanging on the beach and watching you surf."

Mateo laughed. "No, you don't."

She laughed too. She kind of did, but she recognized those feelings as more a nostalgia for a past she could never reclaim than a wish for her future. "Maybe not. But sometimes I do miss other things, you know?"

He held her gaze, letting the moment stretch and float. His voice wistful, he said, "How's H.D.?"

Layla smiled. "Happy. Dating. Did you know he's running the VIP room at the Vesper when he's not painting? He seems to love it."

"And your mom?"

Layla closed her eyes and sighed. "We met for coffee. She might come to New York for a visit. We're taking it slowly. And Valentina?"

The grin that lit Mateo's face was like the sun peeking out from the clouds on an overcast day. "Fully on the mend. She'll be twenty-one any day now, just ask her."

Layla sighed. There was so much to catch up on—so much he deserved to hear. After the scene at RED, she'd holed up at home with her dad for a really long time. Hadn't spoken much to anyone until months had gone by. She'd needed the time to process and heal, but now she realized there might be a price to her silence. "Mateo . . . ," she started.

He leaned toward her and placed a hand on her shoulder. "It's okay. We're good," he told her, and in that moment she knew that they were. Mateo had always been a man of few words.

She watched as a beautiful girl made her way toward them. Her long black hair hung to her waist in soft waves, and she held tightly to a little girl's hand. When she came to stand beside Mateo, Layla got the sense they were dating, and her first instinct was to instruct the girl on just how special Mateo was—that his heart was not to be messed with—that she'd better not even consider treating him the way Layla had.

She was just about to introduce herself when Mateo

nodded and said, "Looks like you have a visitor."

Layla glanced behind her to find Tommy.

She turned back to Mateo, wondering why she suddenly felt so guilty. She was happy. Mateo was happy. So it had all worked out for the best, hadn't it?

Tommy slipped his arm around Layla's waist and planted a light kiss on the side of her cheek.

"Are you Tommy Phillips?" The little girl gazed at him in awe.

Tommy grinned and bent down to her level.

"I am," he said. "And you are?"

She hid her face in her hands. "Violet." She grinned behind her fingers.

"You know I wrote a song about you?" Tommy said, sending her into a flurry of giggles.

As Tommy spoke with the little girl, Layla looked at Mateo. "We're heading to New York tomorrow, but tonight we're all going over to Aster's new place to watch the Oscars. Do you guys want to join us?" She looked at Mateo's friend, making sure to include her.

Mateo looked at Layla, then reached for the girl's hand. "Thanks," he said. "But Maria and I are just going to hang with the family tonight."

Layla nodded, then took one last look at the beach. She loved New York City—the hectic pace was a good fit.

Still, LA would always be home, and nothing could ever replace it.

She leaned forward and hugged Mateo to her. She had so many things to tell him, but none of them mattered. Not anymore.

She and Tommy were heading for the car when Mateo called out to her. "I forgot to ask—am I in the book?"

Layla glanced back with a grin. "Guess you'll have to read it and find out."

With Tommy's hand in hers, she turned away from her past and headed into her future.

FIFTY

THE MAN WHO SOLD THE WORLD

Ira Redman sat behind his desk in his office at RED, looking over the list of potential A-list guests begging for the chance to either form their own narrative, or simply indulge their deepest voyeuristic fantasy.

Thanks to the tragedy, Ira's clubs had never been hotter. But at the moment, none was hotter then RED.

He looked away from his papers and fiddled a bit with his phone, scrolling for Tommy's text. Shame how everything had gone down just exactly as he'd planned, all except for that moment when Tommy was forced to reveal Ira was his dad.

Of course he hadn't controlled the outcome. It had never been his to decide. Still, as a keen observer of people, he found he was rarely surprised. From the moment he determined Heather was behind it, he figured she'd also inadvertently orchestrate her own demise.

It was the cartoon cat that gave it away.

Heather had come to him with an idea for a line of T-shirts, greeting cards—an entire product line—and asked him to help fund it. She wanted to call it Socio Cat, a sort of demented version of Hello Kitty.

Ira had done his best to explain why the idea wasn't one that interested him. But Heather was persistent, and he'd finally taken a meeting where she'd left a prototype behind.

The day it fell from his desk and he saw the way Tommy reacted, Ira knew it meant something more and decided to do a little digging.

Though he'd never intended to be held hostage inside his own club, much less all the bloodshed, he realized now he should've expected as much. Still, the latest rumor that the club was haunted with Heather's ghost had guaranteed that Halloween at RED would continue to be the hottest ticket in town for years to come.

If Ira had one regret, and he wasn't one for regret, but if he did have one, it would be the way Tommy had been forced to say what Ira had known from the start—Tommy Phillips was his son.

What Tommy had no way of knowing was that Ira had spent the last eighteen years watching from afar. Walking into Farrington's that day was anything but random.

Some might say he'd been too hard on Tommy. But Ira would disagree. Maybe he wasn't paternal in the usual way, but there was no doubt he played a large part in the sort of man Tommy had become.

Into his phone, he typed:

Thought I'd stop by and say good-bye before you leave. That okay?

Tommy was quick to reply:

Sure. We're at Aster's new place. I'll text you the address.

Ira wrote:

Got it. See you there.

Tommy now commuted between his place in LA and Layla's place in New York. Though Ira was happy for them, Aster's choice to attend UCLA wasn't exactly the future he'd envisioned at the start.

All along he'd been positioning Aster to be an A-list actress. And yet, while she definitely had the looks and charisma required, she lacked the sort of relentless tenacity needed to make it to the top of the heap. Not everyone could be Madison Brooks. And in the end, there was a part of Ira that was glad of that. Over the course of the summer, he'd come to think of Aster as a daughter. When he saw the look of fear on her face after finding him bound and gagged, he realized she cared for him too. So maybe it had all turned out for the best.

It was like Marilyn Monroe had once said: "Hollywood

is a place where they'll pay a thousand dollars for a kiss and fifty cents for your soul. I know, because I turned down the first offer often enough and held out for the fifty cents."

More than anything Ira liked people to feel indebted to him, and yet he'd grown fond enough of Aster that he no longer wanted that for her.

"Got a moment?"

Ira pushed his phone aside and waved Emerson inside.

Emerson stood at the edge of Ira's desk and handed over the file Ira had requested.

He flipped it open and quickly skimmed the first page. "You sure about them?"

Emerson nodded. "I think you'll like what you find. An Instagrammer on the rise, a model with an impressive number of followers, an up-and-coming actress—and, of course, a musician."

"Any artists? Like a painter, sculptor, graphic arts, anything like that?" Ira regarded Emerson closely. He'd shown a lot of promise when he'd worked in marketing. And when Ira had asked him to take on the additional assignment of keeping tabs on Layla and tracking her whereabouts, Emerson had been quick to comply, no questions asked.

"That wasn't on the list of gets, but I'll be sure to look into it."

"Good," Ira said. "No need to repeat the exact formula, no matter how well it worked before. And what about

James—he ran all the usual checks?"

"Says they're good and ready. He's training Priya to take over."

Ira grew silent. James had been one of his best employees, and though he'd miss him, no one was ever irreplaceable.

"Okay then." Ira closed the file and met Emerson's gaze. "You ready for this?"

"Of course," Emerson said. "Just . . ."

Ira waited.

"How do we top the last competition? It's not like we can actually kidnap anyone."

Ira grew thoughtful. He looked at Emerson. "We may never top it. But I'm not sure we have to. With a list as young, driven, and hungry as this, something is bound to happen."

He reached into his desk to retrieve a stack of flyers. "Start with these. See that they're widely distributed. We're shooting for a record turnout. We want every kid who interviews to think they stand a chance."

"The Hollywood dream," Emerson said.

"Works every time."

FIFTY-ONE

THE PRETTIEST STAR

Madison Brooks sat calmly in her front row aisle seat at the Dolby Theater. With Blue at her feet—she'd taken him as her date—and a fully recovered Paul by her side, life had never felt sweeter.

Six months after the tragedy at RED, Madison's star continued to rise. She'd already won the Golden Globe for this role, and with Heather Rollins now buried and gone, she'd taken Madison's secrets along with her. From this point on, Madison had nothing to fear. She could look forward to living out the rest of her life free of the burden of constantly looking over her shoulder.

Paul nudged her side. The nominees for Best Actress in a Leading Role were being announced. When her name was called, Madison faced the camera with the serene expression she'd been practicing with this exact moment in mind.

Her friends were all watching at Aster's new apartment, and she wondered what they'd make of her gift of the black-and-white photographs that had once hung in her entry. She didn't care if they displayed them or buried them deep in their closets. It was more her way of acknowledging something they'd suspected all along, while thanking them for their continued silence.

It felt strange to have friends. Not that they texted every day or hung out on most weekends. Everyone was busy. They each had their own lives. Still, when they did get together, their connection was deep. Like survivors of something the rest of the world could never comprehend, they were forever bonded after that night at RED in a way that was impossible to explain.

Blue perked his head up, and Madison grinned and leaned down to scratch between his ears. Ever since they'd been reunited, he'd barely left her side. His constant presence gave Madison comfort and also seemed to delight the countless tabloids, bloggers, and glossy magazines that detailed her every move. The same top designer responsible for her pale pink dress had also designed the various doggy tuxes Blue wore during award-show season.

"I'm thinking like Nicole Kidman just after she separated from Tom Cruise," her longtime stylist, Christina, had said when they were choosing between the numerous designs on offer. Madison had wanted to go with a fiercer look to honor all she'd been through, while Christina did her best to sway her in the opposite direction. "You want to look delicate, almost to the point of fragile. It'll convince people to root for you."

"They're already rooting for me," Madison said. "They consider me a hero."

"You've overcome a lot," Christina was quick to agree. "You had to convince the public those blog posts were the result of a deranged mind."

"Which they were." Madison had glared.

"Clearly." Christina blushed furiously and fought to recover. "Still, for a fairy-tale event like the Oscars, you want to be seen as a princess. Soon as it's over, you can put on your Wonder Woman cape and conquer the world."

Madison had halfheartedly agreed. But after walking the carpet and seeing the hushed deference paid to her, she had to admit Christina was right. In a town like Hollywood, the truth didn't matter: perception was king.

Absently, she traced a finger over the place where the tracker had been removed, and focused on the big screen. Luckily, the tracker was only one of many precautions Paul had put into place. Though he'd been shadowing Gerald Rawlins's contacts for the last decade, it was only recently that he'd been able to confirm Heather's true identity. Once that was established, it was simply a game of follow the leader, which had ultimately led him to Death Valley. Madison shuddered to think what might've become of her if Paul hadn't shown up when he did.

Mistaking her shiver for nerves, Paul reached over and squeezed Madison's hand. She was quick to squeeze back. It was probably normal to feel butterflies, but Madison wasn't worried, not in the least. There was no one left to deny her, no one left to stand in her way from claiming Hollywood's most valuable prize.

The clips of all the nominated roles were done playing. She nudged Blue with her foot, preparing him for the moment they'd practiced at home.

The presenters fumbled a joke that didn't quite land. Then one opened the envelope and handed it to the other, who looked into the camera and said, "And the Oscar goes to . . ."

ACKNOWLEDGMENTS

Finishing a series is always bittersweet, but I'm grateful for Katherine Tegen and Claudia Gabel for making Beautiful Idols such a pleasure to write.

I also want to thank the HarperCollins global team for all their hard work. What a thrill it's been to see this series launched all over the world!

And of course, I have an abundance of gratitude for my excellent agent, Bill Contardi, my amazing husband, Sandy, my lovely and supportive family and friends (you know who you are!), and of course my readers, who allow me to live this wonderful dream.